Reviews of Peter: The Untold True from readers around the world

★★★★★
"A wonderfully magical book. It makes you look at life in a different way and how you can still be a kid at heart. We are forced to grow old, but we don't have to grow up. There are always aspects in our life that would be easier if we could just be a little more childish and fun."
Jillian, Colorado

★★★★★
"I thought this story was a breath of fresh air. In the theme of youth this was the cleanest story I have read in a very long time. Peter is a baby when this story starts riding in a carriage with his parents. The carriage comes to a stop in the middle of the enchanted forest and Peter disappears- not to be seen again till age 11, naked and grown up in the wild. Margaret, a young girl, sings and Peter stops to listen. Margaret spots the wild boy. Her family takes him in and everyone who comes to know Peter is enchanted by him. This story includes all the adventures you knew and loved with a different twist. I will be reading this story to my boys. This story moved me to tears. Peter reflects innocence and true genuine kindness unaffected by the world around him and the problems that come with age. Sometimes the fountain of youth is not always a blessing. I enjoyed this adventure and even pictured it coming to life in a movie someday."
Fallon, Age 32, Florida

★★★★★
"Perfect for rainy day reading! *Peter* is the delightful story about the real boy who never grew up... Although the story stays firmly planted in its historical context, the allusions and parallels to Peter Pan are unmistakable and fun to keep an eye out for... Unlike other contemporary Peter Pan related stories that are filled with dark and sinister plots and motives, Peter illustrates the enchanting magic of the innocence of youth."
RT, Age 24, California

★★★★★
"If you are a Peter Pan aficionado, then this is the book for you!"
Roxie, Age 62, Maryland

★★★
"I became emotionally attached to Peter throughout the book. I caught myself trying to find out the secrets of Peter and about his past. The book will never leave me as it is so magical and recommend people to read it, the book will still be in your mind long after you've finished it!"
Hollie, United Kingdom

★★★★

"I really liked this rendition or retelling of *Peter Pan*. I have always loved the story of Peter as it made me realize how wonderful it is to be a kid in a big world full of hard questions and hard decisions. I really liked how the author slowly starts piecing the story of Peter Pan that we all know together, with the feather in his hat and the defeated pirate. I love retellings of my favourite stories so this was a great treat for me."
Dana, Canada

★★★

"This was a very interesting read and take on Peter Pan's story. Granted, it wasn't what I was expecting but in the end I'm happy it wasn't. The book follows Peter, the 'Wild Boy,' being taken away from the forest where he had spent many years of his childhood and then integrating back into civilization. Overall, the book was easy to follow and finish, giving the reader a fresh perspective of Peter's tale."
Anna, Idaho

★★★★

"*Peter: The Untold True Story* is such a wonderful and magical book. You grow attached to Peter and the other characters. It made me smile, laugh, and cry. I think the author did an amazing job writing this. Each chapter was detailed and very well written. This was an enjoyable read and couldn't be read at a more perfect time for me. Reading this made me feel like a kid again. Don't we all just want to be a little bit like Peter? Don't we all want to be forever young? This book is perfect for all ages and I highly recommend it."
Mallory, Age 28, New Jersey

★★★★★

"Well-suited to reminding a reader of any age that a youthful outlook is a valuable thing."
Jake, California

★★★★★

"Wow. I was not expecting this book to be so good. This is one of those books where you simply can't tell if it is fiction or not, it is so well written and so plausible! It feels just fantastic enough to be true. While I spent a lot of time feeling sorry for Peter, I kept reminding myself that he was happy with the path his life took. And whether I agreed with the "civilized" people or not, it was a really interesting twist on the Peter Pan story, one that will stick with me for a long, long time to come. It reads like a superbly written biography, and has characters as well developed as any classic literature I've read. It entertains, while presenting philosophical questions it does not answer. It is a great read, both from a fun standpoint and an enlightening one. Could not recommend this any more strongly!"
Alyson, New York

★★★★★

"Peter's joy, innocence and fire are qualities that we all embody as children and so I found this poignant account rather nostalgic. Memories of my childhood and youth were brought to the fore as I delved into this dazzling novel, containing colourful characters and thoughtful reflections and impacting resonance. Peter is a magical, poignant tale full of love, humor and outstanding courage in the face of hardship and trials. Above all this wonderful book makes you dream and remember how dreams really can come true!"
Lucinda, Age 23, United Kingdom

★★★★

"The story got me from the first few pages making me smile and kept me turning pages till the very end. I liked the way this book was written. Proper attention was given to details from the very start, which ignited my visual imagination, made me to bond with the characters quickly, feel their emotions and environment around them... I liked Peter and sympathized with him. I kept guessing what would become of him, and he made me to look deeper into my soul longing to become a better person. Even after reading the book the urge to be an organic and natural part of the nature, breathe at the same rhythm with it, rather than just remain a passive observer, still persists. Just to stay still for a moment and let the world in, never to stop wondering, smiling and be open to what may come even if it may hurt."
Evija, Age 30, Latvia

★★★★★

"*Peter Pan* is probably my favorite childhood story. I loved the thought of being forever young and loved Peter. And this amazing story made me love Peter even more. When I read the plot of the book it sounded very interesting, but the book itself is so magical, it makes you feel much younger. Characters in the book are saying that Peter is making them remember the child in them, and I think everyone should read the book because it definitely brings back the nice time of being an innocent, careless kid. This book is truly incredible, it's just like I imagined it would be, and even more. Definitely worth reading."
Dorotea, Age 17, Croatia

★★★

Christopher Mechling's debut novel on the true story of Peter Pan is certainly almost as, if not equally, fascinating as the original novel by James Barrie. Mechling perfectly retains the innocence of the original Peter Pan with the disparaging tension between growing up and staying young, along with the genuine relationships forged in the story between characters. A key aspect of Mechling's novel though, which I found interesting, was how he highlighted how human nature inevitably makes a big deal out of the Other. (Peter was Different, and therefore attracted a lot of attention.) The whole story made me wistful, but in a good way. Looking forward to reading his next novel.
Lexine U., Hong Kong

★★★★★

"I liked this book. I love fairy tales and the stories behind them. I thought this book was entertaining and well written. I love the characters and how Peter is remembered by people who actually knew the boy behind the story. My son also liked this book. He is 10 and said that he liked this book and how it was an original story- as in behind the movie, where it came from. He liked how it put Peter Pan in a realistic way."
Lauren, Connecticut

★★★★

I have fallen in love with this book! While it doesn't have much in the action department, the feel of the story more than makes up for it. This will be one of those stories you read over and over and your kids will love it as much as you do! I had my 4 year old nephew overnight and he wanted a story before bed so I pulled this out having just started it. After the first part he begged me to keep reading. He stayed up until halfway through the third part. And when he woke up we had to keep reading! Definitely worth the read!
Melissa, Age 24

★★★★

I thoroughly enjoyed this book. The author's first book turns a historical figure of Peter the Wild Boy that inspired tales of Peter Pan into an easily accessible, charming, and captivating story for all ages. The narrators the author uses, young girls at different points in Peter's life, speak from the heart about Peter and I found it helped let Peter enter my own life as I read this novel. Looking at the story of this boy's life helped bring important things into perspective. The wisdom we find in Peter magnifies well beyond the obvious desire of being forever young. It is a delightful look at human nature and the importance of retaining a childlike innocence and wonder that is all too often lost in today's world. I know I will go forward in my days and try and keep a little piece of Peter with me. So thank you Christopher Mechling for this lovely novel. I look forward to future works.
Jeniece, Age 28, New York

★★★★★

This story was so well written, it was as if it were one of the classics. I loved how it was its own story, wrapped around true events as well as hints of Neverland-like magic. Every time I sat down with this book, I felt like I was being wrapped up in it like a blanket. Toward the end, the author did a good job of portraying the emotion behind saying goodbye to childhood. I may have lost a few tears in those final chapters. It's hard to say which parts are real, and which parts are made up. In the beginning, I wondered this a lot. By the end, it no longer mattered. This was an amazing story, full of love, innocence, and magic. It transported me from my world to Peter's world. The story is what it's supposed to be. Well done, Christopher Mechling.
Crissi, California

Peter

Published by Christopher Mechling
www.christophermechling.com

First Paperback Edition, 2014

This story is based on true events, however some of the characters, names and certain locations and events have been changed, and others have been fictionalized for dramatization purposes.

ISBN 978-0-9891270-2-8

Peter

The Untold True Story

As related by Her Royal Highness
The Princess Caroline of Great Britain
Daughter of King George II and Caroline of Ansbach

With an afterword by her sister, The Princess Amelia

Prepared for Publication by
Christopher Mechling

Contents

For Joseph & Susan Mechling

PREFACE

In preparing to publish *Peter: The Untold True Story*, I am reminded of the influence Ray Bradbury had on me as a writer. My first introduction to Ray was a short quote placed prominently on the back of one of my favorite books- *Jonathan Livingston Seagull*, by Richard Bach. Ray's comment was, "Richard Bach with this book does two things: he gives me Flight, he makes me Young."

Over the course of my childhood, I became acquainted with a number of Ray's books and short stories- *Fahrenheit 451, A Sound of Thunder, The Pedestrian, Zen in the Art of Writing, Dandelion Wine, the Martian Chronicles* and others. I liked his work, but it wasn't until I met him in 2005 that I really had the opportunity to get to know him.

I had been aware of Ray coming to San Diego to give lectures on the Art of Writing for several years, and had wanted to meet him, but circumstances hadn't worked out. When the opportunity came in 2005, my grandmother Annie and I were both interested to attend, so we went together, and listened as Ray shared his life experiences and philosophy.

One of the central themes of his lecture was to, "Do what you love, and love what you do," and that was certainly a maxim he lived by. Ray's loves included comic books, movies, science-fiction, dinosaurs, Egypt, Mars, libraries and librarians, etc. But how had he begun his path in life?

During the middle of his talk, Ray related the following adventure from his childhood: In 1932, when he was twelve years old, Ray visited a carnival and met a man who called himself Mr. Electrico, whose act involved sitting in an electric chair and being "electrocuted". At one point in the performance, Mr. Electrico reached out with a sword and touched Ray on the brow as a king would knight a young man, and the contact gave Ray a jolt. "Live forever!" Mr. Electrico shouted.[1]

Ray's uncle had recently passed away, and so the suggestion of living forever was quite provocative to his young mind. The next day, while driving home with his family from his Uncle's funeral, young Ray looked out the window and saw the colorful pitched tents of the carnival down by Lake Michigan. "Stop the car!" he exclaimed, with such emotion that his father did stop. But Ray did not have the words then to tell his father what was in his heart, he could only leap out of the car and run away from Death, to the carnival, to find Mr. Electrico. His father called after him to stop and come back, but Ray just kept running, and so the family drove on without him.

Ray found Mr. Electrico sitting among the tents of the carnival, and wanted to speak about what was troubling him. Mr. Electrico appeared almost as if he had been waiting for Ray. However, faced with the opportunity, Ray didn't know where to begin. How do you ask someone to teach you how to live forever?

So, instead, Ray pulled a magic trick from his pocket and asked Mr. Electrico how to do the trick, and Mr. Electrico taught him. Then he invited Ray to meet some of the other members of the carnival. Beating the side of the tent, Mr. Electrico called out to those inside to clean up their language, and then led Ray inside to meet the Skeleton Man, the Fat Lady, the Illustrated Man, the acrobats and other characters who would in later years haunt Ray's imagination.

---

1   Mr. Electrico was a magician. This act should not be attempted at home, or under any circumstances by inexperienced individuals without the supervision of an expert of the subject and the proper type of electricity.

Mr. Electrico and Ray ended up sitting beside Lake Michigan talking about life. In Ray's words, "He talked about his small philosophies and let me talk about my large ones. At a certain point he finally leaned forward and said, 'You know, we've met before.' I replied, 'No, sir, I've never met you before.' He said, 'Yes, you were my best friend in the great war in France in 1918 and you were wounded and died in my arms at the battle of the Ardennes Forrest. But now, here today, I see his soul shining out of your eyes. Here you are, with a new face, a new name, but the soul shining from your face is the soul of my dear dead friend. Welcome back to the world.'"

First Mr. Electrico had told Ray to live forever. Now he told him that he had lived before. Ray's mind was filled to overflowing.

Mr. Electrico gave Ray his card, and said Ray could write to him, if he wanted. As he left the carnival, Ray felt that something strange and wonderful had happened to him. He went home, and the next day left for Arizona with his family.

Shortly after his arrival in Arizona, Ray began writing. He loved the works of writers such as L. Frank Baum, Jules Verne, H.G. Wells, and Edgar Rice Burroughs, and had dreamed of becoming either a writer or a magician. Now, ideas poured from his hand to the page. From that time onward, every day for the rest of his life, Ray wrote.

Ray became a master of storytelling, and filled many volumes with his prolific writing. But along the way, he transcended his medium. Ray compared writing fantasy and science fiction to the means by which Perseus confronted Medusa. We look at the monsters in our lives indirectly, through the mirror of our writing, and in this way we take aim and strike.

By the time I met him, Ray was advanced in his years. His glasses were very thick, and he was obliged to sit in a wheelchair. However, his spirit was strong enough to keep an audience of several hundred people spellbound for over three hours as he spoke. The many stories he told, from that early experience with Mr. Electrico, through all the wonderful adventures and challenges he faced in his life, illustrated how he had taken the things he loved and built a life with them.

Listening to Ray, I felt that much of what he said tallied with things in my own heart. During intermission, my grandmother who, like Ray, was in her eighties, said she wanted to ask Ray to sign a copy of *Dandelion Wine* for her, and so we went together to the front of the room to join the line of people waiting there. On an inspiration, I took my sketchbook with me.

When it was my turn to meet Ray, I showed him my sketchbook and told him about the unpublished series of novels I was working on. At that time, I had written several thousand pages in a science-fiction epic. I asked him if he would sign my sketchbook. He looked at me with interest and asked what my name was. I told him and he wrote, "Chris! Good luck," then signed his name, returning my sketchbook with a smile.

I thanked Ray and then wheeled my grandmother back to where we were seated. For the rest of the lecture, I held the sketchbook with Ray's inscription in my hands, full of emotion. I had not come expecting this- I hadn't known what to expect. I'd only read a few of Ray's stories before, but now, I felt I knew him, and more than that, he knew me.

It was as if he had taken Mr. Electrico's place, and I in turn was the young man in the audience. At the end of the lecture, during the question-answer period, I stood up, said, "...Well, I just wanted to say thank you for signing my sketchbook. I am working on a series of novels, or you could say a series of stories, it really is a collection of short stories in a way. I find a lot of what you said today very inspirational, and I wrote you a note; I'll read it. It's basically just- Mr. Bradbury, thank you for signing my sketchbook and wishing me luck, I expect my series of stories will be finished in a few years and I promise I will send a set to you. You are a great inspiration, and I am grateful to have heard you speak. May you live forever!"

"Ah!" Ray said, as everyone joined in applause, "...thank you-thank you."

It should be noted Ray touched not only my life, but many lives. As we stood up after the talk was concluded, many audience members began speaking amongst themselves and to me about their own sense of being inspired by Ray's lecture. Among those people was a woman who came up and spoke with me. She admitted she had been contemplating ending it all, but had been given new hope that day. Without a doubt, listening to him speak changed the course of her life. With all the lectures he had given, and all the copies of his writings that had been circulated around the world, how many people had he helped?

I left the hall charged with a sense of great purpose. I felt I had been touched, as Mr. Electrico had touched Ray. I can still hear Ray's voice when I read his writing. He was one of those rare individuals who are more than the sum of their parts.

In the years that followed, I continued writing, and took opportunities whenever I could to go to events where Ray spoke, at lectures in Pasadena, at the Comic-Con, and later at the playhouse where his plays were staged. I wrote a number of letters to him also.

On opening night of the stage production of Fahrenheit 451 in Pasadena, Ray and I talked. He remembered me, and asked if I was published yet. I told him no, because I wanted to write out the complete series first. He urged me to get something out there—even if it was just a short story for a magazine.

Ray's specialty was short stories. The science fiction project I had taken on was a very large one, which I felt obligated to see through to completion. But I took his advice to heart, and began to work on several smaller projects also, to introduce myself as a writer.

Along the way, life threw some unexpected obstacles at me. My grandmother passed away, then my mother was diagnosed with a serious cancer. I spent sixteen months traveling around the world with her, seeking the best treatments available for her condition. The therapies helped improve her health and quality of life dramatically, so that she was able to take long walks, sing and dance, and focus on positive living. Eventually, however, she had a stroke, and passed away peacefully a few weeks later, surrounded by friends and family.

I am glad for every day spent caring for my grandmother and my mother, as they are now cherished memories. Since my mother passed away in 2010, my brother and I have been putting our lives back together, rebuilding our businesses, and refocusing ourselves. Through all this, I continued writing, but my pace was slowed.

In 2011, my father and I discovered the story of Peter the Wild Boy, and made the connection between his life and the legend of Peter Pan. I've been working on this book since then. It is a story I believe Ray would have enjoyed very much, and it is the first book I have chosen to publish, to introduce myself as an author.

Ray Bradbury passed away on June 5, 2012. I regret that I was unable to complete this work before then. In reviewing Ray's writings, I found he wrote an account in 2001 of his childhood encounter with Mr. Electrico, and concluded that account by saying, "I have long since lost track of Mr. Electrico, but I wish that he existed somewhere in the world so that I could run to him, embrace him, and thank him for changing my life and helping me become a writer."

Thank you Ray, for electrifying me. I hope to see you again.

Christopher Mechling

CHRIS!
GOOD
LUCK

Max
Brooks

INTRODUCTION

This is the true story behind the fairy tale of Peter Pan, telling the adventures of the real-life boy who inspired James Barrie's classic tale. Peter the Wild Boy lived in eighteenth century England, through the reigns of three kings (all named George), and achieved legendary status in his own lifetime. He was not only a popular figure, but also drew intense philosophical and scientific study, and was a subject of interest to literary figures such as Daniel Defoe and Jonathan Swift. Peter retained a youthful appearance throughout his life, and had a joyful, intuitive spirit that was both challenging and infectious.

It took over two years of research to authenticate the manuscript, which was written by the hand of the girl who loved Peter best, The Princess Caroline of Great Britain, with an afterword by her sister, Princess Amelia. This manuscript was unfortunately lost when it was originally produced several centuries ago, and as far as I have been able to determine, only one copy now survives.

Christopher Mechling

PROLOGUE

All children grow up, all but one. His name is Peter and by now, all the civilized world has heard of him. He has captured the public imagination and become a legend, a subject for poets, philosophers and psychologists to write about, and for children to dream of. The children's tales might be lacking in some details, but on the whole they are more accurate than most other accounts, for children will always understand Peter intuitively, as I did when I first met him.

I shall endeavor to tell you the true story of my friend Peter, because he cannot tell it to you himself. Afterward I hope you will love him and defend him as I have for the remainder of your days, and pass on to others an accurate account of the wild boy who would not grow up, who danced with kings and won the hearts of princesses, who defied logic and reason, who lived and loved with an innocent heart, and found peace in the midst of a turbulent world.

The Princess Caroline of Great Britain
St. James' Palace, London

Act I:
Margaret

Chapter 1: The Enchanted Forest

The German city of Hamelin was already familiar to legend when Peter's story began. The forests outside the city were said to be enchanted, and many folk tales were told about events that took place there. The most famous of these tales you have probably heard- that of a Piper whose music had the power to charm animals and children alike, and how the call of his pipes ultimately led many children into the wild, never to return. I do not know the truth and the fiction of that tale, but it has been suggested to me the legend of it may be related to the Greek stories of Pan, God of Nature as well as of Shepherds and Flocks.

Now no one knows exactly when our wild boy Peter was born, but one thing is clear, he left his parents when he was still young, before they could teach him the lessons that turn a little boy into a man. I have always pictured the scene taking place at twilight in the countryside. A covered wagon traveling down the country road headed toward the ancient forest. Since it was summer, there would be fireflies in the air in great numbers, and perhaps one firefly in particular would meander her way toward the wagon. If she were listening, that firefly might have heard Peter's parents arguing:

"I am worried about our boy," Peter's mother says, "It is unnatural for a boy his age to speak so little and not to read or write. It's as if he's made up his mind not to grow up."

"You are worrying too much," his father replies, with masculine confidence and a hint of charm, "Just look at those clever eyes of his, that handsome smile. Surely such a magical child will find his way in this world."

By now our little friend the firefly would have peeked inside to see the parents seated toward the front of the wagon, while their boy is sitting at the rear. The parents pause their conversation to regard their son, and see the firefly enter the wagon. Peter sees it too, and his eyes sparkle. He laughs and puts out his hands playfully, and our lady firefly dances in the air before him. Then, she calmly settles in one of his hands.

"...Speaking of magic, look at that," Peter's father says.

His mother shakes her head, "You know as well as I do that magic does not put food on the table. When will you be serious about our boy's future? What kind of man will he become?"

Peter's mother has now turned her attention back to her husband, but the father's gaze lingers for a moment on his little son and the firefly before he finally looks back to his wife.

"Oh, I don't know," he says, "...whatever he wants, I imagine."

Her tone is sharp, "Whatever he wants?"

He shrugs in response, "...A lawyer perhaps."

She furrows her eyebrows, "I think he should learn to be a doctor."

The father argues, "A doctor's life is miserable- always hanging around sick, injured and unhappy people. Why would you want him to be a doctor?"

"At least it's an honest trade," she says, "Who would ever trust a lawyer?"

"Well, we'll let him choose for himself, when the time comes."

"And when will the time come?"

"Sooner then you think, dear. I've arranged for a tutor to start lessons with him."

"Can we really afford a tutor?"

"I'll find a way to pay for it. And when he starts to speak more, and to read, we'll enroll him in school with the other children, and then he'll grow up so fast you'll wish he had stayed this age forever."

"Oh, I can hardly wait. He is so difficult to manage sometimes."

And then perhaps, by chance, the father's eyes would drift back to where Peter has been seated, only to find the seat is empty. Peter is no longer in the wagon!

"He's gone!" the father exclaims, and both parents rush to the back of the wagon.

"Gone!" the mother cries, "No, no, no- stop the wagon! Stop!" And so the driver pulls in his reins and the wagon halts. "It's so dark now," the mother says, "I can't see anything except the fairies."

"Fairies?" the father asks his wife before grasping her meaning. "Fireflies, you mean. Boy! Can you hear me? Come back!"

"Sweetheart!" she calls, "Where are you?" But there is no answer from the the forest, only the dance of the fireflies. "It's no use," she says, "He never comes when I call. I swear, that boy will never grow up."

"Do you suppose he left because we were arguing about him?" the father asks.

"Don't be ridiculous," she says, "I scarcely think he understands half the things we talk about. It was that fairy, he must have gone chasing after it. We'll never find him now."

"Why do you say that?" he responds. "Boy, come here! Stop playing around."

"Don't you know this forest is enchanted?" she says.

"I thought you didn't believe in magic," he says to her.

"And I thought you did!" she replies.

He shakes his head, "I am a practical man, my dear. Of course I don't believe in magic. Not the kind in fairy tales anyway. Boy! Come back here this instant, or we're leaving without you."

"Leaving?" Peter's mother cries, "How can we leave?"

Her husband tells her, "If we search for him in this forest at night, we'll only get ourselves lost. Many travelers have. That's why they say the place is enchanted."

"But if we leave- we'll never see him again," she says.

He scoffs in disbelief, "Never? How far can a little boy go?"

"When it comes to little boys," Peter's mother replies, "there's no telling."

Peter is amongst the trees where his parents cannot see him, chasing after the firefly.

"Boy!" his father calls, taking up a lantern and getting out of the wagon to search the roadside for his son. In spite of his claims to the contrary, the father had no intention of leaving. He would stay for hours calling out into the dark, if it would bring Peter back.

"Sweetheart!" the mother calls.

Peter turns his head at the sound of his parents' voices, but then the firefly circles around him, and he resumes his chase, which leads him further away from the road, into the Enchanted Forest. And so begins the story of Peter.

❖　❖　❖

From all evidence we can conclude Peter lived for some period of years alone in the forests of Hamelin, surviving through the seasons and finding food and shelter for himself by whatever natural instincts a child is born with, and perhaps with the sympathetic help of the animals as well. It is a mystery to civilized men how lost boys and girls can adapt to life in the wild, but children are capable of a great deal more than men give them credit for.

Peter learned to eat the good things one can find in the forest, and to move about with the grace and agility of the beasts. He quickly found he had no use for the clothes his parents had given him, and so he ran about the forest naked. How he endured the snow in such condition I cannot tell you, but his skin became tanned by the sun, and his curly brown hair grew long and wild. He was as comfortable climbing or running about on all fours as he was walking on his two feet.

It seems through the course of seasons, the animals of the forest came to know Peter and to trust him, for he soon became more attuned to their language and etiquette than to the language of his own kind. The birds sang greetings to Peter daily, the gentle

Deer King and the fierce Mother Bear both fawned over him, and even the surly Boar grunted tolerantly when Peter passed by.

Peter was clever, in his fashion, and so for the most part he avoided encounters with travelers who passed through the forest. The ways of grown-ups did not interest him. Other children, however, sometimes drew his attention. If he heard them playing, or telling each other stories, or singing, he would sneak close to watch or listen and, occasionally, the children would notice. So a little legend began to circulate, among the children of Hamelin, about a wild boy who lived in the forest and never had to bother with school or chores or any of the other bothersome things that parents insist on.

One day, in the summer of 1725, Peter made an encounter that would change his life forever. It happened as he was chasing his way through the forest, leaping over rocks and fallen logs with ease and bounding his way through the trees, sometimes on two legs, sometimes on all fours, in pursuit of a butterfly I imagine, for Peter loved butterflies. In the midst of this pursuit, he did not pay attention to the fact that he was drawing near to the road that ran through this section of forest. But when he heard the sound of travelers on the road, he stopped short and backtracked, climbing a tree to avoid being seen.

From the branches of the tree, Peter watched the travelers pass by, and in the window of their carriage, he spied a girl about his own age, singing to her younger brothers. Peter was transfixed. The butterfly he had pursued earlier crossed in front of him again now, but he paid it no attention.

When the carriage had passed by, he climbed down from his perch in the tree and kept pace with it from a distance, being careful to stay out of view while listening to the sound of the girl's voice. Getting ahead of the carriage, he stopped and climbed a tree once again to listen and watch. However, the new tree he chose proved not to be the best hiding place, for the girl sitting in her window spotted him. Their eyes met and she stopped singing. How strange to see a wild, naked boy, sitting in a tree!

5

"Father!" she spoke out. Peter instantly disappeared from view, climbing higher into the tree branches like a squirrel.

"What is it?" a man's voice answered. "What's wrong?"

"I saw him- I saw the Wild Boy of the Forest. I think he was listening to me sing. He is perched up in the tree over there, like a squirrel."

"What did he look like?"

"He was small, and brown, and- and he wasn't wearing any clothes. He was just like the girls in town described. I thought they were just telling tales, but he's real."

"Did he frighten you?"

"No, Father- he's just a boy. But I think he was frightened, when I saw him, because he immediately climbed higher in the tree, out of view. He must be very timid. I wonder how he came to be living out here in the forest."

"Gunther," the man called, "stop the carriage."

The carriage stopped and the man inside, a doctor, stepped out. He turned back to the window and asked, "Where did you see him?"

The girl answered, "Over there, in that tall tree."

"And you say he had no clothing?"

"None that I could see."

"Give me that blanket and some chocolate." Taking these items from his daughter, the doctor walked from the carriage toward the tree, whistling. At the base of the tree he looked up, and saw the boy looking down. He smiled and said, "Here boy, come down from there. Everything is all right. See? I have chocolate for you." But Peter was not ready to come down- instead he climbed higher into the tree. The doctor sighed. "Gunther, come here. The boy is quite high in the tree and I cannot reach him." Leaving his post at the front of the carriage the driver came over and, after taking a quick glance up, started to climb the tree, prompting Peter to scramble up higher. "Gently now, Gunther. We don't want to frighten the boy. Here, take this chocolate to him."

6

Gunther took the chocolate and resumed climbing. Peter tossed something down at him. "Ow!" he cried out. "He's throwing acorns at me!" Peter laughed, and Gunther bristled. "You think that's funny, do you?"

"Easy, Gunther. Take a bite of the chocolate and then offer it to the boy."

Gunther took a bite from the chocolate, which seemed to calm him slightly, and then looked back up at the boy, and said, "Here, boy. Chocolate. It's good." When Peter hesitated, Gunther took another bite from the chocolate. "You don't want to let me eat all of this, do you?" Peter did not move. "It's no use, Doctor. First time I've ever seen a boy turn down chocolate."

"Perhaps he doesn't know what it is," the girl said.

The doctor looked surprised to see his daughter standing beside him. "What are you doing over here? You ought to be waiting in the carriage."

"I thought I might help. I was the one who discovered him after all."

"The boy is naked."

"I know- and he's probably frightened too."

"Go back to the carriage dear. It isn't proper-"

Just then, Gunther came crashing down out of the tree branches to the ground, landing just beside the girl, who shrieked in surprise. "Are you all right, Gunther?" the doctor asked, rushing forward to stand over him.

"I'm fine, just a bit sore," Gunther said. "...Cocky little rascal."

"What happened?"

"I tried to climb higher and grab him but he slipped free."

"Oh Gunther, you shouldn't have done that," the girl said.

"Hello there!" a new voice called from the road. "Is everything all right? Why is your carriage stopped in the middle of the road?"

The doctor sighed and set the blanket he was holding down. Turning, he told to his daughter, "I must go see who that is. Stay here with Gunther."

7

"If you insist, Father." The girl watched her father go and then looked up at Peter and smiled. He looked down at her, and smiled back. Sitting down on the blanket, the girl looked off in the direction her father had headed and she began to sing.

Out on the road, three hunters on horseback hailed the doctor as he approached "Hello," he said, "…sorry for any inconvenience. There is a lost boy up in the tree over there, and we can't convince him to come down. Perhaps you gentlemen could help?"

"The boy is some relation of yours?" the lead hunter asked, dismounting and then taking his horse by the reins.

"No," the doctor said as they began to walk toward the tree, "…my daughter saw him from the carriage window. He is naked, and appears to have lived in the wild for some time."

"There have been rumors of a wild boy living in the forest," another one of the hunters mentioned, following behind.

Peter, up in the tree, saw the doctor returning with the hunters and looked around for a way to escape. Swiftly, he swung himself downward, from one tree branch to another, and then dashed easily on all fours out the length of a long branch and jumped off, landing on the hillside behind the tree.

Observing Peter's action, the girl halted her singing and gazed at him. He looked back at her solemnly, and once again their eyes locked with each other. But the hunters also saw Peter drop from the tree and they called and pointed at him.

Peter turned his head and looked at them, just in time to see them start to run toward him. Then the serious expression on his face broke, a cocky grin spread over his features, and he sprang from his position, racing into the forest at such a pace that you might have thought he was flying.

In a moment, both Peter and the hunters were gone from view. "Do you think they'll catch him, Father?" the girl asked, staring in the direction they had gone.

"Yes I imagine so."

"I hope they don't hurt him."

"That makes two of us," the doctor answered, "but they seemed like decent fellows- I wouldn't worry too much."

As the doctor and his daughter sat down beneath the tree to wait, a heated chase was happening beyond the green veil of the forest. Peter loved chases- regardless of which side of the game he was on, and the hunters were giving the most exciting chase of his young life.

"YAHOO!" Peter cried as he leaped onward, narrowly escaping the clutches of his pursuers, who scrambled tenaciously over obstacles to lunge headlong after him.

Peter was accustomed to racing with deer, and so he ought to have been able to escape these men easily, but he was enjoying himself too much to simply bolt away and disappear. Careless and overconfident, he took risks he should not have, playing hide-and-seek with the hunters amongst the trees, and running them in circles after him.

Over the rolling terrain of the wilderness he led them, repeatedly showing off his ability to evade capture by jumping and dodging after letting them come too close. But in spite of Peter's enthusiasm, the hunters were hard on his heels, and soon he realized he might not be able to continue to outpace them in this manner.

Peter finally bolted at full speed, hoping to put distance between himself and the hunters. Behind him, he heard them giving chase doggedly. They were falling further and further behind, but still they followed. So after several minutes sprinting, he scrambled up a tree like a squirrel, thinking he would elude them that way.

The hunters, however, were not ready to give up their pursuit. Two of them followed Peter up into the tree while the third stayed on the ground, watching the action. Peter sprang from branch to branch, laughing at the hunters' efforts to follow him, until finally they began to close on him- at which point he disappeared into a small hole in the tree trunk.

The tree Peter had chosen was hollow- something the hunters had failed to notice initially. Peter crowed at his own cleverness as he slipped down inside the tree until he reached the ground and sprang out of a hole at the base of the tree, ready to continue running. But the third hunter, who had remained on the ground, caught Peter and held him fast.

"I've got him!" the hunter called to his fellows. "Come give me a hand."

Peter wriggled in the man's arms, trying to free himself, but to no avail. Presently, the other two hunters dropped down from the branches of the tree and joined their friend in restraining the boy.

They had no choice but to prepare to carry Peter out of the forest, for he would not come willingly. He thrashed and kicked inside their arms and became increasingly agitated until it finally became clear to him he could not escape, at which point he began to cry at the unfairness of his position.

Thus Peter was brought out of the wild against his will and in tears. Poor Peter at that time could not have known what adventures lay ahead of him, or that it would all come right in the end. He only felt that a terrible injustice was being done to him.

The doctor, standing with his daughter beneath the tree as the hunters carried Peter down the slope out of the forest, saw the state Peter was in and rushed forward to comfort him. "What have you done to the boy?" the doctor demanded.

"We didn't do anything to the imp. He's just sore because we caught him."

"Here," the doctor said, holding out the blanket in his hands, "cover him with this, and set him down so I may speak with him." The hunters did as the doctor asked, setting the boy down and wrapping the blanket around him, but they kept a hold on him still, so he wouldn't run off again. "Now then boy, what is your name?"

The tearful boy stared at the doctor but did not answer.

"Perhaps you would like to try some chocolate now," the doctor said, pulling a chunk from his pocket and offering it to the boy, who gazed blankly at it.

"I told you Father," the girl said, coming to join the group, "…
he doesn't know what it is. Here, let me." Taking the chocolate
from her father, she looked at the boy and smiled prettily. Biting
gently from the chunk, she then put it to his lips, and said, "Try it-
you'll like it." Peter opened his mouth and bit into the chocolate.
"There," she said, taking his hand, "now come with me to our
carriage." She stepped away and his arm stretched with her but
he did not move. She looked back. "Well he can't move with you
holding him like that," she said to the hunters.

"I went to a lot of trouble to catch this boy," one of the hunters
said, "I'm not inclined to go through all that again."

"Well we can't stay here all day," said the leader of the hunters,
"let's give her a chance to try and get him in that carriage. Keep
an eye on him though." Thus resolved, the hunters released Peter,
and the girl led him forward, with them following close behind.
The leader of the hunters addressed the doctor, "We'll travel with
you into town. There may be a reward for the boy."

"A reward?"

"Certainly. The boy's parents must be looking for him."

"Maybe," the doctor said, "but it looks as though the boy has
lived in the wild for several years at least. I would guess he is
eleven or twelve now, but when he went missing he must have
been much younger, and his parents may have given up hope of
finding him."

"Then his parents will be all the more happy to see him. And if
his parents are not looking for him, perhaps the King's guard are."

"I can't imagine why the King's guard would be looking for
him. He doesn't seem like he could have done anyone any great
harm."

"You didn't see what we had to endure to carry him out here
after we captured him. The boy has a wild side. Anyway, we did
all the work, so I expect a fair reward."

"Of course, you are welcome to it," the doctor said. "I want
only to make sure the boy reaches the authorities safely."

The girl was happy to ignore the conversation of the adults. She squeezed Peter's hand in hers and swung it gently to and fro as they walked to the carriage. Peter, for his part, was not entirely at ease in the present circumstance, being uncertain of where he was being led to, but the slender, gentle hand of the doctor's daughter was certainly preferable to the grip of the hunters- and then there was the possibility that she might give him more of that chocolate- so he walked onward to the carriage with her.

At the door of the carriage, the girl stopped. Her brothers looked out the window and stared at Peter curiously. "Is he going to ride with us?"

"Yes of course," their sister replied, "…if you will be so kind as to open the door."

The boys complied, and the girl let go of Peter's hand to climb up the steps. Peter watched her go and then glanced over his shoulder. The doctor and the hunters towered over him. He looked back at the girl, and then at the ground.

The girl began to sing again- the same enchanting song that had caught Peter's attention earlier. He looked up at her, and she smiled, continuing to sing. A twinkle appeared in Peter's eye, and he grinned, then sprang like a cat up into the carriage, bypassing the stairs. The boys inside the carriage cried out in astonishment, and the hunters shook their heads. "He's a wild one, that's for certain," the chief hunter said, "but your daughter seems to have charmed him."

"Indeed," the doctor said, gazing at his children, who were all on their feet inside the carriage, circling the wild boy with curiosity. Thankfully, the doctor thought to himself, the blanket had managed to stay wrapped around the boy during his dramatic leap. "Then again," the doctor said, "perhaps it is he who is the charmer."

"…I say," asked one of the boys in the carriage, illustrating with a hop as he spoke, "how did you jump like that?"

"Yes, yes," said his younger brother, jumping up and down repeatedly, "tell us how."

12

"He learnt it from the fairies," said the girl, halting her singing and rising from her seat to join in the fun. "Didn't you boy?"

By way of answer, Peter began to dance. The children clapped and laughed, bouncing about joyfully. It would be impossible for a group of adults to carry on inside of a carriage in this way, but for the children there was plenty of room to jump and dance and no reason in particular not to. Suddenly, with a great flourish, Peter ceased dancing and cast off the blanket that had been wrapped around him, tossing it so that it flew into the doctor's face. The children roared with laughter.

By the time the doctor had pulled the blanket off his head, the boy Peter was gone from view, having escaped apparently through one of the windows on the opposite side of the carriage. The children were all gathered at the windows looking in the direction he had gone. "How does he do that?" one of the boys asked in wonder.

"He's gone!" exclaimed the doctor. The hunters circled around the wagon and gave chase to Peter, disappearing into the forest in the direction they imagined he had gone.

The children turned away from the windows to look at their father. "He's gone," they said, clearly disappointed that the wild boy would not be their traveling companion. Then there was an unnatural sound that made the doctor and his children all freeze.

It was the sound of a rooster. But it was midday! Why should a rooster crow so late? Gunther was the first to understand, and he fell over laughing. The doctor looked at him and asked, "Gunther what is it?"

Gunther could not bring himself to stop laughing, so in order to answer he pointed. There, on the roof of the carriage, stood the wild boy Peter. When Peter observed that the doctor had seen him, he began to dance, which caused the children to all poke their heads out of the windows in curiosity.

"Cocky little rascal!" Gunther exclaimed, still laughing.

Peter quickly became bored with dancing on top of the carriage, and so leapt to the ground. He might have run off then, and thus avoided a great many adventures to come, but the girl cried, "Wait!" and he turned to face her. "Please," she implored from the window. "Don't go. Come with us. I promise you won't regret it."

For a moment, Peter stood in the road indecisively, staring into the girl's eyes as if trying to penetrate a great mystery. The doctor approached, and took Peter's hand gently. "Come boy," he said. "There is a long road ahead."

Chapter 2: In the Hands of the Authorities

Peter rode in the carriage together with the doctor and his family, all the way into Hamelin, escorted by the hunters on horseback. The hunters kept a close eye on Peter through the windows of the carriage, believing that he might at any moment attempt to escape again. But Peter made no such attempt- he was enjoying himself so much.

The doctor and his children were splendid company for Peter, who was fond of laughter and music. They all sang and joked together, with the doctor playing upon a flute. From a basket he kept at his side, the doctor also produced the most delicious morsels that Peter, in his short life, had ever tasted.

Once they reached the city, Peter rushed to the window- which had been closed to keep him inside. But Peter was not trying to get out; he was only interested to see the sights of the city, for Peter had never entered the city before. As he gazed out the window with great interest, and the girl came over beside him. "It will be all right," she said, "…you'll see. Don't be afraid."

❉ ❉ ❉

Peter was taken to the court of Hamelin to be examined by the authorities there. The doctor and the hunters stood by as Peter was questioned- first in German, then in English, French, Spanish, Polish, Russian, Italian, and Gypsy. The boy listened attentively for the most part, but did not answer, and did not seem to understand the meaning or purpose of the questions.

"It seems you have found a feral child," the chief examiner said, after an hour of questioning had passed with no success.

The chief hunter shifted uncomfortably. "Feral, you say?" He was mostly familiar with that term being applied to cats that had lived for too long in the wild.

"Yes- quite unusual. The boy appears to have lived alone in the wild for years, surviving by whatever natural instincts he may have, and if he was ever acquainted with human language, he has since forgotten it. Unfortunately, there will be no way for us to determine who his parents are."

"What will happen to him then?" the doctor asked.

"What I'd like to know is if there will be any reward for finding him," the hunter said.

The public servant turned and regarded the hunter. "Yes of course," he said after a moment. Reaching into a drawer, he withdrew a bag of coins and gave it to the hunter. "…For your trouble."

The hunter felt the weight of the bag in his hand, looked inside, then nodded. "It isn't as much as I'd hoped for, but I'll accept it and be on my way. Keep an eye on the boy, though. If he escapes again, it'll take more coins than this to get me to help recover him."

"Thank you, but I don't think we will be needing your services again."

"I'll be on my way then," said the hunter, withdrawing.

The chief examiner faced the doctor. "What about you, doctor? Are you waiting for a reward of some kind?"

"No sir," the doctor said, "I would only like to know what will happen to him next."

"We will put out news that a lost boy has been found in the forest, and if his parents are still looking for him, they will come to us for more information. In the meantime, he will be sent to the juvenile department of the House of Corrections at Celle."

"A prison? But the boy is no criminal." In spite of having just met Peter, the doctor felt protective of the boy, having seen Peter relate so amicably with his own children.

"It is a secure facility, there will be no risk of his escaping into the wild again, and perhaps they will be able to get him to speak.

They are accustomed to dealing with difficult cases there. Anyway he will have food, shelter and a chance to become educated, if he is willing to learn."

"The boy is quite harmless, sir. He could stay with my family until-"

"You did the right thing by bringing him to us, Doctor. We will see to it that the boy is safe and properly handled. You understand that if his parents are indeed searching for him, it will be best if they find him in the care of the authorities."

"...I understand, yes. But, I believe that boy is special, and if his parents do not come for him, I wish to see to it that he is cared for, that he is not left to rot in a prison cell. Now, I am presently on my way to Hanover, where I will be attending to a member of the court, but on my return journey I shall visit the House of Correction at Celle, and I expect to find the boy in good health and good spirits."

"I shall make a note on the boy's record that you will be looking in on him from time to time, and that you have volunteered to take care of him, if his parents do not claim him and if he is deemed safe for release."

"Thank you."

❋   ❋   ❋

Now Peter was not expecting to be left in the care of the authorities by the good doctor, and so when he saw the doctor leave, he got up from his seat to follow. Much to his surprise, a firm hand gripped his arm, and held him in place. Peter turned, looked up and gazed into the unsympathetic eyes of the guard who now held him.

"Don't be alarmed boy," said the chief examiner, approaching Peter. "No one is going to hurt you, unless you misbehave. Karl here is going to take you to a room where you will stay until we can arrange transportation to the House of Corrections." His words were the sort that one might use to be reassuring, but his tone was cold and clinical. Peter regarded the chief examiner's face, which showed no hint of emotion, and their eyes met for the first time.

17

Up until now the chief examiner had somehow avoided looking directly into Peter's eyes- not by any direct intention, but by habit. The chief examiner was a man who felt he had seen everything- that there was nothing within the scope of human nature that could surprise him, and so he seldom bothered to hold eye contact with anyone. And yet... Peter's fierce, vulnerable, innocent eyes held his attention. He stared at Peter, and Peter stared back at him, and for a moment, the chief examiner felt completely naked and utterly ignorant, as if everything he knew about the world, about life, was nothing more than a fragile veneer- an eggshell that had just now been broken through by this boy. He felt this, and then he stepped back, retreating from Peter's blazing gaze. His feelings were illogical, irrational. There was no reason why his spirit should feel unclean at this moment, no sensible explanation why he felt wrong in taking custody of the boy. Everything he had said and done was proper.

Karl gripped the boy's shoulders and turned him around, away from the chief examiner and toward the door leading to the place where Peter would be kept. "...Karl," the chief examiner said, finally able to speak again, "-please speak with the head matron and see to it the boy is given a bath, a good dinner, and some warm clothes." There was an unusual touch of emotion in the chief examiner's voice, which caused Karl to turn his head and look back.

Karl noticed something had changed in the chief examiner's countenance. He looked... human. Karl paused, and then smiled. "Yes sir."

❖ ❖ ❖

The chief examiner did not visit Peter in the room where he was kept, nor did he take any other opportunity to see the boy until the morning he was to be transported to the House of Corrections. He did, however, take the time to write a report to the administrator of the House of Corrections regarding the circumstances of Peter's capture and his present condition. It was, for the most part, an unremarkable report like any one of the hundreds of others that the chief examiner had written, except that the chief examiner, having no name to use in reference to Peter, seemed to struggle to find a proper way of referring to him, calling Peter alternately, "a feral child," "the wild boy," "the boy in question," "a most unusual boy," and "a human tabula rasa." The chief examiner also made note that the doctor would be coming to look in on him, and that the staff of the House of Corrections should take care to treat the boy well, give him a room to himself, and try to get him to speak, if possible. The chief examiner also drafted a public notice, describing the boy's appearance, how hunters had caught him in the forest outside Hamelin, and asking for the boy's parents or anyone with information about the boy's origins to come forward.

On the morning when Peter was to be sent away, the chief examiner came to see him. Karl was already in Peter's room, squatting to help the boy get dressed with the assistance of a matron. "How is he?" the chief examiner asked.

"He's fine sir," Karl said, rising.

"Do we have to send him away, sir?" the matron asked, looking at the chief examiner hopefully. She pressed, "The other women and I, we've all grown terribly fond of him since he was brought here, you see. It's true he's not like other boys, and we'd have to teach him many things but-"

"This is a police station, not an orphanage," the chief examiner said gruffly, "we have neither the authority nor the facilities to keep him here."

"I know that sir, but sending him to a prison hardly seems fair."

"Until a more suitable location is found, the House of the Corrections at Celle is the safest, most appropriate place to send the boy. If we sent him to a common orphanage they wouldn't know what to do with him. He is a charming boy, but completely without education. If he is improperly handled, he might escape into the wild again, or become violent."

"He's not been violent with us," the matron said.

"That doesn't mean he isn't capable of violence," the chief examiner said, "...remember, he survived alone in the wild for years."

"But he seems very gentle."

"Supposing he meets someone who is cruel to him- what will happen then? A boy such as this could be capable of anything." The chief examiner shook his head. "Believe me, I have considered the situation carefully."

"So," the matron asked, "why did you come to see him before he leaves?"

"The boy is an unusual case," the chief examiner said, sinking to one knee before Peter, "and as such, I feel a greater sense of responsibility to be sure he is properly taken care of. There is no telling what destiny has in store for him." He looked into Peter's eyes again. This time, the boy smiled at him, reached out, and pinched his large nose. The chief examiner laughed, and pinched Peter's nose in return. Karl and the matron looked at each other in surprise- they had not seen the chief examiner laugh before. But the levity was brief; in the next moment, he rose and said, "Come on then. The carriage is waiting."

If Peter had known where he would be taken next, he might have tried to escape- but innocent Peter did not suspect that he was being taken out of one prison cell only to be taken to another, more permanent one. So he went quietly out of the Hamelin police headquarters and was transported by police carriage to the city of Celle, where he would be kept until the authorities decided his fate. The House of Corrections at Celle was a destination for many troublesome characters, and we can only imagine what Peter saw there when he arrived. Certainly there were all manner of scoundrels and villains present, as well as any number of unfortunate men and boys who had been arrested for lesser crimes. Thankfully, the guards whisked young Peter past the rogues' gallery before any one of them could lay a hook on him, and led him straight to the Juvenile Department, placing him in a private cell there, where he would remain for the indefinite future.

There is not much to say about Peter's time in the House of Corrections other than the fact that it was dreadfully dull. Poor Peter had gone from a carefree life in the wild to the dreary, mundane existence of a prisoner. He had no idea why he was being kept locked up, but he longed for the freedom of the forest, and had no way of knowing when, or if, he would ever be able to enjoy such freedom again. Of course, Peter's tale was not fated to end in the House of Corrections- already wheels were in motion that would guide him far, far away. Our dear friend the doctor had not forgotten about Peter.

Chapter 3: Intervention

When the doctor reached Hanover, he settled his children at a comfortable apartment that was his to use while he was working for his patron, my grandfather, King George. Having seen to it they were properly situated, he then went directly to Herrenhausen Palace, where he was informed that his services would not be required for several days, and that he should return to his apartment and await a summons. This seemed somewhat strange, considering that the letter which had brought him to Hanover had stressed the urgency of his visit, but he was at the King's disposal, so if the King wished for him to wait to be summoned, he would wait.

❊ ❊ ❊

The doctor's relation to my family began eighteen years prior. My mother, after giving birth to my eldest sibling Frederick, had fallen ill with small pox and then pneumonia. My father, George Augustus, out of devotion to my mother, had remained at her side during her illness, until he too contracted small pox. Thankfully, at that time, there was a master physician present in Hanover who knew how to treat the lethal disease, and with the help of his son, he cured my mother and father. Naturally, my family was grateful to the physician, and the House of Hanover kept him in their employ for a number of years, until finally he announced his intention to retire and recommended his son to serve as his replacement. So the physician's son became a doctor to the House of Hanover- the very same doctor that would later discover our wild boy Peter.

The good doctor was favored by my mother, and therefore was present for the births of my sisters, Anne and Amelia, and for my birth as well. When my family had moved from Hanover to London in 1714, a year after my birth, he had been invited to come along, but he had chosen to remain in Germany, having recently started a family of his own. However, he continued to correspond with my mother about scientific and medical matters about which she was interested, and in 1722 advised her to inoculate Frederick, Anne, Amelia and me against smallpox by means of variolation, a technique that was gaining popularity at the time.

In general, because of his history with the family, whenever anyone at Herrenhausen Palace became ill, the doctor was among the physicians who might be called on to help. At the present time, there was an apparent outbreak of influenza that was causing some concern at the Palace, and so the doctor had been asked to come and check on the health of the King and a few courtiers.

The doctor waited for several days at his apartment for a summons from the King. During that time, he played with his children and passed the time by reading the newspapers. One day there was an article that caught his attention. It was about the Wild Boy who had been found in the forest outside Hamelin. Somehow, the doctor and his daughter's role in finding the boy did not make it into print, but the hunters' difficulties in capturing him were described in some detail. The next day, there was more writing about the Wild Boy in the newspaper, and on the following day, the Wild Boy was mentioned in two newspapers. It seemed that the public notices written by the chief examiner had been widely circulated, and had caught the imagination of the German newspaper publishers.

After more than a week of waiting, a summons arrived from the Palace. The King was requesting a private visit from the doctor. The doctor prepared himself quickly and set out for the Palace.

King George greeted him with a smile and said, "Good afternoon, Doctor."

"Your Majesty, it is good to see you again. You look well- how do you feel?"

"For a man of sixty-five years, I feel fine. Your presence here is more a formality than anything else. You see, some of my subjects would like me to return to London soon, but Walpole has things well in hand at the moment, and I have it in mind to remain here a while longer. I am very fond of this place you know."

"Yes of course, Your Majesty. Well you know influenza is an unpredictable illness- it can last for a short time, or a longer time, and even when you seem to have recovered, it can come back again with full force. So I would not make any immediate travel plans until you are fully healthy," the doctor said with a grin.

"We shall have to sit here a while," the King said, "so that no one will doubt you have given me a full examination."

"I could, of course, examine you while we are waiting, if you wish."

"No, that will not be necessary. I would rather hear any news you might have- it is always valuable to hear what people are talking about, outside of the Palace."

"Well," the doctor asked, "have you heard about the Wild Boy who was found in the forest of Hamelin?"

"…No, I have not."

"They are writing about him in all the newspapers now, Your Majesty. But I know more about him than you will read on any of those pages, for I was there was when he was captured, and I helped deliver him to the authorities. It happened while my children and I were on our way to Hanover, and the Wild Boy ended up riding with us in our carriage into the city of Hamelin."

"He rode with you, you say? He is not dangerous then?"

"I don't think so, Your Majesty."

"Well if he isn't dangerous, why do they call him the Wild Boy?"

"Because, Your Majesty, it seems that this boy grew up alone in the wild, without any help. No one knows who his parents are, and he doesn't seem to speak a word of German, English, French, Gypsy, or any other European language. It may be that he knew some words when he was younger, but if so, he has since forgotten

24

them, which means he has survived on his own for years. His skin is tanned from the sun, as he is accustomed to going about naked, his hair is long and unruly, and he seems just as happy walking on all fours as he does on two legs. He can scale a tree as fast as a squirrel, and can leap up high in the air with the grace of a cat. But he is not a beastly character; on the contrary, he is a handsome child, with a charming smile and intelligent eyes. He is quite remarkable, really."

"Indeed. I would imagine the boy would be fascinating from a scientific point of view as well."

"Certainly, Your Majesty."

"How old is the boy?"

"I would guess he is about ten or eleven years old."

"Where is the boy now?"

"It is my understanding that he is being held in the House of Corrections at Celle."

"The House of Corrections? Why? Did he do something wrong?"

"No, Your Majesty. As far as I know he has done nothing wrong. But the boy has no parents to claim him, no home to go to. I offered to take care of him until a permanent solution could be reached, but the authorities-"

"I see." The King paused, and then said, "I think I would like to meet this boy."

❈ ❈ ❈

Later that morning, the Warden at the House of Corrections was making his rounds when he received the surprising news a contingent from the Palace had arrived and was requesting to speak with him immediately. He stopped short and turned his head, looking curiously at the guard who'd brought the news, "From the Palace, you say?"

"They are the King's men, sir. You'd better come quickly."

"Just a moment," the Warden said, pausing and straightening his tie, "...tell me did they say why they had come?"

"No sir."

25

"Did they seem friendly, or hostile?"

"I don't know sir," the guard said. "They didn't seem hostile, but they said it was urgent. King's orders."

❖ ❖ ❖

As he made his way through the House of Corrections, the Warden couldn't help wondering whether this visit would be good news for him, or bad news. It was unusual, that much was certain. Approaching the place where the King's men were waiting for him, the Warden saw there were half a dozen people present. He slowed his pace, wishing to appear calm and unhurried.

"Gentlemen," he said, "welcome to the House of Corrections. I am the Warden. To what do we owe the honor of your visit?"

From among the group of soldiers, a doctor stepped forward and presented himself. "Greetings, Warden. The King has requested that a certain boy currently in your care be released to me, that I may convey him to the Palace to meet the King."

"The King wishes to meet one of our boys?" the Warden asked. "What for?"

"That is the King's business," the doctor said gently.

"Of course, of course," the Warden said, wiping his brow with his handkerchief, "Tell me the name of this boy, whom the King wishes to meet, and I shall have him brought out at once."

"His Majesty wishes to meet the Wild Boy of Hamelin."

"The Wild Boy? You mean the child found recently in the forest of Hamelin?"

"Yes, and I would prefer that you lead me to the place where he is currently being kept, so that I may see if he has been properly cared for."

"...As you wish, doctor."

❖ ❖ ❖

"I arranged for the boy to have a room to himself," the Warden said, as they walked through the prison to the Juvenile Department where Peter was being kept. "He has been fed three times a day, and given periodic opportunities for exercise."

"Has he begun to speak?"

26

"The staff has attempted to communicate with him, even to teach him words, but so far he has shown no capacity for learning. We have had some luck, you know, reforming wayward young people, but I am afraid we are not equipped to educate this boy. I hope it is the King's intention to find a more appropriate home for him." The Warden stopped and said, "Here we are. Guard, please unlock the door."

The guard stepped forward with his keys and opened the door inward. There, squatting bare-chested in the middle of the cell, was the Wild Boy, Peter. When Peter's eyes met the doctor's, a grin immediately spread across his face. Seeing the doctor kneel down, Peter quickly scrambled forward on all fours to meet him. Rising to stand on two feet in front of the doctor, he reached out to touch the doctor's face gently, and laughed. The Doctor gripped Peter's shoulders, smiling. Peter then looked at the other men gathered round, most of whom were dressed in the colorful uniforms of the King's guards, and his eyes widened with interest.

"Have you two met before?" the Warden asked, surprised by Peter's warm reaction to the doctor.

"Yes we have," the doctor said, producing something from his pocket. Peter looked back at the doctor, and saw he held a bar of chocolate in his hand. "Here boy, I have some chocolate for you."

Peter wasted no time in taking the confection from the doctor's hand and happily wolfing it down. "Well he seems to know what chocolate is," the Warden said. The doctor laughed and stood up, taking Peter's hand in his.

"Yes," the doctor said, "...but the first time we met he didn't know. So it would seem he is capable of learning if his interest is sufficiently aroused."

❖   ❖   ❖

Making his way out of the House of Corrections with Peter holding his hand, the doctor was uneasy. On his way to fetch the boy, he had been so focused that he did not take in much of the atmosphere of the prison. But now, walking out with Peter beside him playfully swinging his hand to and fro and dancing

27

gaily, the doctor became acutely aware of his surroundings- the heavy smells, the sounds, the dirt and the faces of the criminals behind bars staring out at him. They were not all bad men- many of them no doubt, had found their way to this place because of desperation and misfortune- but among them there were some who seemed to have lost themselves long ago; men whose eyes glittered like the eyes of serpents, men whose faces had lost all trace of innocence, men whose hands would forever be restless because of the evil they had done. Peter had been kept apart from these men, thankfully- but how long would that have continued, if the doctor had not come to rescue him? Clearly the staff at the prison were ill-equipped to care for the boy and educate him. How long would it have been, before they gave up trying to teach him and condemned him to a life among these ruffians?

Even though he had the King's men with him as he passed through the corridors, the doctor was much relieved when he and Peter were safely out of the House of Corrections. At the gate, he said good day to the warden, then squeezed Peter's hand and headed out toward the carriage that was waiting for them.

A happy sound met Peter's ears as they came into view of the carriage. There, in the windows of the carriage, were the faces of the doctor's three children, gazing out at him and calling to catch his attention.

The doctor's daughter, whose name was Margaret, later wrote of seeing Peter emerge from the prison: *The gates of the House of Corrections opened with a crack, and out of that grim, unhappy place, Peter emerged like a bright spark, bringing warmth and light.*

As soon as he saw us, Peter flew from Father's grasp. We threw open the door of the carriage, Peter bounded inside, and everyone let out a great cheer, surrounding and congratulating him with laughter and smiles. Peter, exultant, tilted his head back and crowed like a rooster.

Climbing up into the carriage after Peter had made his entrance, Father smiled and said, "All right, children- all right. Please sit down now so we can be underway."

28

We all obeyed, except Peter, who stood alone in the center of the carriage, watching as the rest of us sat down. His expression was not one of defiance, but rather of innocence- and after a moment he sat down in the center of carriage, looking curiously around him.

"Come here, boy," I said, tapping the seat cushion beside me gently. Peter smiled, but did not move. The carriage meanwhile, had begun to move. "Come on," I repeated, beckoning him to join me. He imitated my gesture, tapping the floor with one hand and beckoning to me with the other. I laughed. "Father, what shall we do with him?"

"Let him sit on the floor for a while, if that is what he wants. He'll come around eventually, I'm sure."

"May I sit on the floor, Father?" asked Thomas, my younger brother.

"No you may not. Our aim is to educate the Wild Boy, not be educated by him."

Peter had turned his head to listen to Father, and now he crawled over to where Father sat. He stood up and began to pick at Father's clothing, inspecting it with great interest. Father observed this with mild amusement for a few moments, until Peter fished his hand into one of his pockets and drew out what he had been searching for, apparently: a large piece of Father's prized chocolate!

Peter hummed with pleasure at this discovery and Father burst out laughing, but then he snatched it quickly from Peter's hands and said, "Very clever, but this is to be shared." Breaking the chocolate into pieces, he tossed a piece to each of us children and then gave a piece to Peter. "Now then, children," Father said, drawing out his flute, "let us pass the time with some music."

* * *

The trip from Celle to Hanover was as joyful and mirthful as our previous carriage ride had been, and the Wild Boy Peter seemed not to have been at all affected by the time he had spent at the House of Corrections. There was no anxiety in his expressions, no hint of fatigue or desolation in his eyes. If the experience of being imprisoned had troubled him in any way, he seemed to forget it easily enough. Full to the brim with the innocence of youth, he seemed only interested in the present moment, without a care for the future or a worry about the past.

The music of Father's flute fascinated him, and more than once he reached for it, imploring the doctor with his eyes to let him try the instrument. When Father relented and let Peter try his luck with the flute however, Peter was the only one who was pleased with the results. Eventually, Father took the flute back from Peter and asked me to pull out the food basket. This blunted Peter's disappointment at losing the flute, and his attention quickly turned to the contents of the basket, which I was beginning to dole out. He crossed over to where I sat and peered into the basket, sniffing the air with interest. "Here," I said, offering him a small chunk of cheese. "Try this."

Peter was quite hungry as it turned out- which was something my father had expected- but Father had not anticipated the depth of Peter's appetite. It seemed the boy had a bottomless stomach. He chewed upon the food brought from the King's kitchens until there was nothing left, and still he seemed hungry at the end of it all, looking deep inside the basket hoping to find a little bit more.

When it was clear there was nothing to be found in the basket, Peter sank to the floor, disappointed. I could not help but laugh at how pitiable his expression was, but then my heart turned to sympathy as I saw the sincerity in his eyes. "Poor boy," I said, "... they didn't feed you enough in there, did they?"

"They said they fed him three times a day," Father said, "... but we may never know the truth of that. Anyway, I wonder if we had more food, whether he would have stopped eating, even if he was full, or if he would have tried to stuff himself further. Having lived so long in the wild, he might have developed a habit of eating as much as he could when there was good food available, so that his body might have some reserves available, when food became scarce."

"I think I shall sing for him," I said, "...to take his mind off of his appetite." Lowering my head for a moment, I took a deep breath, and then lifted my eyes to meet Peter's and began to sing. It was a good melody- one the whole family knew, and before long we were all singing. Peter smiled and listened for a while, gazing up at me and humming along with the song, then he laid down to rest on the floor of the carriage, curling himself up into a comfortable

position. He continued to look up at me for a few moments, then his eyes closed, his head sank, and he was fast asleep.

"Is he sleeping?" little Thomas asked, in an offended tone.

"Yes he is," I said, "...do keep your voice down."

"How can he sleep at a time like this?" Thomas asked, not lowering his voice one bit.

"Hush!" I hissed at my brother. "He may not have had a good night's sleep since we saw him last. How well do you think you would sleep in a prison cell surrounded by thieves and murderers?"

"Your sister is right," Father said, bending over Peter and covering him with a blanket. "That prison was no place for an innocent child to be kept. Don't be upset that he has fallen asleep so quickly- it is only a sign that he is at ease among us." Taking his jacket off, Father folded it up and placed it beneath Peter's head.

Father resumed his seat and everyone was silent for several moments, until Thomas spoke up again, this time more softly, "... Do you think the King will let us keep him?"

Father looked up at Thomas. "I don't know. But the King is a good man- I am certain he will want to do whatever is best for the boy."

Chapter 4: Herrenhausen Palace

Peter was indeed very tired- he slept for almost a full day after his departure from the House of Corrections. When he finally woke, he found himself in a bed unlike any he had ever known before. After years of living in the forest, he was accustomed to sleeping on rough surfaces- which was why it had not been difficult for him to fall asleep on the floor of the carriage- but this new bed was anything but rough; it was as soft as feathers, and as smooth as silk. It felt strange. Peter sat up, and looked around.

The room that Peter found himself in was richly ornamented in the Baroque style, which meant very little to Peter, but was nonetheless visually stunning. Peter's eyes widened as he gazed at all this opulence, and then he saw the doctor sitting in a chair at the foot of his bed. The doctor smiled at him and said, "Good morning! Welcome to Herrenhausen Palace. You have been sleeping for a long time. Are you hungry?"

Peter did not understand a word the Doctor said, but smiled back at him just the same. Slipping out from under the covers, Peter stood on his bed and hummed briefly. Reaching up with both hands, he touched the top of his head and found a woolen cap.

Taking off the cap, he turned it around in his hands and looked at it with curiosity. Crawling across the bed to where the doctor was seated, he swung his feet off the edge of the bed onto the floor and stood. Holding out the cap, Peter looked at the doctor inquisitively.

"Thank you," the doctor said, accepting the cap from Peter and putting it on his own head. Peter smiled. Standing up, the doctor offered Peter his hand, "Come- let us go and find some food for you."

❖ ❖ ❖

The serving staff of the palace was surprised by the appearance of Peter and the doctor making their way to the kitchen hand in hand. Peter was dressed in his nightgown and danced barefoot down the hall humming loudly, while the doctor, wearing a wool cap that was obviously too small on his head, matched Peter step for step, singing a popular folk song in his fine baritone voice.

"Good morning," the doctor said merrily as they entered the kitchen. "I hope we have not come too late to have some breakfast."

"Begging your pardon, doctor," one of the women there said, "but it is two in the afternoon. Perhaps we could interest you in an early dinner meal?"

"Have you heard about our distinguished guest- the Wild Boy of Hamelin?" the doctor said, still smiling. "He is to meet the King for dinner this evening. I think breakfast is what is called for now. Perhaps some fruit and porridge?"

"This is the Wild Boy?"

"Of course he is," said another one of the women, "just look at that hair of his. Doctor- have you spoken with a tailor about some suitable clothing for the boy?"

"I have," the doctor said. "...Whether the boy is willing to wear the clothing is another matter."

"What about trimming his hair?" the first woman asked.

"Why, so that he will look like all the other boys?" the second woman asked.

"Well I just thought- never mind. Don't you worry doctor, we'll have some breakfast ready for you and the Wild Boy. He's a handsome one, that child."

❖ ❖ ❖

The doctor led Peter into another room to sit down and wait. A few minutes later, the serving staff brought out two platters of food and set them down in front of the guests. Peter's eyes widened as he saw the arrangement of fruit on his platter, and immediately he

33

snatched up a handful of berries and popped them into his mouth. "Mmm," he hummed approvingly, his mouth full.

"Oh my!" one of the serving maids said, shocked by the Wild Boy's lack of manners. "I suppose nobody in the forest ever taught him polite table etiquette."

Peter looked up at the maid, swallowed, and offered her a berry. He smiled, eyes twinkling.

The maid, a petite brunette about nineteen years old, looked uncertain of how she should respond. "I admit I am not an expert on forest etiquette, but I think the polite thing to do would be to eat it," the doctor said, smiling.

Accepting the berry, the maid said to Peter, "Thank you very much." Then she delicately put the berry into her mouth. Peter grinned, and immediately offered her another one. "Oh no- this food is for you!" the maid protested.

Peter still held out the fruit. "Perhaps you had better sit down with us," the doctor suggested, rising from the table and offering the maid a chair.

"Oh no, I couldn't!" the maid said, shaking her head, "I'll get in trouble if I don't report back."

"Please," the doctor said, "accept the fruit and have a seat."

The maid looked back at Peter and sighed, smiling. Taking the berry from Peter's hand, she bit into it and sat down, looking both embarrassed and amused. As she slipped the rest of the berry into her mouth, she bowed her head and confessed to the doctor, "I have never, ever sat down at a table inside the Palace."

Peter's hand appeared before her again now, holding another piece of fruit- a slice of apple this time. The maid looked at it with indecision.

"You hesitate to accept," the doctor said, "...there is no sin in this. What you see here is the fruit of innocence. Eat of it, and you shall be forever young."

The maid smiled at the doctor's words. Turning her head to look at Peter, she accepted the apple. Peter grinned.

It seemed Peter was more interested in watching the maid eat than in eating breakfast himself, and so after she had eaten the piece of apple, the doctor proposed to her, "Perhaps you should offer him something to eat. "

Happy to think she might be able to shift the attention away from herself, the maid picked up a piece of food from the tray and offered it to the Wild Boy, who happily accepted it. The maid, taking a cue from the way he had kept her supplied with food, found another morsel for him immediately. As soon as he had taken this item from her, she had another ready for him. He laughed, and so did she.

In this manner, the Wild Boy finished eating his breakfast. When the maid had fed him the last available bit of food, she rose from her seat, her cheeks still rosy from laughing, and she bid the doctor and the boy farewell. "I really must go now, but thank you- thank you both."

"Thank you, miss," the doctor responded, rising from his seat. "I doubt I could have gotten him to eat all that food so quickly without your help. May I ask your name?"

"Rose," she said, curtsying, "...my name is Rose."

"Thank you Rose. Do you have any plans for the evening?"

"No sir."

"We are scheduled to have dinner with the King. Perhaps you could be persuaded to join us?"

"Sir, I couldn't! A maid eating dinner at the King's table. What would people say?"

"The focus will be on our King and probably Peter. I doubt that their attention will divert to you, Rose. For better or worse, I believe the novelty of the Wild Boy will eclipse any concern regarding your presence at the table."

"But sir-"

"I appreciate your sense of etiquette and decorum, but you must understand by now that the Wild Boy does not share such considerations. Don't you think it would be good if he had a companion to provide some balance?"

35

Rose looked at Peter, who had just now climbed up from his chair onto the table and was reaching toward the chandelier. "I see your point sir."

"Ah," the doctor said, fishing out his pocketwatch. "Here, boy. Have a look at this."

Peter turned his head, saw the gleaming gold pocketwatch, and stopped reaching for the chandelier. He crossed the table and danced up to the doctor, who held out the pocket watch for him to examine.

"It will be a night to remember, I'm sure," the doctor said. "If you are willing to help, I shall make the arrangements for you to attend."

Gazing at Peter and smiling, Rose answered the doctor, "I am willing, sir. Thank you for inviting me."

❊ ❊ ❊

When Rose was gone, the doctor said to Peter, "You seem to have quite an effect on the ladies, Peter."

"Hmm," Peter said, lifting his gaze from the watch to look the doctor in the eyes.

"My daughter can't stop talking about you."

"Hmm."

"Some will dismiss a boy like yourself, with no modern language or trade skills, as a simpleton- an idiot. But how did you manage on your own for so long? No common child could survive as you did alone in the wilderness. No, to be sure, you are no ordinary boy. All the creatures of the forest must have admired your gentility, your courage, your innocence." Peter listened to the doctor's musings, smiling. "Did you ride on the backs of bears, or make the acquaintance of the wary deer? Did you share acorns with the squirrels, as you shared your breakfast with Rose?" Peter laughed. The doctor continued, "...In the wild you must have been a prince." Having said this, the doctor paused for several moments, looking at Peter critically. "We must take care and make sure the King sees that tonight. They were right about your hair-cutting it would be a mistake at this point. The hair is part of your image. But we must strike a balance with your clothing. Yes, we must go to the tailor at once."

❅ ❅ ❅

Twenty minutes later, they were in the office of the Palace tailor. "...Prince of the Forest, you say," the tailor said, circling the Wild Boy and appraising him.

"That's the look we're aiming for."

"Maybe something in green?" the tailor asked. "A bit of red?"

"I will trust your judgment. But the outfit must be ready in a very short time."

"I understand. Normally we do not do work this quickly, but I think we have some items on hand that can be modified to suit the purpose."

"Thank you."

"Thank me when the boy is famous," the tailor said, still gazing at Peter.

The doctor smiled. "The boy is already famous."

Shaking his head, the tailor replied, "Today, all of Hanover is talking about him. But tonight, the Wild Boy dines with the King. Tomorrow, all of Europe will know his name." He paused, and looked at the doctor, "Does he have a name yet?"

The doctor replied, "The King shall give him a name."

"Of course!" the tailor exclaimed. Rubbing his hands together, he said, "...Have no fear Doctor. We shall make sure the Wild Boy is suitably dressed for this momentous evening."

❅ ❅ ❅

While waiting for the tailor to complete his work, the doctor had it in mind to take Peter on a tour of the Great Garden of Herrenhausen. Covering an area equal to fifty city blocks, the Great Garden is one of the largest and finest Baroque gardens in all of Europe, and in the center of it sits a spectacular fountain, which shoots water over a hundred and twenty feet into the air and can be seen from far away. As soon as Peter stepped out of the Palace, spotted the Great Fountain, and heard the sound of the crashing water, he took off running toward it. The doctor, taken

37

off guard by Peter's sudden speed, could do nothing to stop the boy.

The path to the fountain was long and straight, so it seemed there was no danger of losing sight of Peter, but the doctor was soon out of breath and had to slow his pursuit. When the doctor finally did reach the fountain, Peter was nowhere to be seen. His nightclothes, however, had been discarded, and so the doctor could guess easily enough where he was.

Approaching the water, the doctor looked around and just then, Peter popped up at the center of the pool near the fountainhead. Spray from the fountain cascaded around the boy, which frightened the doctor, but Peter did not seem worried by it. The doctor called out to him, "Boy! Come out of there! It's not safe." Peter turned his head and looked at the doctor, but showed no interest in leaving the fountain. Shaking his head, the doctor took his jacket off, jumped into the pool, and waded over to where Peter was swimming. Taking hold of Peter's hand, he said, "I'm sorry, boy, but you must get out of the water. If anything happens to you, I am responsible."

Peter did not resist as the doctor led him out of the pool, but when the doctor wanted him to put his clothes back on, Peter balked. And so the two of them stood there at odds, Peter standing naked and the doctor in his dripping wet clothing, until finally the doctor reached into his pocket, removed his pocket watch, and gave it to Peter. This made Peter happy, and the doctor bent over, picked up his dry jacket from the ground, and put it over Peter's shoulders.

"Come on then. We shall have to tour the Garden another day."

❊   ❊   ❊

The doctor returned Peter to the guest bedroom, took back his coat and then went to find a dry set of clothing for himself. In spite of his sympathy for the Wild Boy, the doctor found himself feeling irritated at Peter for acting so wildly!

He did not have any spare clothes at the Palace, and there was no time for him to return to his apartment, so he went to see the tailor again. When the tailor saw the doctor, his eyebrows lifted in surprise.

"I need some dry clothes," the doctor said, stripping off his wet shirt. "Nothing special, just basic formal clothing."

"What happened?"

The doctor smiled a little as he answered, "The Wild Boy ran off and went swimming in the Great Fountain, and I had to fish him out."

"You don't think he's too much trouble to deal with?" the tailor asked.

Shaking his head, the doctor laughed, "He's a rascal, that's for certain. But I cannot blame him for wanting to swim in that fountain. If I were a boy, I would probably want to do the same." Taking a deep breath, he asked, "How is his new costume coming along?"

"It will be ready in time," the tailor said, going to the shelf and pulling out some items. "...Here, these should fit you well enough."

"Thank you."

❈ ❈ ❈

Dressed in dry clothes now, the doctor returned to the Great Garden without Peter and strolled around for a while. Eventually he came back to the fountain, and sat down.

"Even I, seeing myself as the boy's advocate, lost patience with him here. Was he in any real danger, or was that only an excuse for me to be angry with him? I was annoyed that he made me chase him, annoyed that he disrupted my plan to have a peaceful tour of the Garden, annoyed that I had to fetch him from the water and get my own clothes wet in the process... but did I really have to fetch him out? Having survived for so long alone in the wild, would he really have perished here, had I not intervened?" He sighed and fell silent for a time. "He may be a wonderful boy, but he is still a boy, and he has been taken away from everything that is familiar to him. For better or worse, I am responsible for what happens to him now."

A feeling of sobriety came over the doctor, as he reflected on the events that had led to this point. Was he leading the Wild Boy toward a better life, or had he become swept up in the public fantasy, and ushered the boy into a world that would never accept such unbridled innocence? There was no way to tell, but much would depend on the King's reaction to the boy tonight.

Chapter 5: The Grand Banquet

"Your Majesty, I am pleased to present to you the Wild Boy of Hamelin, Prince of the Enchanted Forest and adopted son of the Fairy Folk."

The Wild Boy stepped forward, dressed in a white silk shirt with a red tie and a fine forest-green velvet suit with brown accents. The King rose from his throne and approached the boy. "Prince of the Enchanted Forest. Adopted son of the Fairy Folk. Wild Boy. Your reputation precedes you, child. All of Germany has been talking about you lately. And yet, no one knows your name." The boy looked up at the King and smiled. The king smiled back, and took a deep breath. "...Henceforth, you shall be known as Peter." Reaching out to take the boy's hand, he shook it and said, "Peter. It is good to meet you."

The boy smiled and said, "...Peter."

The King and the doctor both looked surprised. "That is the first time I have heard him speak, Your Majesty."

Touching his chest, the King bent forward slightly and said to Peter. "King George."

"King George."

Laughing in amazement, the King said, "This is remarkable. Peter, *sprechen sie Deutsche? Parlez-vous Francais? Do you speak English?*" The boy laughed, but showed no sign of understanding the King's words. "No, apparently not. But evidently you are capable of learning to speak." The king paused and said, "Please, let us adjourn to the banquet hall. Dinner is waiting."

"Mmm," Peter said, eyes wandering.

The King walked hand-in-hand with Peter to the banquet hall, followed by the doctor, the maid and a number of courtiers. "...

You know Peter," the King said, looking down at the boy as they walked, "I have a granddaughter in England who is about your age. In fact I have seven grandchildren in England- two boys and five girls. The one I am thinking of is named Caroline, after her mother. The elder boy, Frederick, is almost a man now, and two of the girls are also in a hurry to grow up, I think. But like you, gentle Caroline is in no hurry to become an adult- and that I think, is wise." Entering the banquet hall, Peter gasped at the sight of the feast that had been laid out for them. "I didn't know what type of food you would enjoy, Peter, but I understand you have quite an appetite, so I asked them to prepare a bit of everything for you." Glancing at the doctor and the maid, he asked, "Shall we sit down?"

Rose and the doctor stepped forward to take hold of Peter so that the King could assume his place at the head of the table. After the King had sat down, they helped Peter to be seated. The doctor appeared calm and composed, but the maid was acutely conscious of all the people who were staring at them. She had never been at the center of so much attention, and she felt terribly nervous.

"Tonight," the King said, "We are honored to have Peter, the Wild Boy of Hamelin, as our guest. It seems that he has lived apart from human influence through many of the formative years of childhood, with only wild beasts and fairies to keep him company. In this age of reason and science, he offers us a rare and valuable opportunity to study the raw elements of human nature." The King paused, and smiled, noticing Peter was reaching for some of the food on the table and the maid, Rose, was attempting to stop the boy. Laughing lightly, the King said, "Apparently our Wild Boy Peter is eager to begin eating. Let us not delay then, but let him feast to his heart's content. Doctor, while we begin, perhaps you could share with us a brief account of how Peter was found, and your impressions of him."

"King George," Peter interjected.

"Yes?" the King asked, turning his head to see who had spoken, "Oh, it is you, Peter!"

Peter smiled, holding up a gravy covered morsel in his hand. "King George."

King George stared at the grinning boy and realized, somewhat belatedly, that although Peter had an utter lack of knowledge of the proper uses of tableware, he was nevertheless displaying a natural sense of politeness by offering the first bite of his food to the King. Glancing quickly at the faces of members of the court looking scandalized by Peter's innocent behavior, King George smiled and accepted the food from Peter's hand, and ate it without utensils. "Thank you Peter." He then said to everyone assembled, "In honor of the customs of the Fairy Folk who raised Peter, tonight we will all eat without utensils." At a gesture from the King, the Palace serving staff collected all the forks, knives and spoons from the table. For the most part, everyone accepted this in good humor, and then the King said, "Doctor, you may proceed."

"Certainly Your Majesty," the doctor said. "It was my daughter who found him, actually. She was singing as our carriage passed through the forest of Hamelin, and her voice must have stirred something in Peter's soul, for he came to the edge of the trail and hid himself in a tree to listen to her.

"He was not dressed then as you see him now, but rather was as naked as Adam before the Fall. My daughter spied him there, among the tree branches, and cried out to me that she had seen the Wild Boy!

"Apparently Peter had been seen before, never by an adult, but by other children, and a variety of legends had developed about him, that my daughter had learned from the other girls in our village. It was said that he had been raised by fairies and spoke to animals in their own tongue, as if they were his kin. And he appeared to my daughter just as he had been described, small in stature, tan all over, with unruly hair and the poise of a wild creature, but with bright, piercing eyes that seemed almost magical.

"We stopped our carriage, and tried to fetch Peter down from his tree, but he was unwilling to come down. It was a stroke of good fortune then, that a group of hunters chanced to approach on the road. They agreed to help get Peter out of the tree.

"Peter did not make it easy for the hunters to capture him, however. He escaped the three of them and led them on a chase through the forest, up to a tree where he was sure they would not be able to catch him. You see this was a hollow tree, and so he led them up high into the branches, and then cleverly slipped into the inside of the tree and squeezed himself down to the bottom again, where he emerged and very nearly got away, I am told, but one of the hunters had not gone up into the tree after him, and so was able to catch hold of him, and with the help of the others, lifted Peter up and carried him, wriggling and kicking and tearful, out of the forest and back to the carriage, where my daughter helped calm him down. Together with the hunters, we transported Peter to Hamelin and presented him to the authorities there, who ruled that Peter should be kept in the House of Corrections until a more suitable and permanent arrangement could be made.

"My children- I have two boys and one daughter- all love Peter. To them, he is a fairy tale come to life. I can think of no worse place for such a child to be kept than in the House of Corrections. If no other accommodation can be found, I would gladly care for him myself.

"Peter is to me the very image of human innocence on the verge of knowledge- like Adam and Eve before the Fall, he sees everything without prejudice. When he is generous, it is not because he has been taught that this is good and proper, it is because it is in his nature to share, as you see him even now sharing his food with Rose." The doctor paused, smiling as Rose blushed. "...When he seems heartless, and behaves in ways that are amusing only to him, such as when he abandoned me this morning during our walk only to lead me on a heart-pounding chase culminating in a struggle under the geyser of the Great Fountain, it is not because he has any intent to cause distress, but rather that he is full of joy, of life, and does not comprehend an adult's reluctance to let go of decorum and propriety.

44

"We have all heard tales of the so-called savages found in the New World- how gentle and courteous they are. To be sure, there is a warrior spirit within them, but it is a warm, pulsing, human spirit that breathes universal compassion and goodwill. There is none of the calculation, discrimination and falsehood- what we call sophistication- that we find embedded in the daily intercourse of our society. And we hold the Red Man as inferior to ourselves, because he lacks sophistication. Peter also, shall be viewed by some as inferior to other children, until he has received the same education that our children do. But we know that mere sophistication does not infer excellence. We hold that excellence rests not in the raw elements of human nature, nor in the refinements of society, but in the triumph of spirit transcending the artifice of civilization.

"Thus the Progress of Man is from purity of nature, to education of intellect, to perfection of spirit. But how many in our time can be said to have gone beyond calculation, discrimination and falsehood- how many among us are truly far advanced from the savages? Perhaps we have become too enamored of our sophistication, perhaps we have fallen to the sin of pride and we need to remember that art should not simply be for art's sake, that it should always be aimed at the soul.

"Perhaps," he said in conclusion, "...we have as much to learn from Peter as he has to learn from us. Peter-" the doctor stopped, and looked around quickly, "...where is Peter?" Somehow, Peter had disappeared without anyone noticing.

Rose quickly discovered where Peter was- he had slipped down from his chair and was sitting under the table. "Ah ha," she said, reaching in to try to get him out. But this only caused Peter to crawl away quickly on all fours.

Foolishly, Rose followed Peter under the table. Peter loved to be chased. The two of them raced between the legs of the courtiers from one end of the banquet table to the other, where Peter emerged, minus his shirt and jacket, which he had somehow removed while down there.

45

Someone else, a courtier, tried to catch Peter as he came out from under the table, and so Peter leapt up onto the table to escape the man (Peter was very good at jumping), and flew back across the table to the place where King George sat. Gracefully, Peter managed to avoiding stepping in the food as he ran, but all along the way, the maid and other people tried to catch him, and they made a mess of things.

Landing in front of the smiling King, Peter laughed triumphantly and did a little victory dance. He looked supremely happy.

The King, motioning for Peter's pursuers to stand down, reached out with both hands to help the boy down from the table. Seeing this gesture, Peter also spread his arms, and stepped forward to hug King George.

The King was surprised, but did not reject the hug. Smiling, he hugged Peter back, and then noticed Peter's weight shift, and heard a little snoring sound. "The boy has gone to sleep!" King George said in surprise.

"Here, Your Majesty, I will take him," the doctor said.

"That's all right, let the boy rest as he is, but help me to sit down again." So King George settled himself back in his chair, with Peter's arms still wrapped around him, and the dinner went on a while longer. Eventually, it was time for everyone to retire, and so, with the doctor at his side, the King carried Peter out of the banquet hall.

Chapter 6: Wild Boy

To serve at the Palace was an honor accorded only to individuals of high character, outstanding merit, excellent qualifications, or high family status. Rose was known to the King be a kindhearted, well-intentioned young woman, whose father's work as an Ambassador had kept him away from home for much of her childhood.

Rose had been just thirteen when her father died, but she took it on herself to seek employment at the Palace, to help support her mother and younger siblings. Working at the Palace, Rose had earned a handsome wage for her family for the past six years and learned many valuable lessons about life at court.

Now, in the aftermath of the banquet, in view of the colorful disarray that she had created trying to catch Peter, one would expect Rose to be transferred from her duties as a Palace maid. But the King, in his wisdom, felt that Rose had made a genuine connection with Peter, and took her role as his companion seriously. Therefore, after conferring with the doctor, who agreed, King George decided to appoint Rose to help look after Peter.

Peter would not be invited to a banquet again for some time, but he became a familiar face to everyone in Herrenhausen Palace, because the King had decided to keep him as a ward under the doctor's supervision. For his part, Peter was mostly well behaved in the period that followed the banquet, and by the King's orders, he was granted freedom to wander the Palace. This brought him into contact with a variety of personalities. The kitchen staff, for the most part, doted on Peter, offering him sweet treats, fruit and other attractive morsels, whenever he wandered into their midst. When they tried to usher him out of the kitchen, treat in hand,

47

Peter was compliant, but later he would sometimes slip back in for seconds, or even thirds. The guards of the Palace, who stood in place and did not move or change their expression through most of the day, greeted the Wild Boy with a friendly smile, "Hello, Peter!" and some added, "Hello Rose!" which made the pretty maiden blush. Over the next several months, people became accustomed to Peter's presence and the mood in the Palace brightened considerably. Smiles were more frequent, and laughter could be heard from one room or another throughout the day. The stately Palace and the elegant Baroque gardens that surrounded it took on a happy atmosphere, as people began to approach each other with warmer expressions and gentler tones.

What had happened at the dinner table was not forgotten, but people in the Palace mostly looked back on it lightheartedly, and in a way, the epic disaster of the banquet made it easier to forgive Peter for any small mistakes he may have made afterward.

❀ ❀ ❀

Peter had some odd habits, which revealed themselves over time. For example, he did not stay in his bed at night. In the evening, he would be carefully tucked under the covers by the doctor or by Rose but in the morning he could always be found curled up on the floor. Out of concern for Peter's health, the doctor decided to set a plush rug in the corner of the room, where Peter was often found sleeping, to make this a warmer and more comfortable location. Peter also seemed to not like clothes very much, and to shed them whenever possible. The Palace tailor made outfits for him that were as comfortable as possible, but after some consultation with the doctor, also began to consider ways of securing his clothes more effectively.

There was one incident, not long after the banquet, that caused a minor stir. Somehow, while covered from head to toe in bubbles from his daily bath, Peter slipped past the doctor and ran down the hall, with the doctor chasing after him. Rose, who had been waiting outside, joined the pursuit and eventually caught hold of Peter, but slipped on the trail of water and bubbles that Peter had left behind him, and the two of them fell to the floor and slid a short distance before coming to a stop. When the doctor was able to catch up with them, he helped Rose to her feet, then led Peter back to the bath while putting his jacket over Peter's shoulders.

❊   ❊   ❊

The doctor and Rose made efforts to teach Peter to speak, but these efforts met with limited results. Of course they understood that Peter had lived in the wild for many years, and so it would take him time to adjust, but sometimes it was troublesome that he could not tell them what he was thinking. For example, one day Peter became very anxious, and spent much of the day and night huddled in the corner of his bedroom. They had tried to console Peter and to understand what was troubling him, but there didn't seem to be anything specifically wrong with him.

The doctor stayed with Peter through the night, and watched the Wild Boy toss left and right restlessly, until eventually, the doctor fell asleep in his chair. He was awakened by a touch on his shoulder. The doctor opened his eyes and Peter smiled at him, then ran to the window and touched the glass. The window glowed bright white. Rubbing his face with his hands, the doctor rose and went to look out the window. As he approached, he saw that the window sill was white, and the world outside had been blanketed with snow. In the air, snowflakes still drifted gently down. "It snowed!"

Peter looked up at him and grinned, taking his hand and pulling toward the door. It dawned on the doctor that perhaps Peter had known the snow was coming, as animals are often able to sense storms days in advance.

Following Peter toward the door, the doctor said, "…You knew the snow was coming, didn't you? That's part of how you survived all those years in the wild- by learning to sense the changes in weather, the way the animals do. Knowing when to seek shelter, before a snowstorm."

Peter reached for the doorknob and twisted it. Pulling the door open, he gave a shout and began leading the doctor out into the hall.

Peter's tug was insistent and the doctor had to move quickly to keep up, but still the doctor could not help but wonder aloud, "Here we have been trying to teach you our language, Peter. If only you could teach us yours. We think of the air about us as merely empty space, but it speaks to you. You are the only one who knew that the first snow of winter would come today, Peter." They reached the doors that led out to the Great Garden before the doctor stopped to consider that Peter was dressed only in a nightgown. "Wait," he said, "you should be dressed more warmly before you go outside." But Peter let go of his hand, opened the door and slipped out before the doctor could stop him.

"YAHOO!" he cried out, throwing off his nightgown as he ran out into the falling snow.

The doctor looked to an attendant who happened to be nearby. "Your name is Albert, isn't it? Go and fetch me a coat, please. And tell Rose to join me in the Garden."

❖ ❖ ❖

When Rose ventured out of the Palace into the new, moist snow, she saw the doctor standing stiffly in the midst of the garden, clutching his coat around him tightly, while bare-skinned Peter danced and rolled about in the snow, tossing clumps of snow into the air and laughing. "How long has he been out here like this?" Rose asked, coming up beside the doctor.

"Almost a quarter hour, I think," the doctor said.

"Aren't you afraid he'll catch cold?"

"I suspect I am more likely to catch a cold than he is," the doctor said. "Think how many winters he spent out in the forest. He knows what snow is. He knew it was coming before any of us did. Remember how he curled up yesterday, the way dogs sometimes do before a storm?"

Rose's eyes widened, "But how-?" Her question was cut short by a snowball pelting the side of her coat. She turned to see Peter

50

laughing and preparing another. "Peter, you rascal!" Quickly she bent down and scooped up some snow for herself, packing it into a ball. She was not quick enough, however. Peter's second snowball hit her before she could launch her retaliatory attack.

Peter roared with laughter, until Rose's snowball caught him square in the chest. Then Rose laughed, and Peter shook himself. Of course, Peter was not put off for long- he soon had another snowball at the ready, as did Rose. The two of them pelted each other with snowballs for several minutes before Rose tired of the sport, and approached Peter. "Peter," she said, taking his hand in hers, "Peter. Come inside now. We shall have some hot chocolate and sit by the fire. I will read you a story."

The doctor watched as Rose led Peter back to the Palace. "Oh- it's that easy, is it? He wouldn't come inside when I asked him," the doctor grumbled.

Rose smiled and said, "Lend Peter your coat doctor, so he won't be so much of a spectacle when he gets inside."

The rest of that day was spent indoors, bundled up with blankets beside a warm fire. As promised, Rose read to Peter, and though we don't know for sure how much he understood of the book, he listened to her voice and watched her face intently until he gradually fell asleep.

❃ ❃ ❃

Over the holidays, Rose and Peter spent a good deal of time together. The King invited Peter to breakfast or lunch occasionally, and sometimes the doctor's children came to visit in the afternoon, but besides the doctor, the person who was with Peter most often was Rose.

All through the winter months, Rose kept up the practice of sitting by the fire with Peter and a book telling him stories. The doctor stopped to listen one afternoon out of curiosity, and heard her say, "...then the Mermaid said to the Pirate, 'I would rather perish with the boy than go with you.' And the Pirate said, 'So be it,' and sealed them both up inside the treasure chest. Then the pirate's crew got together to lift the chest up, and with a nod from their captain, they cast the chest overboard into the sea. The chest was so heavy, it sank in the water in spite of the air inside, and in seconds it was gone from view, disappearing into the deep blue depths. If the boy and the mermaid were unable to free themselves, they would surely perish." Peter's eyes were wide with interest. "But- I can't tell you what happened- you'll have to find out next time." She stopped and closed the book. Peter shook his head and put his hand on the book. She laughed and said, "You want to hear more now, do you?" Raising her eyes, Rose saw the doctor and said, "Hello. I was just telling Peter a story."

"Don't stop on my account," the doctor said. "What book are you reading?" Rose smiled and offered up the volume for the doctor to examine. He read the title aloud, "*Erucarum Ortus Alimentum et Paradoxa Metamorphosis*- a study of the curious life cycle of butterflies by Maria Sibylla Merian. I did not realize that pirates and mermaids factored into this book." He handed it back to her.

"Yes well, Peter likes the pictures."

"He seems to like the story too."

"It is a story about him."

"About him, you say?" the doctor sat down.

"Yes well, we ran out of adventure books to read some time ago. I wasn't sure what to do. There were some books we read more than once- *Robinson Crusoe* in particular we have reviewed many times."

"You mean the new book by the English author, Daniel Defoe?"

Rose nodded, "I found a copy in the library. Peter never seems to tire of that book, but for me life on Mr. Crusoe's island was getting stale. Then I thought- Peter is not the sort of boy to have a boring life. He must have had a great many adventures before he came to stay with us. So I began telling him about his own adventures."

"...Which involve pirates and mermaids?"

"Among other things, yes."

"I did not realize Peter's range of experience was so broad."

Rose smiled, "Neither did I, until we began exploring together. Peter's not much of a talker, as you know, but he gives me hints, and gradually I have been piecing the story of his life together. The mermaid for example came into the story as Peter and I were reviewing the legend of *Melusine*. He kept pointing to the picture of the girl with the fish tail, as if he knew her. And the pirates, well- for some reason King George seems to have a number of books involving pirates, not only *Robinson Crusoe*. And Peter is fascinated by the pirate pictures."

"Some time I should like to hear more of this story. But I think it is time for Peter to go to bed."

❖ ❖ ❖

One afternoon Peter came into a chamber where the King and a number of his advisors were discussing a letter from Emperor Charles VI of Austria. "If Charles doesn't like that we have made alliance with France and Prussia, then he should not have allied with Philip of Spain and promised him Gibraltar." Noticing Peter had entered the room and was solemnly listening to the conference, King George stopped and said, "Why hello, Peter."

"Begging your pardon, Majesty, he slipped into the room before I could stop him," Rose said.

"Is the Prince of the Enchanted Forest not our guest? Did I not grant him freedom to wander about this Palace? There is no need to apologize, Rose. Now Peter, come here and let me show you Europe."

Seeing the King beckon to Peter, the courtiers stepped aside, allowing the boy to approach the conference table, where a grand map of the world was spread, with various points marked. King George put a hand on Peter's shoulder, pointed and said, "This is Hanover, where you and I are now. And this is England, the heart of the British Empire, where our Parliament has recently ratified a mutual-defense treaty I signed last year, together with France and Prussia. Our treaty was precipitated by an alliance formed in Vienna between Charles of Austria and Philip of Spain. Philip is an unhappy man who thinks that he ought to have been allowed to wear two crowns at once- the crown of Spain and the crown of France- and his wife is even more ambitious than he is. But the French shall keep their independence, and the British Empire shall not be eclipsed by the Spanish. You see Peter, in foreign affairs, there is usually more than one way to solve a problem, and strategy involves knowing which pieces to move, at what time."

Peter, who had been watching as King George gestured here and there on the map, now pointed to a different location. "Ah," the King said, "America. The New World. You see we have some colonies along the Atlantic coast there, and then you see Newfoundland and Rupert's Land up in the north, and further down in the Caribbean and along the Gulf Coast we have other colonies. I think you would like America, Peter.

"In America there are vast expanses of wild territory, ruled only by the native Indians, who live in harmony with nature. Like you, the Indians call the animals of the forest their brothers, and do not spend their lives constantly worrying about empires and warfare- or at least that is how they seem to have lived until we arrived. But on the whole they are a peaceful lot, and there is so much empty land in America that there needn't be conflict with the Indians for some time to come."

Peter pointed to small markers scattered across the Atlantic. "There you have our trade routes, and those of the French and the Spanish, across the high seas. The ships of the British Navy guard our routes, against our rival governments and against pirate ships, of which there are many.

"Pirates are men who believe it is more profitable to work for themselves than for any particular king or country, and for a lucky few, this is true. For the rest, the profits gained are quickly offset by the hazards of their lifestyle. A pirate's life is full of dangers and uncertainty, but for the last seventy-five years, while the trade routes have been growing, there have been many young men willing to take such risks. Some are Englishmen, some are Arabs, Frenchmen or Spaniards. A handful of these pirates, such as Henry

Morgan of Jamaica, were useful to us at one point or another, but now the age of pirates is being brought to an end. Most of the clever ones have already retired. The economic interests of all nations demand an end to piracy, and so all pirates who still dare to sail the trade routes are being systematically hunted down. As King of England, I support this. But one cannot help but consider the future- what will it be like when all the wild places of the earth have been taken over by civilization, and there is no more room for Indians, Pirates, and Wild Boys?

"The world is changing Peter, and we must be prepared to change with it. There was a time when Europe was all we knew, all we could ever hope to conquer. Now, although we must guard our land in Europe, the future lies in the colonies, and in control of the sea trade routes. Whoever controls the seas controls the wealth of all continents. Which is why Philip desires to regain Gibraltar, so that he can control access to the Mediterranean Sea, and why we shall ensure that he never does."

King George patted Peter's shoulder, and offered him a bit of chocolate, "Here Peter, you have been a very good listener, and have allowed me for a few minutes to set aside my concerns about the machinations of Charles and Philip. Now, thanks to you, I am ready to write my response to Charles. But a boy should not be troubled with a king's worries, so it is time for you to go with Rose."

Munching on the piece of chocolate, Peter smiled at the King, and then looked at Rose, who had stepped forward to take Peter's left hand. "Come along, Peter," she said.

"King George," Peter said, holding out the chocolate in his right hand for the King to take back.

"Thank you," the King said, accepting it back from Peter. After a moment's hesitation, he took a small bite out of it and smiled. Peter grinned, and then turned to leave with Rose.

❖ ❖ ❖

At times when King George had something weighing on his mind, he would pace the halls of the Palace, with his hands drawn

55

behind his back and his head bowed slightly, deep in thought. The King, like every other person, needed time occasionally to be alone with his thoughts, and the staff of the Palace was usually sensitive to this. By his posture and his expression, the staff knew not to disturb him, or even acknowledge his presence, if possible. One day in early spring, however, as King George was walking with the usual posture and expression that told everyone he needed privacy, he noticed people staring at him and smiling. So, he smiled back and said good morning. They responded to his greeting warmly, and then, still smiling, they resumed whatever it was they had been doing, and the king resumed his thoughtful walk, his expression becoming somber again. This same thing happened several times during his walk, and the King quietly wondered aloud if he wasn't doing something properly, because no one seemed able to ignore him as they usually would.

What the King did not realize was that somewhere in the midst of his pacing, Peter had fallen in behind him, and was walking with the very same pensive expression and posture that he displayed. What was more, Rose was following behind Peter, anxious that the Wild Boy would cause some sort of trouble but also unsure whether she should intervene or not- for the King had said Peter should be allowed to wander free.

Finally, Peter gave himself away. The King said good morning to a wide-eyed courtier, and before the courtier could respond, Peter filled in, "Guten Morgen!"

King George stopped and spun around. "Ah-ha!" he cried out. Peter halted walking and looked up at King George curiously, his arms still crossed behind his back as the King's had been. King George grinned at the boy's posture, and inquired, "Just how long have you been following me like this, Peter?"

"Several minutes sir," Rose answered. "He fell in behind you and I didn't know what to do."

"Well don't worry," the King said to Rose, "there's no real harm in it- I just came to realize why everyone was smiling as I passed them this morning."

"Shall I take him away now, sir? I'm sorry if he's embarrassed you in any way."

"No- not at all. If Peter wishes to walk with me, let him walk with me." Crossing his arms behind his back again, King George resumed walking, this time with Peter at his side.

"You are very kind, Your Majesty," Rose said, following from behind. "...I always worry that somehow Peter will make you lose your temper and send him away, and I would be very sorry for that, because I have grown rather fond of him. And because I am responsible for him, of course."

"Is that what is always worrying you?" King George asked, glancing over his shoulder as he walked. "Well, Rose," he said, continuing forward, "I am glad you are concerned for Peter. But, I have also grown rather fond of the Wild Boy. He helps me remember what it is to be young. Do you feel that also, Rose?"

"I would like to think that I am still young, Your Majesty."

"Ah! Yes, of course. We would all like to think that of ourselves. But the truth is that one needn't be long in years to have left childhood behind. The innocence of youth is a condition of the heart. If we cannot put aside our worries, our cares and desires, if we cannot breathe the fresh air and recall our original proportions, then it is merely vanity to think of ourselves as being young. As long as we can remember, then we are not far from Peter's age. But to remain young- not to drift from our natural condition- that is very difficult to do. Being like a bright, clear mirror, reflecting always the innocence and joy of our creator- that is the original state of mankind. You can see it in the eyes of a child- it is a kind of brightness. But by the age of ten or twelve, the light has faded for most boys and girls. By nineteen or twenty, the light may be totally obscured. So, Rose," the King said, drawing to a halt, and turning back to face the maid, "...take care that you keep your heart clean and bright. Do not think, simply because you are given to watch over Peter, that you have nothing to learn from him." Pausing, King George looked down into Peter's eyes and asked,

57

with a smile, "How many boys born of common parentage have walked side by side with a King? Peter is special."

Peter smiled back at the king, then threw his head back and crowed like a rooster. "Uh-oh," said Rose, anticipating Peter's next move. "Peter, wait!"

In a flash, Peter was gone, and Rose started after him. "Excuse me, Your Majesty!" she said, as she raced past the King. Bemused, King George watched her go after Peter, and then, after a pause, he resumed walking and returned to his private thoughts.

❂ ❂ ❂

Peter liked Rose. Though older, she was not much bigger than he, and when she looked into his eyes, she always smiled. She tried her best to keep him out of trouble and to teach him sensible things, like how to use table utensils, but there was a part of her that seemed to appreciate him as he was, wild and untamed. She became more of a friend than a nurse to him, and often walked or danced hand in hand with him through the halls of the Palace or down the paths of the Great Garden. At midday, they would sit in one of the big, cozy, cushioned chairs and she would read to him from a storybook (or at least she would tell him a story using the book as a reference), and Peter always listened attentively, looking back and forth between the book and her face.

Rose had competition for the Wild Boy's attention, however. The doctor's children came to visit on a number of occasions, and had picnics in the Great Garden with Peter, Rose and their father. At such times, the children, and Margaret in particular, would monopolize Peter's focus. They played chase in the open spaces of the garden and hunted each other amongst the hedges of the Labyrinth, and tried to teach Peter a variety of other games with varying degrees of success. Rose and the doctor would occasionally be drawn into whatever game was being played, but more often they sat on the grass or on a bench, entertaining each other with conversation as they watched the children. When the children were tired enough, they would return, breathless and happy, and Rose would tell them an episode of Peter's apocryphal

58

adventures. This was something the doctor had encouraged, after he had discovered her skill as a storyteller.

Rose liked the doctor. She might not have gotten the chance to know him, had it not been for Peter, but she appreciated his wit, his sense of compassion, his calm presence, and his ability to relate to children. Rose had come from a large family, and her father had often been absent from the home. While her brothers and sisters had married, Rose remained single. Of course she'd had suitors try to win her affection, but she'd never been convinced to marry one, partly because she doubted they would be good fathers.

Sitting beside the doctor one afternoon, Rose reflected that his wife had been very lucky to find him. Then it occurred to Rose that she had never met the doctor's wife. "Doctor," she asked, "where does your wife reside?"

The doctor glanced at Rose, and then looked away, and said, "My wife passed away several years ago. She is in Heaven now."

"Oh!" Rose exclaimed, "...I am so sorry. Then, you have had to raise Margaret and the boys all on your own?"

"Correct." The doctor looked back at Rose and said, "I miss Edith, but then I look at my children, and I see her in them. They are her greatest gift to me, and my source of consolation. They sustain me, as much as I sustain them."

"It must be hard though," Rose said, "...My father was seldom at home, so my mother had to do most of the work of raising us children. I helped, as much as I could, but I always thought, a house ought to have both a father and a mother in it."

Looking away again, the doctor said, "I couldn't bring myself to marry again, after my wife's death. Maybe I just didn't meet the right person." After a moment, he turned his gaze back to Rose, and acknowledged in his mind for the first time what had been gradually formulating in his heart. He liked Rose. He didn't yet know how to express this to her, but it was clear to him now, and a choice suddenly loomed large in his mind. He worried what it would mean, if he told Rose how he felt.

Rose and the doctor were both silent, then Peter interrupted, appearing out of nowhere. He was soaking wet, and grinning ear to ear. "Peter, what have you gotten yourself into?" Rose asked, laughing at Peter's appearance and expression. In lieu of an answer, Peter reached for her hand and the doctor's and drew them to their feet. Then he began to dance between them, and swung their arms to and fro, encouraging them to join him. The other children, having caught up with Peter, laughed and joined in, taking up hands with each other and with Rose and their father.

So the adults were thus drawn to cast their cares aside and dance together with the children, and the conversation sparked by chance between them would not be addressed again for some time. But each looked at the other differently from that point on.

❖ ❖ ❖

"Have you noticed the change in the palace since Peter has arrived, Doctor?" the King asked the doctor one morning at breakfast.

Roused from private thoughts, the doctor responded smartly, "I have, Your Majesty. It seems Peter has cast a spell over all of us. Even the most stonefaced courtiers have begun to smile."

"I wonder if the boy might be able to have a similar effect on the English court."

"…I suspect he would, Your Majesty."

"And what are they saying about Peter in the local newspapers?"

"The Wild Boy continues to be a popular subject of journalistic inquiry," replied the doctor. "If anything, fuel has been added to the fire now that he is living in the Palace and has been given a name."

The King said, "Apparently news of Peter has spread to England already."

"Really?"

King George nodded. "The English are apparently becoming as enchanted as the Germans by the stories being printed in the newspapers about Peter. Something about him has captured the public imagination."

"Well, just the idea of Wild Peter dining with King George is so novel, so fantastic! And of course, how Peter was able to survive in the wild is a question everyone is proposing their own answer for. Some having him being raised by wolves, others put forward bears or deer, and some are entertaining the idea of fairies. But what everyone really wants to know is what will happen next."

"In all the talk about Peter, I have also noticed that newspaper editors seem to have finally forgotten about the South Sea Bubble collapse of 1720."

"Well, how long can a story about a bubble last anyway?" the doctor said, eliciting a smile from the King. "Peter is a much more fascinating topic." Pausing, he asked, "Are you considering a return to London soon?"

"Not just yet," King George said, "but soon, I think."

"What will become of Peter, when you go?"

"I haven't decided yet."

❖ ❖ ❖

One day in early spring, the doctor invited Rose to join him for dinner with Margaret, Samuel, and Thomas at their apartment. Rose happily accepted the invitation, and volunteered to help with the cooking. "Another time perhaps," the Doctor said. "This time, just be our guest. Margaret and I will prepare everything." Rose consented and promised to come at the appointed hour. "But what about Peter?" Rose asked.

"Find someone responsible who can look after Peter for the evening," the doctor said.

Rose had a friend, Josephine, who also worked at the Palace. So Rose asked Josephine to keep an eye on Peter that evening, and went home early to decide what to wear to dinner.

❖ ❖ ❖

When Rose arrived at the apartment, the doctor opened the door and drew in a deep breath at the sight of her. "Hello-" he began to say, before being interrupted.

"Rose you look beautiful!" little Thomas said, having come to the door with his father.

61

The doctor laughed and Rose smiled. "…He took the words from my mouth."

Blushing, Rose asked, "May I come in?"

"Yes- yes, of course. The meal is almost ready. Please come in and make yourself at home."

"Hi Rose," Samuel said, standing at the dinner table with plates in his hands.

"Dinner's almost ready," Margaret called from the kitchen.

A few minutes later, Rose and the family were all seated together around the table. Rose complimented Margaret on the feast she'd prepared. Margaret beamed. The candlelight in the dining room danced and flickered in the eyes of the children and around the soft, cosy dining room. Then the doctor invited Rose to say grace. Everyone put their hands together and Rose, bowing her head slightly, said, "…Thank you Lord, for this food, for your enduring kindness, and for leading Peter into our lives."

"Amen."

The meal was full of jovial conversation and laughter. Everyone was as happy as if Peter was right there amongst them, for you see, it was true what the King and the doctor had observed- Peter had a way of infecting people with happiness that lingered even in his absence. The effect was stronger for some people than it was for others, but all of the company gathered here had come to love and trust Peter, and therefore his influence on them was very strong- strong enough, perhaps, to last them to the end of their days.

After dinner, everyone worked together to clean up the dishes, and then the doctor and Rose put the children to bed. "Good night Rose," said Thomas.

"Good night, Thomas."

"Good night Rose," said Samuel.

"Good night Samuel."

"Good night Rose," said Margaret.

"Good night Margaret," Rose said, "and thank you for dinner."

"You can come over again for dinner any time you like," Margaret said.

"Thank you," said Rose, "I'd like to come again. Maybe next time I'll help with the cooking."

"That would be nice," Margaret said.

"Good night children," Rose said.

The children responded, "Good night Rose. Good night Father."

❊ ❊ ❊

The doctor closed the door to the children's nursery, and then returned with Rose to the living room, hand-in-hand. Finally they were alone, and the doctor searched his thoughts for the words he had planned to say to her, "Rose, I-"

At that moment a knock was heard at the door. Rose looked at the doctor curiously, "Who could that be?"

"I don't know," the doctor said, releasing her hand and going to answer the door, "Who's there?"

"Albert, sir- from the Palace, sir."

The doctor opened the door, "Albert, what brings you here at this hour?"

"Terribly sorry sir, but it's about the Wild Boy, Peter. He's missing."

"Missing?" Rose said, coming up beside the doctor, "but I left Josephine to watch over him."

"I know- I mean- Josephine had Peter in the Palace library and he was sitting very peacefully, so she- I didn't think it would matter if she left him alone for a few minutes. You know, he's been very well-behaved recently. Josephine and I- well, when we came into the room again, Peter was gone- escaped out the window."

"Out the window? Are you sure?"

"The door was shut."

Rose's eyes widened. "The door was shut?"

"We should go," the doctor said, "I'll fetch my coat and your shawl."

As quickly as they could, they set out with Albert for the Palace. A search team had already been mobilized, but the doctor

63

and Rose joined in the effort, searching the area surrounding the Palace long into the night.

❊   ❊   ❊

Morning came, and still Peter had not been found. Rose was distraught. "I'll never forgive Josephine," she said to the doctor, as they returned wearily to the Palace.

"Honestly, Rose," the doctor said, "though I am worried that we do not know where Peter is, when I think about it, I am surprised something like this did not happen sooner. Peter is accustomed to living outdoors alone, with no one to prevent him from wandering from one place to another. These past few months, he has lived completely out of his element. It would seem perfectly natural for him to be curious about his life in the forest and want to go there again. Certainly, if Josephine had been more watchful, he might not have slipped away last night, but it could just as easily happened another day. All of us had begun to take Peter's presence in our lives for granted."

"We've been with him every day since his arrival at the Palace," Rose said. "...Do you think he might have left because we weren't there yesterday?"

"That is my point, Rose," the doctor said, coming to a halt. "We will not be able to be there every day of Peter's life. We can only do our best in the time we have. I feel terrible that he is missing, but we must remember that Peter came from the wild, and we have no way of knowing precisely what goes on in his mind. We searched all around near the Palace, because a normal child would be unlikely to travel very far from home, but Peter isn't a normal child, and this isn't his home. Who's to say he hasn't gone back to the Enchanted Forest?"

"How could he know where Hamelin is?"

"How do the birds know where to fly at the turning of the seasons? I don't know. But spring is in the air, and that could have as much to do with Peter's sudden departure as any other reason you can conjure." The doctor paused, "Rose I am sorry that Peter is missing, but- I am not sorry to have had dinner with you last night."

Rose paused, "...Well, I had a wonderful time too, right up until the news came about Peter. I trusted Josephine to look after him, and obviously that was a mistake I regret. I feel awful right now. I guess I need to get some rest."

"We both do," the doctor said.

"I hope they find Peter soon," she added.

Nodding, he told her, "They are planning to expand the search this morning. Hopefully it won't be long before they locate him."

❖ ❖ ❖

That day, search parties spread out over all of Hanover, trying to find Peter. But Peter was nowhere to be found. By order of the king, the search continued the next day, and the day after that.

Where had Peter gone? What had inspired him to leave the Palace? No one but Peter knew the answer to these questions- and he wasn't telling.

Several days after his disappearance, Peter was said to have been spotted in the forest amongst a group of deer. The deer were perfectly at ease with the Wild Boy in their midst, but they took flight when someone called out to Peter, and Peter fled as well. The people in the search party were not as fleet of foot as Peter and the deer were, so they lost sight of the Wild Boy, and almost despaired, but they pressed forward into the forest and finally discovered Peter at ease in the branches of a tree, eating a piece of honeycomb and watching the search party come toward him.

Having been given clear instructions, the search party did not immediately try to force Peter from the tree. Instead, they had some chocolate at the ready, and attempted to lure him from the tree with it, while sending one of their number back to town to report. However, Peter was not easily lured, and eventually, they had to bring an axe to cut down the tree in order to get hold of him.

Peter did not immediately understand what the people were doing as they began to cut at the tree, but was ready to bolt as the

65

tree began to fall. To his dismay, he was not quick enough in this case, and the members of the search party were able to catch and hold him. He struggled with them briefly, and then waited to see what was going to happen next.

Thankfully, Rose and the doctor arrived soon afterward, and Peter was visibly relieved to see them. Thus his return to the Palace was not an unhappy experience. Wrapping him in a warm blanket, they comforted him with food and song, and held him gently as they walked back to the carriage. They were met on the road by other members of the search party who were happy that Peter had been found and was all right, and so eventually they all found their way back to the Palace.

❊   ❊   ❊

What Peter had done in the time since he left the Palace was something no one could account for, but I believe the doctor's intuition regarding Peter's motives was not far from the mark. Rose was also of this same opinion.

Knowing Peter, I imagine that for the past several weeks, he had indeed felt the changing of the seasons, as all creatures of the wild do. Though he was far from home, he knew that the ice that covered over the brook in winter had melted long ago and the crystal water was now burbling merrily through the Enchanted Forest. He knew the ducks had returned from their winter vacation, and that their splashing and frolicking and quacking in the brook was putting the wild boar in a bad mood. Peter looked forward to the boar's bad moods, because they always ended in the most exciting chases. The squirrels, meanwhile, had emerged from hibernation, and would be out foraging for food, having exhausted their winter supply of nuts. The Mother Bear and her cubs also would have woken from their winter sleep by now, and would be sniffing about the forest, seeking the nest of the honeybees. Peter could not help but lick his lips at the thought of the broken honeycomb. The bears always left a little share for him when they were done- would that share go to waste now?

All these memories danced in Peter's mind in his quiet moments at the Palace. Yet he was happy with all the new friends he had made, and there were so many pleasant things to do at the Palace that it was easy to forget what was happening back in the Enchanted Forest. Ultimately, I imagine, it was not the thought of the bears and the honeycomb, or the squirrels, or the wild boar, or the ducks in the burbling brook that had roused Peter that fateful evening and made him leave his newfound friends at the Palace behind. It was the call of the Deer King.

Now, normally deer are not particularly vocal animals, but on that evening, the Deer King was restless. He was restless because the does were restless, and the does were restless because they missed Peter. Peter had been a friend to the whole deer herd, and for the last several months of winter, he had been absent from their lives. With spring beginning, the herd needed to start preparing for a new generation of fawns, but first, the Deer King had to put the does' hearts at ease, and for that, he wanted to resolve the question of what had become of their beloved Wild Boy.

So, the Deer King had wandered far from his usual range, bellowing Peter's forest name into the wind, and when Josephine had carelessly left Peter alone by the open window, the wind carried his voice to Peter. "PAAAN... PAAAN..." and the Wild Boy lifted his head to listen.

The rest followed quite naturally. Peter climbed out of the library window, then leapt to the ground and vanished into the night. He stripped off his clothes as he went, for they restricted his movements uncomfortably and it would feel awkward, going to the Deer King dressed in such a fashion.

You may wonder how Peter would have known which way to go to reach the forest. That I cannot tell you, other than as the doctor observed, wild creatures often have a better sense of direction than their domesticated kin. I imagine Peter knew precisely which way to go, and would not have stopped running until he reached the edge of the wood. Then he might have paused, to breathe in the scents that greeted his nose and listen to the sounds of the forest.

Peter would have navigated the forest as one navigates in a dream, not by conscious logic but by intuition. He felt the Deer King's presence, and that feeling guided him through the dark wood.

The Deer King snorted when Peter drew close- the Wild Boy smelled different now than in months past. Peter snorted too, and then held out his hand. After a moment, the Deer King approached him, sniffing, and then nudged Peter's hand with his head.

"Mmm." Peter said, holding his hand gently on the great deer's head.

Both the Wild Boy and the stag were still for several moments, getting a sense of each other. Then the Deer King made a noise and shook his head. Peter then circled around and mounted the deer's back.

Away they went, into the night. Eventually, they met up with the rest of the deer herd, and the does all gathered happily when they recognized the Wild Boy's presence. For the next several days, Peter eased himself back into the deer herd. He had spent so many months watching and living his new life among people. Now suddenly he was back in his forest. His body responded, tensing, stretching, reliving the joys he felt running with the deer.

Peter and the deer herd ranged over the forest together, and without words, Peter told the deer about his new life at the Palace, amongst people. The scents that lingered on him told a hundred stories. His expressions and movements too, echoed foreign influences. And in Peter's eyes, the story was told plainly. They sensed that he had grown not just physically, but in his being he was bigger, more mature.

The deer wanted the Wild Boy to return to the Enchanted Forest with them, but they were uncertain he would come. They called him by his forest name, and he replied, "Peter." The strangeness of this intonation puzzled them.

The Wild Boy too, felt the competing forces and was uncertain what his plans were. He had never consciously faced a choice like this before. When he had left his birthparents behind, so many years ago, it was done carelessly, unconsciously. This was different.

For a while, Peter avoided thinking much about the choice- it was easier, and preferable, to simply wander with the deer herd and enjoy their company. When they ran, he ran and when they rested, he rested. Their speed was invigorating- to keep up, his mind had to be clear, his body focused. And when they grazed or rested, the deer were so peaceful and silent that he could hear all the subtle sounds of the forest, and smell the rich wild odors around him. He would stand still in the warm sunlight, arms spread and head lifted to face the sun, for long stretches of time, soaking in the goodness of nature. I can picture him distinctly in this stance, for later, when I came to know him, it is a pose I saw him assume frequently when he was at ease, whether by himself or with others he knew well and trusted.

As Peter and the deer ranged together through the woods on their private trails, Peter was happy not to consider the future. But when the search party finally caught up with him, Peter knew he had to make a decision. He decided to lead the search party in a different direction than the path the deer had taken.

❖ ❖ ❖

The entire Palace was much relieved when Peter was returned safely to them. As Peter did not understand the trouble he had put everyone through, the King saw no point in punishing him for escaping, but instead put out a great feast of food for Peter to welcome him home. To be sure, in the future, people would be more careful about which windows they left open.

Chapter 7: Changes

Soon after Peter was found and returned to the Palace, King George called the doctor to meet with him privately. "I have decided, doctor, that I have idled long enough at Herrenhausen Palace and that it is time to return to my responsibilities in England. Therefore, it is time for my influenza to be abolished."

"I see." The doctor paused thoughtfully, and then said, "What this calls for, Your Majesty, is several days out of doors. Sunlight and fresh air have been known to work wonders for the health. After three days, I think, there should be no question but that you are ready to go to England."

"I shall take the Wild Boy with me when I go," the King said.

"Of course- some time out of doors will do Peter some good also."

"I mean to London, Doctor."

"Oh!" the doctor said.

"I was wondering if you would like to come along as well."

"To London."

"Yes."

"...I shall have to give it some thought, Your Majesty."

"You have three days to make a decision. I shall take your advice, and spend some time out of doors with Peter. Then we will begin making preparations to depart."

❊ ❊ ❊

The next three days passed quickly. On the first day, Peter and the King took an extensive walking tour of the Royal Gardens, accompanied by members of the serving staff who brought with them chairs and refreshments and various other luxuries so that the King was able to halt from time to time and rest. The serving

70

staff followed from a respectful distance as the King walked, but at his slightest gesture of invitation, they were ready to assemble themselves around him. Rose and the doctor came along with the group as well, but for the most part, their presence seemed unnecessary. Though the entire serving staff stood ready for Peter to try to engage in mischief of one sort or another during this trip, the Wild Boy defied their expectations and was well behaved the whole time.

Peter seemed to have sensed the King's stature almost from their first meeting and this carried through in little ways Peter behaved throughout his time with King George. His demeanor was calm and pleasant, and he was attentive to the King. Something about King George inspired focus and clarity in Peter.

During one of the early stops on the tour, the King complimented Peter for having learned to use a fork (even if his technique was not quite perfected yet), and Peter smiled, holding up the fork for the King to see. "Fork," he said with a grin.

"Rose taught him that," the doctor commented.

"Congratulations, Rose," the King said.

"There's more, Your Majesty," the doctor said. "Peter, come here," he said, beckoning with one hand. Peter got up from where he was sitting and went to take the Doctor's hand. "Good," the doctor said, shaking Peter's hand. "Now," he said, releasing Peter's hand, and gesturing toward Rose, "Peter, may I present the lady Rose."

On cue, Peter bowed low toward Rose, took her hand, and kissed it elegantly.

"Wonderful!" the King said, clapping and laughing. "Very good, Doctor. Very good, Peter. But will it only work with Rose?"

The doctor shook his head, "As Shakespeare said, Your Majesty, a Rose by any other name will still smell as sweet. What is your name, dear?" he asked one of the serving staff.

"Marie, sir."

"Peter," the doctor said, "May I present the charming Marie."

71

Peter turned, and as before, made a grand bow, took Marie's hand and kissed it.

The doctor explained, "The magic words are- Peter may I present," he paused, and then, noticing Peter was looking at him attentively, "Marie and Rose," he finished, with a gesture to the two of them. Peter bowed and kissed Marie's hand again, and then returned to Rose and repeated the gesture.

"Well done, Peter," the King said. "We shall have to remember that trick."

The tour resumed, and Peter walked hand in hand with King George. More convinced than ever that the Wild Boy would some day become able to engage in conversation, the King pointed out various flowers and trees that he admired and also spoke at length regarding the horticultural significance of the four gardens of Herrenhausen, the Great Garden, the Berggarten, the Georgengarten and the Welfengarten. Peter's language abilities at this time were not nearly sufficient to follow such an oratory, but he nevertheless listened with interest, as the King was being unusually vocal and expressive. Peter liked King George.

❖ ❖ ❖

When they returned to the Palace, everyone- even Peter- was ready for a rest. "Tomorrow," the King said to the doctor, "I should like to go for a carriage ride with Peter, to make a tour of the sights of Hanover. Perhaps your daughter, Margaret, would like to come along with us. After all it was her charms that first brought him to us aboard a carriage."

"I think she would enjoy that very much, Your Majesty."

❖ ❖ ❖

The next day, Margaret came to the Palace with her father and met the King, who was seated on his throne. Peter was close by. She curtsied politely to King George, and he said, "I have heard you have an excellent singing voice, Margaret. Let us hear a song, before we go."

So Margaret bowed her head slightly, collected herself, and then lifted it and began to sing. Her voice, though youthful, was

72

strong, sweet, haunting and utterly captivating. Not only Peter, but everyone present, was transfixed by the sound of her voice, and when she finished, King George led the applause. "I know now, why Peter could not help but come out of the forest. Will you join us in a carriage ride today, as we say farewell to Hanover?"

"Farewell?"

The King nodded, "I will return to London soon, and Peter will come with me. Before we leave, I wanted Peter to have a chance to see the sights of Hanover, and I thought it would be appropriate if you came along for the ride."

"...I see," Margaret said. Taking a deep breath, she said, "Yes, I would love to join you today."

So the King, Peter, Margaret, and an accompaniment of guards and servants assembled and proceeded to where the Royal Carriage stood waiting. The King welcomed Margaret and Peter to enter the carriage first, and then he climbed up himself, followed by a servant. When all were aboard, the guards standing outside signaled the driver, and with the sounding of his horn, the tour began.

"If you children are hungry or thirsty at any point," the King said, "we have brought with us plenty of food and drink."

"Thank you, Your Majesty," Margaret said. Then, glancing out the window, she added, "Peter, look!" and pointed. Peter went to the window, and Margaret joined him. "Wave, Peter- like this," she said to the Wild Boy, teaching him to wave to people who lined the sidewalks, watching the Royal procession pass by. Surprised and smiling, people waved back, which encouraged Peter to wave more.

Normally King George was very reserved in public, but inspired by the joyful conduct of the children, he decided to join them in waving. As they continued on the road, he pointed out various sights to Peter and Margaret and told them facts that he considered interesting. The people who lined the roads wondered at the sight of the King and the children at the window, and happily cheered greetings to them.

The tour lasted several hours, and encompassed all the historic locations around Hanover. King George, Peter and Margaret enjoyed the food that had been prepared for them, and stayed perched at the window for most of the trip.

❊ ❊ ❊

While Margaret rode with Peter and the King in the Royal Carriage, Rose and the Doctor took Samuel and Thomas for a picnic in the Great Garden. After eating lunch, Samuel and Thomas went to play in the Labyrinth, leaving their father and Rose to themselves.

"So," Rose said, standing beside the doctor admiring the flowers, "...the King is returning to London, and he is taking Peter with him." The doctor nodded. "It felt as if our time with Peter might never end," she added, "and now, all of a sudden, it seems our time is almost over."

"Yes, it seems that way," the doctor said. "Rose, what if you could go with them, to London? If the King invited you along. He knows that you have been very dedicated to Peter, these past few months."

Rose shook her head. "I couldn't. My mother, my sisters, everything I know and care about is here in Germany. I love Peter, but I know nothing about England. I would have to learn a new language, new customs... I don't think I could be as much of a help to Peter there as I am here."

"I was invited to go to England with Peter and the King," the doctor said, "but like you, I am not certain how easily I would adjust to life in London. I think, I will have to decline the King's invitation." He sighed. "I will be sorry to say goodbye to Peter though."

"Me too."

"Peter is the reason we have come to know each other," the doctor said. "...Even though I must say goodbye to him, Rose, I do not want to lose you also." Taking Rose's hand, he sat down with her on one of the garden benches and asked her, "...I have

74

been wanting to ask you this for some time now. Rose, will you marry me?"

Startled, Rose nodded, with tears in her eyes. "Yes," she said, breaking out in a smile as she wiped her tears away. "I will."

The doctor slipped the ring he had been saving for this moment onto Rose's finger and then got to his feet. She laughed and he leaned in, kissing her for the first time. It was a sweet, delicate kiss that seemed to cause time to stand still for an eternal moment, and in that moment, their hearts began to beat as one.

❖ ❖ ❖

When the King returned to the Palace with Margaret and Peter, Margaret saw her father and Rose holding hands, and noticed the ring on Rose's finger. A happy expression lit her face and she rushed forward to hug Rose. Looking up at her father, Margaret said, "You did it! You finally asked her."

"And I said yes," Rose said smiling.

"Asked her what?" Samuel and Thomas asked. The boys had been oblivious up until this point.

"Rose is going to marry father, and be our new mother," Margaret said.

"Oh," Samuel said, looking relieved. To Rose he said, "We have been terribly in need of a mother."

"Terribly," said Thomas.

Rose laughed and spread her arms to hug the boys. "Well you shall have one, from now on."

"Will you tell us stories at night?" Thomas asked.

"Yes," she said, "I will."

"Perfect," said Samuel.

Peter looked on at this exchange with some curiosity, while the King congratulated the Doctor, "Well done, Doctor. Well done." Then to all who were present, the King announced, "Tomorrow we shall hold a celebration in the Great Garden, and I shall see these two fine people married. The next day, I shall depart for England."

❖ ❖ ❖

75

From the moment the King made his announcement onward, Herrenhausen Palace was buzzing with activity. To organize a wedding, a celebration and a departure all at once, the entire staff had to be active. To their credit, the staff of the palace performed their duties admirably, and the following day, a grand event was ready to be held.

Invitations to attend the king's celebration had gone out to all of the notable people of Hanover, and so, late in the morning, carriages began to roll up, delivering their passengers to the Palace. Ushers directed them to the garden, where the orchestra was beginning to play.

❉ ❉ ❉

The air in the garden was fresh with the fragrances of spring, and the mood was festive. When all the guests were seated, the processional began. Rose's mother and grandmother walked down the aisle together, looking radiant and proud. They took a seat of honor at the front, then came the Bishop and the doctor, followed by the bridesmaids and groomsmen.

Next came the children. Margaret and Peter walked hand-in-hand together down the aisle, with Margaret holding a bouquet of flowers and Peter bearing the wedding rings upon a pillow. Thomas and Samuel followed behind, tossing rose petals here and there as they went.

Finally, Rose and the King appeared together at the archway. Because Rose's father had died several years prior, the King had volunteered to serve as her escort for this occasion. With her hand on the King's arm, facing the assembled guests and the wedding altar, Rose passed through the archway and began the procession down the aisle, feeling as if she had somehow entered a fairytale. Ahead of her, she saw the Doctor waiting for her, together with the children, the groomsmen and her bridesmaids, and she could not help but smile and shed a tear.

At the altar, Rose let go of the King's arm, and stepped forward to join the doctor. The bishop greeted her with a gentle smile, and the music became quiet. Opening his book of rites, the Bishop said, "In the beginning, the Lord God said, 'It's not good that man should be alone; I will make him a helper fit for him.' And thus He has created us in pairs ever since. Dearly Beloved, we are gathered here today in the sight of God to join this man and this woman in Holy Matrimony, an honorable estate not to be entered into by anyone lightly or unadvisedly, but solemnly and reverently, considering the causes for which matrimony was ordained..."

Sitting with the other children beside Rose's mother and grandmother, Peter watched and listened intently to the proceedings. He may not have understood the words of the wedding ceremony, but sitting next to the smiling matrons, and beholding the expressions on the faces of Rose and the doctor, he sensed the gravity of the occasion. Thomas and Samuel fidgeted somewhat in their seats, but Peter was very still and focused, so much so that Margaret, interested as she was in the ceremony, could not help but turn her head and look at him. His eyes were smiling, his attention solely resting upon the sincere and emotional words being spoken at the altar.

"...take this woman to be your lawfully wedded wife, to love, honor, cherish and comfort, in sickness and health, forsaking all others, as long as you both shall live?"

"I do." the doctor said.

"Mmm," Peter said appreciatively, smiling and still staring at the Doctor and Rose. The sound Peter made drew Margaret's attention to him again, as the Bishop began to address Rose.

"And do you Rose, take this man to be your lawfully wedded husband, to love, honor, cherish and comfort, in sickness and health, forsaking all others, as long as you both shall live?"

Margaret turned her gaze in time to see Rose flash a beautiful smile from beneath her veil and say, "I do."

"Mm-hm," Peter said.

Rose and the Doctor received the rings Peter had brought for them. Then the Bishop blessed their union, and gave them permission to kiss as husband and wife.

"Eww!" Thomas said quietly, covering his eyes.

Rose and the doctor happily turned and walked down the aisle together away from the altar hand in hand. Everyone watched with interest, and then in an orderly procession, withdrew out toward the entry.

❖ ❖ ❖

The celebration that followed the wedding was a joyful mix of food, laughter, music and dancing. Peter was allowed to attend, under the watchful eyes of Josephine, who had begged Rose for this chance at redemption. Margaret too, had promised to help keep Peter happily engaged.

Josephine and the children had a table to themselves, so none of the other guests were troubled very much when Peter took a platter full of food and disappeared beneath the tablecloth. On the contrary, Margaret, Samuel and Thomas copied Peter, and took the rest of the food that was spread on the table down with them underneath the table. When Peter saw them do this, he laughed, and offered Margaret a carrot, which she accepted.

Everyone knew that Peter had become more skilled with utensils in the past few months living in the Palace, but thankfully for this occasion, the Palace staff had chosen to make delectable, finger-friendly dishes for the children's table. Thus, Peter, Josephine and the children were able to engage in Peter's preferred method of dining- sharing food with each other- without making too much of a mess of things.

While they munched happily beneath their table, hidden from view by the tablecloth, someone outside announced that Rose and the doctor would now perform the first dance. When Margaret heard this, she rose up with a sudden start and hit her head on the underside of the table, eliciting some laughter from the boys. Josephine looked concerned that Margaret might have hurt herself, but Margaret simply said, "Hurry! We don't want to miss the first dance." Following Margaret, the boys climbed out from under the table and got back into their chairs to watch as the newlyweds stepped out onto the dance floor together.

Peter visibly enjoyed the music and dancing, rocking side to side in time with the melody and humming to himself. Margaret glanced at Peter and smiled, but her attention was mostly fixed on her father and Rose, as they swirled blissfully together. With both her hands in her lap, she gazed dreamily at the pair. She was very happy for her father, and she was glad that Rose was now part of their family.

Margaret was so enchanted by the dance that she did not notice when Peter left her side. Josephine did see this, but she was not quick enough to stop him as he strode out to the floor to join the dancing pair. Margaret let out a little squeal. "Oh no!" she exclaimed.

"What?" Samuel asked, before recognizing what was happening.

"Peter is going onto the dance floor!" she said, standing up in alarm, but reluctant to go out and cause a bigger spectacle. She had heard about the disaster at the Great Banquet.

Josephine caught hold of Peter's hand before he reached Rose and the doctor. Peter turned his head, saw Josephine, and smiled. Making a bow, he took her hand and kissed it, then stepping toward her, he put his other hand at her waist.

Rocking side to side, Peter hummed and Josephine laughed, putting her hand on his shoulder and dancing with him. Rose and the doctor saw this and smiled, continuing their own dance a short distance away.

When the assembled guests saw the Wild Boy and Josephine dancing beside Rose and the Doctor, there were a few titters and laughs, but Josephine was a skilled dancer, and realizing that she and Peter were now just as much onstage as the newlyweds, she decided to put on a show. She had to improvise her steps and movements to adjust to Peter's untrained style, but he was a willing partner, and soon laughter turned to applause.

Margaret, who had feared for the worst when Peter got up, now stood stiffly at the edge of the dance floor, watching the Wild Boy dance with Josephine. Her mouth hung open in amazement, and she was uncertain what to do. Finally, she sat down in her chair again, looking cross, as more couples began to step out onto the dance floor, joining in the fun.

Margaret glowered and stared at the merry figures of Josephine and the Wild Boy until a great big hand fell in front of her eyes and gestured invitingly. She lifted her gaze and saw King George standing before her, smiling. "May I have the pleasure of this dance, Margaret?"

Margaret swallowed. Rising from her seat, she curtsied and said, "It would be an honor, Your Majesty." Accepting his hand, she took a deep breath and stepped bravely onto the dance floor. When she looked back over her shoulder at her brothers, she saw two ladies of the court inviting Samuel and Thomas to dance with them. She smiled, and looked up at King George appreciatively.

Margaret and the King danced together through a full song. The old King guided Margaret very gently, and moved with a friendly, graceful power that held Margaret's attention almost entirely on him. "Margaret," the King said, after dancing for a while in silence, "...I know that Peter is your friend. You and your family have helped him to adjust to life outside the forest. You know that Peter and I will be leaving for England tomorrow. Once there, your father has recommended Peter be placed into the care of a friend of his, Doctor John Arbuthnot."

"Yes," Margaret said, her face falling slightly at the thought.

"I know that your home is here, in Germany, but I would like you and your family to have a bit more time with Peter. Therefore I have asked your father to come visit England for a few weeks and bring your whole family along. He has agreed that it would make a wonderful honeymoon."

"Yes, but our home is here in Germany," Margaret said dejectedly, before stopping and asking, "-wait, what did you say?"

"I said that you all are going to come with us to London and be my guests for a few weeks as Peter adjusts to his new life there."

Margaret's face lit up with joy. "Oh, thank you, Your Majesty!" she said.

King George laughed. "You're welcome, Margaret. I am looking forward to introducing you to my granddaughters. They are close to your age." Twirling Margaret around with one hand, he said, "Now, let us finish our dance, shall we?"

Margaret's face was flushed with happiness at the news the King had given her, until out of the corner of her eye, Margaret saw Josephine and Peter dancing. Then her stomach twisted. But, as the King calmly and masterfully led her through a challenging sequence, her attention shifted again to the dance.

By the end of the song, Margaret was so overcome by the King's awesome manner that she had completely forgotten her jealousy toward Josephine and was simply enjoying herself. Then the King stopped, and said, "Perhaps we can trade dancing partners, Peter?"

Margaret was surprised- she had become so involved in her own dance with the King she had not realized Peter and Josephine were now dancing right beside them. Once again, she curtsied and said, "Thank you, Your Majesty."

"Thank you, Margaret," King George said. "You are an excellent dancer. I always say that the lady's part is more difficult. You made me look as if I knew how to dance. Now perhaps you can help Peter, as Josephine has been doing."

Josephine and the King looked on as Margaret took Peter's hand, and the two children began to dance. "Shall we?" King George asked Josephine, smiling.

Moving gracefully with Peter, Margaret glanced over at beautiful Josephine dancing with King George and wondered idly what she herself had looked like a few moments ago, when the King had danced with her. Then Peter stepped on her foot.

"Ow!" she said, now conscious of her distraction. The expression on Peter's face told her it had been an accident, and the King's words came back to her. She smiled at Peter and said, "That's okay, Peter. It was my fault. The lady's part is more difficult, you know." Peter smiled, relieved that Margaret was not angry with him.

They danced together happily for several minutes, with Josephine and the King close by, and then the music changed, becoming faster paced, and Peter whirled, catching hold of Rose's hand as she was dancing with the doctor. He drew the four of them together and swung Margaret and Rose's hands to and fro, indicating he wanted everyone to dance as a group. The doctor smiled and joined hands with Margaret, making a ring. The four danced in a circle together for several moments until Thomas and Samuel led their lady partners over to join in, and then there were eight of them dancing together. Next the King and Josephine joined in, and the ring grew bigger still, until all the couples on the dance floor participated.

Rose and the doctor were reunited at the center of the dance floor for one more dance, while the rest of the dancers circled round. It was a lively dance, and at the end, everyone clapped and cheered. "Obviously," King George said, looking down at Peter with a smile, "…the Fairy Folk taught you a thing or two about dancing."

❊ ❊ ❊

Josephine took the children to retire from the party early, but none of them were unhappy when they left. Peter's only reluctance had to do with the food he had left under the table, and Josephine was thoughtful enough to pick up a tray and take it with her, immediately drawing Peter's attention.

As they headed down the corridor of the Palace together, the children were all full of conversation about the afternoon's adventures. "Did you see me dancing with the King?" Margaret asked Samuel.

"Of course I did," Samuel said, "everyone saw. Did you see me dancing with Ingrid?"

"Who?" Margaret asked. Samuel looked disappointed.

Josephine smiled, "…I saw you Samuel. You were quite a dashing figure on the dance floor. I think Ingrid had a very good time."

"You and Peter were great," little Thomas said.

82

"Thank you," both Margaret and Josephine said, each assuming that Thomas had meant her. The two girls looked at each other for a moment, surprised. Then they both burst out laughing. "You were amazing Josephine," Margaret said to the older girl.

"And you and Peter were really charming together," Josephine responded.

"Thank you."

That evening, the boys shared Peter's room at the Palace, and Josephine and Margaret occupied another guest room, just next door. The next day, they would depart for England.

Chapter 8: Fire on the Sea

Josephine said goodbye to Margaret, Peter and the boys the next morning, wishing them a safe and happy journey. Waving goodbye to her, the children climbed up into a carriage, together with Rose and the doctor. "This is exciting," Thomas said, looking out the window of the carriage at the bustling scene around them. A procession of carriages was being prepared for departure, some filled with luggage, others filled with members of the King's entourage.

Though the King's departure had not been announced until very recently, plans had been made weeks in advance to allow him to depart when ready. So, it wasn't long before the carriages were all filled up, and then the King himself appeared, striding out of the Palace dressed in blue for the sea voyage. He climbed up into his own Royal carriage, and then with the blast of a trumpet, the procession of carriages set out.

The journey to the seaport by carriage took several days. Along the way, King George called for the procession to stop at various scenic locations. At each of these stops, everyone disembarked and enjoyed a picnic meal together. There were also a few places where the horses were exchanged with fresh ones, so that the carriages were able to continue onward without slowing down.

❊ ❊ ❊

Finally, on the morning of the third day, they reached the city of Hamburg, and made their way to the docks, where the King's ships were waiting to set sail. The air at the port was crisp and the water was still gray from winter, but the sky was clear and there was a pleasant wind. In the distance, a group of seagulls could be seen practicing their aerobatics.

When the King's procession arrived, the ships' crew and serving staff were already aboard making preparations for his arrival. The King entered the ship first, accompanied by his attendants. Peter followed after, together with the doctor's family. Aboard the ship, they were shown to their cabin, and rested there until one of the king's attendants came to inform them that the ship was about to leave port, and their presence had been requested on deck.

❖   ❖   ❖

"Ah Peter," King George said, seeing the Wild Boy emerge from the cabin area. "Come up here. We are about to get underway."

The King was up on on the quarterdeck, standing behind the wheel of the ship. Peter turned and saw him there, and immediately sprang up the steps to join him. "King George!" Peter said happily.

The doctor's family followed Peter up the steps at a slower pace. "Good Morning, Your Majesty," Rose said.

"Good Morning, Rose," King George said, smiling.

"Guten Morgen," Peter said.

"Have you ever steered a ship before, Doctor?"

"No, Your Majesty, I haven't."

"And I suppose you children haven't either," King George said.

Margaret, Thomas and Samuel all shook their heads. "We've never been on a ship before," Thomas said, holding his stuffed bear in his arms. "Will we be meeting any pirates or mermaids?"

King George laughed, "I don't think anything quite so exciting as that will happen on this voyage, but perhaps, once we are out of harbor, you can try your hand at steering this ship. How does that sound?"

"All right. I didn't really want to meet a pirate anyway."

The crew was making final preparations for departure, shouting directions to each other. Looking down at Thomas, King George said, "…But you might have liked to meet a mermaid? Well I don't blame you. Long ago, I fell in love with a mermaid."

Thomas' eyes grew wide. "You did? What happened?"

"Her name was Melusine, and she came from the Elbe River. She was very thin, you know, but she was also beautiful, and she

85

loved me very much, enough that she was willing to leave her river home behind."

"Did she die?"

"No. She now resides in Middlesex County, in England."

"Are you telling a fib?"

King George smiled, "I never tell fibs, Thomas. I only occasionally elaborate upon the truth. Now, here we go!"

The ship had been loosed from its moorings, and now moved away from the dock gently. King George, with the help of the ship's captain, used the wheel to guide the vessel's movement in the water.

The children watched with interest as the King, the Captain and the ship's crew worked together to bring the ship out of harbor and into the sailing channel. "There!" the King said, when they were finally sailing freely upon the Elbe. "Now children, one at a time, you may try your hand at the wheel." King George watched carefully as Thomas, Samuel, Margaret and Peter each took a turn, and then he invited the Doctor and Rose to take a turn together.

After that, King George let the Captain resume control over the steering, and he led Peter and the doctor's family on a tour, pointing out all the key features of the ship to them. Then he went inside with them to have breakfast and afterward everyone went to their separate quarters to rest.

❀ ❀ ❀

The voyage to London was to last over a week. On the afternoon of the third day, storm clouds appeared on the horizon. By nightfall, the ship was in the midst of a storm.

A fearsome wind howled and buffeted the ship, creating whining sounds in the rigging. The drumming of rain was constant, except when waves washed the deck of the ship. After trying unsuccessfully to go outside (Margaret stopped him) Peter huddled in a corner of the room, looking miserable.

Hoping to add cheer to the atmosphere, Rose suggested that they all sing together. Margaret and her brothers joined in with their father and Rose willingly, but Peter, who normally enjoyed music very much, sat uncomfortably in the corner, not joining in.

Then a knock came on the door, and the King entered. "Excuse me," he said, "I just thought I should check in on you all, to see how you are faring in the midst of this storm."

"Well, we are passing the time by singing, Your Majesty. Would you like to join us?"

"Perhaps. How is Peter?"

The doctor responded, "Peter is-" and then he stopped, "where is Peter?"

Peter was no longer huddled in the corner of the room. The door behind the King stood open. Everyone looked around the room and then at each other quickly, before rushing to the door. The King went into the passageway first, and the doctor followed, after telling Rose, "You'd better stay here with the children, to keep them safe."

Rose followed and watched the King and the doctor go, and then stood at the threshold watching the rain fall and the water slosh for a short time. "You three are perfectly safe here. I'm afraid Peter's got himself in some trouble and they may need my help to get him out of it. Stay here," Rose told the children before following the Doctor and the King outside.

Margaret, Samuel and Thomas obediently stood at the threshold for a moment, anxiously waiting for the adults to return with Peter. "I hope Peter's all right," Margaret said.

"Maybe he fell overboard," little Thomas suggested grimly.

Then Samuel said, "Well I'm going to have a look," and he stepped outside. "You two wait here," he added.

In frustration, Margaret said, "Rose said we should stay here. I'm older than you are. Samuel don't go!" but truthfully she wanted to go and have a look as well, so she turned to Thomas and said, "Thomas you wait here with your bear."

Holding his stuffed bear toy in his arms, Thomas pouted and watched his sister go, and then walked back to his bed. Putting the bear down there, he said, "Someone has to wait here. Looks like it's going to be you." Then he turned and dashed out to see what was going on.

On deck, Thomas saw everyone standing motionless in a group. He could not see what they were looking at, so he pressed forward, between their legs, to get a better look. Immediately, he felt hands gathering to restrain him, holding him back from going further. "Thomas stop! Look!" his father said in his ear. His father's voice seemed just barely more than a whisper in the midst of the raging noise of the storm, and it seemed to have a ring of fear in it. For a moment, Thomas did not understand. Then he saw what everyone else was looking at, and he froze, the same way the others were frozen.

The masts of the ship were on fire. The fire was bright white with a touch of blue. The air above them buzzed, crackled and popped, and balls of white light pulsed above the ship. At the bow of the ship, Peter stood bare-chested, facing into the wind with both arms spread. Around him, a cluster of the glowing white balls danced and exploded in the air.

Witnessing this spectacle were members of the ship's crew and passengers, standing beneath the glowing lights in wonder and fear. There were also several large albatross watching from the air, gliding at high speeds amidst the storm winds around the ship. The birds swooped and circled round with interest, as curious as the people were about the blaze.

"Wha- what's happening?" Thomas asked.

"It is St. Elmo's Fire," the King said, "a rare event. I have heard of it but never witnessed it until now."

"Is it dangerous?" asked Margaret. Lightning flashed over the darkened sea and thunder rumbled ominously, as if in answer to her question.

"It can be," the King said. "We cannot risk going out there to recover Peter now. We can only pray for his safety."

Peter's figure was surrounded by a pale, eerie light. As Peter raised his arms higher, the light around him became brighter, and then Peter threw his head back and crowed loudly. Thomas

88

gasped, for suddenly streaks of lightning sprang from Peter's hands, joining the energy cloud that circled him. In what seemed an eternal moment, the group of children and adults gathered in the dark stood transfixed, beholding the Wild Boy bathed in that eerie light, united with the power that had taken over the ship.

"Peter!" Margaret cried out.

The Wild Boy whirled, and for a moment they thought Margaret's voice had reached him, because they saw a smile on his face. But he did not stop whirling- he only crowed again, and continued spinning, dancing with the balls of lightning that crackled in the air around him.

Overcome with curiosity, and less fearful than the other witnesses, an albatross came to land on the foredeck where Peter was dancing. As soon as it landed, the bird was enveloped in light. The albatross called out dramatically and spread its wings, the tips of which shown most brightly, as if they were burning, but it seemed unharmed by the experience.

"I'll get him down from there, Your Majesty," a crewman said, stepping forward bravely.

"Be careful," the King said.

The crewman crept carefully across the deck, wary of the energy pulsing overhead, and eventually came up to the stairs at the bow. Reluctant to climb the stairs, he called out, "Boy! Come here. Boy!" but the Wild Boy paid no attention to him. "Peter!" the crewman called more sternly, climbing the steps. "Stop that and come here!"

They saw Peter turn and face the sailor, and he stopped for a moment, looking at the sailor, who was now standing on the bow with him. The ball lightning still danced noisily in the air around them. Abruptly, the sailor lunged forward, ducking under the electricity and reaching out with both hands, attempting to catch Peter. But Peter ducked under the crewman's beefy arms and crossed over to the other side of the bow. Having fallen to one knee trying to get hold of Peter, the crewman now turned and rose to face Peter again. He said something they couldn't make out from across the ship, but the tone of his voice was clear.

"Oh no," Rose said, "Peter's got him angry now. He's going to go after Peter, and that will just encourage Peter to prolong the game."

"Game?" asked the King.

"Peter loves to be chased," Rose said. At that moment, the sailor lunged again, and Peter dodged sideways. Everyone gasped, because the direction Peter dodged led straight off the edge of the raised foredeck.

They thought in that instant he would surely fall and break his neck on the deck below, but instead, Peter sprang into the air, and caught hold of a rope, pulling himself up into the rigging of the ship. The children cheered.

More sailors stepped forward to help capture Peter now, without waiting for orders from the King. While Peter walked the length of a spar casually, as if it were a tree branch, they swarmed up the foremast rigging to get to him. When they were starting to get close, he darted from his position up to the next level of rigging.

"Your Majesty," Rose pleaded, turning to King George, "you must tell them to stop. They're only making him more reckless."

Just as Rose said this, the men were reaching up to the level where Peter was perched. To avoid them, Peter scrambled up higher, and then leaped out into empty space.

Margaret screamed. Everyone froze.

Death seemed to be the only possible outcome of this fearless leap Peter had made, but somehow, the Wild Boy flew across the void, and caught hold of the rigging attached to the center mast. Scrambling up the rigging with agility that would have been envied by the most experienced sailors, Peter found his way to the crow's nest and climbed inside. Once again, they heard Peter cry out like a rooster.

"Tell the men to stand down," the King said to the foreman.

"Your Majesty?"

"Now!"

"Yes, Your Majesty," the foreman said, hurrying off to give the King's orders to the other sailors.

"What will we do about Peter?" Margaret asked.

"Let him be," said the King.

"What about the fire?"

"St. Elmo's Fire is not the normal sort of fire which burns things, it is a holy fire," the King explained. "Sailors usually consider it a good omen."

"You said it could be dangerous," Margaret responded.

"It can be, but we all saw Peter was unharmed in the midst of it. I am more worried about him flying about amongst the rigging of the ship the way he has been. If he fell, he would surely break his neck. Better that he stays up there until the storm is over. Then we can get him down safely."

"Won't he catch cold up there?"

"My dear, I am more concerned that you will catch a cold down here than Peter will up there," the King said. "Think of all the winters he spent alone in the rain and the snow. For all the time he spent living in trees, he is probably more at home up there than down in the ship's cabin. Come along- come inside now." To the ship's captain, the King said, "Station a few men out here keep watch, in case Peter decides to come down. We don't want him to have an accident, but don't chase him or restrain him."

"Yes Your Majesty."

Following the King's orders, the crewmen took turns standing watch below the main mast, in case Peter decided to climb down. But Peter was quite happy up in the crow's nest, and was in no hurry to descend.

The Wild Boy stood and watched the show of lights for some time, and then settled down on the floor of the crow's nest and put his feet up, making himself comfortable. Looking up, he watched St. Elmo's fire pulse at the top of the mast above him for several minutes more, and then fell asleep.

❧ ❧ ❧

Peter was awakened at sunrise by an albatross- perhaps the same one who had landed on the foredeck the night before. The big white bird hopped up from the floor of the crow's nest to the railing and perched there, alternately looking at Peter and out at the horizon.

Peter smiled and got to his feet, joining the albatross in looking out at the sunrise. The sky was clear- the storm had passed. Peter let out one of his signature rooster calls. Then the albatross lifted his head, and made a trumpeting call of his own. Peter, not to be out done, crowed again.

The albatross bobbed his head approvingly, and made another loud call. Then he spread his great wings and took flight. He circled the ship several times, exchanging vocalizations with Peter, and then finally flew off, toward an island home where men never set foot, but where Peter might be welcomed, if only he could go.

Peter stood and watched as the albatross flew away until he heard a voice call out to him from below. "Peter! Good morning! I trust you slept well?"

Peter looked down and saw who had called to him. "King George!" With alarming speed, the Wild Boy sprang from the crow's nest and descended via the ship's rigging to the deck below.

Landing lightly on the deck, Peter came to join King George at the port railing. King George patted Peter on the shoulder and pointed south, "England is another two days journey, but it should be smooth sailing from here."

"Mm." Peter said, smiling at King George.

❖ ❖ ❖

Whatever the reasons may have been for the storm, it seemed the old god Neptune had no disagreement with King George. The sea and sky, which had come to life so dramatically in the storm, now offered clear passage to the travelers. The cold, dark waters of the North Sea were pacified, the sun shone warmly overhead, and a strong, favorable wind carried the ship southwest, toward the English coast.

Time passed quickly aboard the ship, and soon they found themselves approaching the mouth of the River Thames. The green shores of England were a welcome sight that buoyed the spirits of everyone aboard.

The children watched with interest as the ship's crew navigated the winding course of the Thames. Their progress brought many sights, but perhaps the most striking was the six hundred year old London Bridge. Nine hundred feet from end to end, with a drawbridge at the center and gatehouses at both sides, the great medieval structure was taken for granted by most Londoners, but for Peter and the doctor's family, the bridge was a wonder. Covered with more than two hundred buildings, some up to seven stories tall, London Bridge looked as if it could be a town unto itself.

Beyond London Bridge, they saw the fortified castle walls of the Tower of London, then sailed onward, to make landing at Whitehall. News of their approach spread quickly, leading a number of people to gather along the banks of the Thames to watch their progress.

At Whitehall, I waited, together with my mother and siblings, to welcome my grandfather the King home. I had heard from my mother that he would bring with him a Wild Boy, but I had no idea the adventures that would follow.

Act II:
Caroline

Chapter 9: Introducing Peter

Among the political figures gathered at Whitehall awaiting the return of the King, the Whigs were strongly represented by notables such as the Prime Minister Walpole, Lord Townshend, and Lord Hervey. Townshend, I remember, seemed tense and reserved, while Walpole laughed loudly and talked easily with the other men of the court. Lord Hervey, meanwhile, seemed to find the ladies' company to be of greater interest. Hervey was a handsome man, and there were few who could match his wit or his charm, but he lacked the strength of a man like Robert Walpole. It was not by mere good fortune that Walpole had become the most powerful politician in England.

My father, George Augustus, and my mother, Caroline, were both in attendance. Walpole and my father did not see eye-to-eye with each other about very many things, but Lord Hervey was on good terms with my mother, and his presence helped to ease any tensions that might have existed between Father and the Prime Minister.

Also present were five of us children- my brothers Frederick and William, my sisters Anne and Amelia, and myself. Mary and Louise, my youngest siblings, were not there. Being only thirteen at the time, I was not particularly interested by the adult discussions that were taking place around us, and therefore cannot report much of their contents to you, but in my view that is of little consequence for the purposes of this narrative.

Frederick, at nineteen years old, was eager to be counted among the adults. Therefore, he did his best to avoid standing near William, Anne, Amelia and me, spending most of his time in the company of Lord Hervey or chatting with the young ladies of the court. I remember that Frederick often spiced his sentences with swear words. I believe he did this to sound more grown-up. Some of the young ladies, for reasons I will never understand, pretended to be charmed by his manner. They knew, for their mothers must have told them, that spice is best used sparingly, but instead of turning up their noses at his indelicacy, they smiled and laughed attractively as if he had been clever. Meanwhile, the adults in the room lifted their eyebrows, but were too polite to tell the young Prince that using these words did not really make him seem very grown-up.

Thankfully, though Anne was just two years younger than Frederick, she did not yet feel the need to distance herself from her younger siblings. So, the four of us kept each other entertained while the group of adults (and the young people wanting to be adults) conversed in small clusters. Our mother kept an eye on the four of us, but mostly from a distance, trusting Anne to look after Amelia, William and me.

I cannot remember what we children talked about that day, while we waited for our grandfather to arrive. I do remember Anne, while never neglecting her conversation with us children, simultaneously captivated the attention of a young man who kept us supplied with delicious hor d'oeuvres. Hers was the subtlest technique, one that I did not think I would ever grasp, let alone master. It seemed to have something to do with her smile, or perhaps just the corner of her mouth- I could not tell.

At some point, Mother came over to where we were sitting and said, "Anne dear, could you go to the harpsichord and play something for the assembly?"

Anne was quite skillful at playing the harpsichord, having studied for the past six years with our music tutor, the great composer George Friedrich Händel, who called her the "flower of princesses." Showing no sign of discomfort upon being asked to play, Anne smiled and asked, "Can Amelia and Caroline help?"

Mother looked at Anne curiously, "Three of you playing at the same time? I don't know…"

"Many hands make light work," Anne said. "Trust me Mother."

Mother smiled and said, "Very well. Come William, let us watch your sisters play together."

Anne was grinning as she exchanged glances with Amelia and me. Joining hands with us, and whispering her choice of music in our ears, she gracefully glided across the room to the harpsichord. The three of us sat down together, and after a moment's pause Anne started to play. Once the melody was established, Amelia joined in on the left side of the keyboard, and I joined in on the right.

This was a game the three of us had been practicing together for some time, but we hadn't shown anyone yet, and we couldn't help but feel excited to now have a chance to make an exhibition of it. The music of Händel issued forth from the harpsichord, drawing the attention of the assembled guests, and when they turned to see who was playing, they were surprised to see three pairs of young hands working together in harmony.

We kept at our game for some time, and all the guests gathered round to watch with interest. When we finally finished the melody, everyone applauded, and Sir Robert Walpole called for an encore. So we put our heads together and conspired in whispers regarding our next musical selection, then began playing again.

About a minute into our encore, it was announced that the King had arrived. The attention of our audience immediately shifted to the entryway, but Mother told us to keep playing, as she thought our grandfather, King George, would be pleased by our performance.

As my attention was focused on the keys of the harpsichord, I cannot tell you all the details of my grandfather's entry to the hall where we were all gathered waiting, but I remember there was a great cheer as he came in. It wasn't long then before he appeared beside the harpsichord, smiling.

We stopped, and scrambled out of our positions on the bench to embrace him. "Grandfather!" I exclaimed, hugging him as Anne and Amelia joined with me.

"Caroline!" he laughed, returning our embrace, "Anne! Amelia! That was a wonderful performance. I see you have been taking your studies with Mr. Händel seriously. Now, there is someone I would like you to meet. He has a had a long journey, and so today's meeting shall be brief, but I think you will find him fascinating."

Together with our mother, and our brother William, we followed King George across to the entry, where a small group of newcomers stood waiting. Extending his hand, the King beckoned, "...Peter."

Then, for the first time, I laid eyes on the Wild Boy, as he stepped out of the group to approach my grandfather. The King had seen to it that Peter was dressed stylishly for this occasion, but Peter's hair remained long and wild. It was a vestige of his old life, and the King had decided not to have it cut. He was unlike any boy I had seen before.

What caught my attention the most was Peter's eyes. There was something different about them, which made me curious. Then his eyes locked with mine, and the best way I can describe what I felt is to say it was if I was looking into the eyes of a horse. His wild, vulnerable, intense, innocent soul was present and visible in his gaze. For a moment, I did not breathe, but stood transfixed. Then Peter turned his gaze back to my grandfather and put his hand into the King's hand.

King George shook Peter's hand, and then released it, before turning back to face us. To my mother, the King said, "This is the Wild Boy I have written to you about. Peter, may I present Her Royal Highness, The Princess of Wales." On cue, Peter stepped forward, bowed and kissed Mother's hand.

"He is more mannerly than I imagined from your letters," she said.

"Well we have been practicing that recently. Now, Peter, may I present my granddaughters, Anne, Amelia and Caroline." One by one, Peter bowed and kissed the hands of all us princesses, in order, ending with me. I laughed as he kissed my hand, and he looked up at me and smiled.

The King touched Peter's shoulder and said, "And Peter, these are my grandsons. Frederick and William, this is Peter, the Wild Boy, Prince of the Enchanted Forest of Hamelin and adopted son of the Fairy Folk."

"There's no such thing as fairies," Frederick said under his breath.

The King looked at Frederick sharply and said, "I see you've gone and grown up while I've been away, Frederick. Congratulations." But Frederick's remark had not troubled us children, as we were all crowding around Peter to ask him questions and examine him. We all thought the Wild Boy was very interesting.

Peter's eyes wandered and he looked distracted as Anne, Amelia and William pressed him with questions he could not understand or answer. But then his eyes met mine again and I smiled at him, which made him smile back, and for what felt like a long time, we both stood smiling at each other.

My grandfather interrupted, saying, "Now children, Peter must be tired from his journey, so your questions will have to wait. Come Peter, I want to introduce you to John Arbuthnot." And with that, Peter was led away to be introduced to John Arbuthnot, who was to be his guardian.

Arbuthnot was a learned polymath, almost sixty years of age, respected not only as a physician, mathematician and man of science but also as a satirist. He counted among his friends the physicist Isaac Newton, the poet Alexander Pope and the writer Jonathan Swift.

Having received letters written by the good doctor in Hanover describing Peter's unique character and condition, Arbuthnot had agreed to become Peter's guardian. Therefore, while the Doctor and Rose were in London, Arbuthnot would work in close association with them to become better acquainted with the Wild Boy.

❧ ❧ ❧

Peter's next public appearance was at a banquet held in honor of the King's return at St. James Palace on April 7, 1726. I was not old enough to be present at this banquet, but I heard about it from my mother and sister. It was announced that Peter would be a special guest that evening- *after* the dinner. Members of the Royal Court had been hearing a lot about the Wild Boy recently and were eager to meet him.

Thus, all the King's courtiers were gathered in the drawing room after dinner, engaged in lively discussion when, at the King's word, the doors of the drawing room were opened, and Peter entered in style, carried up high by a brace of footmen. "Ladies and gentleman, it is my pleasure to present to you, Peter the Wild Boy!" Peter heard the King's voice and the smile on his face broke into a grin.

Spotting the King as the crowd parted, Peter stood up on the platform he was riding on and cried out happily, "King George!" And with that, he leaped into the air, drawing a gasp from the crowd. He landed on the floor without a sound, as a cat would, then scampered on all fours right up to the King. "King George!" Peter said, standing and holding his arms out to the King.

The King took Peter's hands and shook them, smiling. Then he said, "Peter, may I present to you again, the Princess of Wales, my daughter-in-law, Caroline." Peter bowed and kissed Mother's hand, and found that she was wearing a sparkling glove. Peter held up her hand and examined it, looking up at her and the King with interest. Mother smiled and slipped the glove off, which surprised Peter. He looked at the glove in his hands and turned it over and around for several moments in curiosity, put his hand inside and showed the King, then smiled and took off the glove, offering it back to the Princess. Reaching into his pocket, Peter drew out a pocket-watch that had been a parting gift from the good doctor, held it up to his ear for a moment, and then offered it to Mother. She took it from him and respectfully looked at it. Peter pointed out to her the fast-moving second hand, and then put his hand to

100

his ear. Mother understood and put the watch to her ear, smiling, then gave the watch back to Peter.

My father, George Augustus, was watching all this and fished his own pocket watch out for Peter to look at. After making a couple of quick adjustments, George Augustus said, "Here Peter, have a look at this." It was a very ornate watch, and Peter admired it greatly. As he stood examining it, the hour hand of the watch struck the hour mark, and the watch began to sound the time. Peter's mouth fell open in surprise, and everyone laughed at his expression.

"Peter," King George said, drawing the Wild Boy's attention, after George Augustus had recovered his watch, "may I present the young Lady Walpole, daughter of the Right Honorable Robert Walpole." Peter bowed and kissed the fragrant hand of lovely Mary Walpole, who was fond of wearing Jasmine Ittar perfume from India.

Something about her exotic perfume bewitched Peter, and after kissing her hand, he sniffed her delicate wrist, then stepped forward, sniffing the air about her. Mary, being simultaneously charmed and amused by Peter, remained still for a moment as he sniffed her neck.

Then King George called to the Wild Boy, "Peter!" which made Peter immediately turn, leaving a breathless Mary to wonder what might have happened next, if his attention had not been drawn away. The young ladies of the court tittered with amusement and perhaps some small amount of jealousy. Meanwhile, my grandfather was saying to Peter, "This is Charles Fitzroy, Lord Chamberlain." Peter bowed, and then shook the Lord Chamberlain's hand.

Fitzroy held in his left hand the white staff of his office, and this drew Peter's attention. After shaking Fitzroy's hand Peter reached out to touch the staff. The Lord Chamberlain smiled and held out his staff for Peter to examine. Without hesitation, and to the surprise of the Lord Chamberlain, Peter promptly took the staff from his hand. Examining the staff and feeling its weight,

Peter spun it in loops around himself briefly, causing people nearby to step back with concern. Then he smiled, and offered it back to Fitzroy, causing everyone to sigh in relief.

The gathering continued with everyone in good spirits until late in the evening. Peter was well-behaved most of the time, except for a bit of pickpocketing he engaged in, which no one was really bothered by, once the King explained that the boy was searching for edible items, preferably chocolate or fruit. He also had a curious habit of alternating between walking on two legs and walking on all fours, which drew curious stares from the courtiers. And I am told he licked at least one person's hand, but that may only be a rumor, for my Mother and sister did not see it themselves. For the most part, Peter was very charming, and therefore held the interest of the assembled guests. Eventually the discussions surrounding Peter took a serious turn, with someone asking, "What will become of the boy? Can he be educated?"

The King asked Dr. Arbuthnot what he thought, after having spending a few days with Peter. Dr. Arbuthnot said, "...I believe it is possible, but it will take dedicated effort over a long period of time, and much depends on him. I have never encountered a boy like Peter before- a boy who knows no human language, who does not understand the purpose or value of clothing, who can stand before the King and not feel humble, who can be amused by a trinket in one moment, and then in the next moment look into your eyes with a depth of spirit one only finds in an infant, an elder, or a lover. I cannot decide yet whether he is simply an extremely charming idiot, or something more. Somehow, he has lived for the past eleven or twelve years without being taught the basic lessons that lead a boy to become a man and he has survived- alone, without help from any adults. It leads one to wonder just how much of our behavior and our logic is inherent, natural, and how much of who we are is a result of what we are taught at an early age. What would we be, what would any of us be, without a family, without an education, without even words to construct what we call thoughts? Is a man's soul born in him, or is it planted and cultivated by civilization?"

The philosophical questions raised by Peter's presence kept the men talking for a long time, but eventually Peter grew tired and went to find a place on the floor where he could curl up to rest. My mother, who at that time was standing aside speaking privately with the King, observed this and went over to him. He looked up at her and she extended her hands, so he got up to his feet, and she led him gently over to a big chair, where she sat down with him in her lap. Patting him gently on the head, she sang a lullaby to him, and soon he was fast asleep. "Look at that," King George said good-humoredly, "it seems we have put the boy to sleep with all of our philosophizing. Perhaps it is time to draw this evening to a close." The courtiers all agreed with the King and began saying their goodbyes.

"Doctor Arbuthnot," Mother called, when she was confident her voice would not disturb Peter. When the doctor came over to where she sat, she asked him, "Doctor Arbuthnot, do you think the boy might learn more advantageously if he were in the company of other children? So that it might seem less like a chore, and more like play?"

"...Perhaps. He does seem responsive to social interaction. If the other children were very well-behaved, it might inspire him to imitate them. But I suspect he would also need at least an hour a day of direct one-to-one teaching."

"What you said earlier, about the soul, moved me. I have spoken with the King, and Peter is to be transferred into my care, but I shall still rely on you to help the boy. We should have Peter baptized next Sunday. Then I would like you to begin giving him regular lessons beginning Monday. If it is possible for Peter to become educated, it is our duty to provide him that opportunity."

Arbuthnot bowed, "As you wish, Your Highness."

"As you may be aware, my children, Anne, Amelia, Caroline, and William, take their lessons in the mornings here at St. James' Palace with their tutors. The King and I have agreed that Peter

103

shall take his lessons here as well, and after his lesson with you, the children may join him for a while."

"Very good, Your Highness."

❖ ❖ ❖

The next day, Mother brought me, Amelia and William to Kensington Gardens, where we met with John Arbuthnot, Peter, and the Doctor's family.

Margaret and Rose were both wearing beautiful new outfits that the Doctor had bought for them here in London. I saw them smiling radiantly at us as we approached in our carriage. Samuel and Thomas were also dressed smartly- but being boys, their moods were not improved by fine clothing. Samuel appeared pensive, and little Thomas had a doubtful expression on his face.

Peter wore a comfortable-looking green velvet jacket and pants. He stretched and flexed inside this garment, feeling its form. He had not yet gotten fully adjusted to wearing clothing.

When he saw us step out of the carriage, Peter's face brightened. My mother saw this, and smiled. "It seems he remembers us," she said, opening her parasol.

As we all stepped out from the carriage one-by-one, John Arbuthnot moved forward to greet Mother. "Your Highness, good afternoon."

"Good afternoon," Mother said, smiling, and extending her hand.

Arbuthnot bowed and kissed her hand respectfully, then seeing we were all assembled, he took a breath and said, "And good afternoon to each of you, as well, Prince William, Princess Anne, Princess Amelia and Princess Caroline. I believe you have all met Peter recently," he said, gesturing toward the Wild Boy, who had come up beside him. Pausing for a moment, Arbuthnot said, "Peter, may I present-"

But Peter was already a step ahead of Arbuthnot. He stepped forward and took Mother's hand, bowing and kissing it delicately, then turned and did the same with each of us- Anne, Amelia and

104

myself. He did so with great poise and elegance, or so it seemed to me.

"Ah- ha ha," Arbuthnot said, watching Peter. Arbuthnot looked slightly deflated. I believe he had just learned the magic phrase *May I present* and had been looking forward to making good use of it, but Peter stole the moment. "Well... I would also like introduce the good doctor who discovered Peter in the forest of Hamelin, his lovely wife Rose, his two sons, Samuel and Thomas, and the charming Margaret, whose singing voice was the siren sound that drew Peter out of the trees and into civilization."

Margaret and Rose curtsied, and the Doctor and his sons bowed. "It is a pleasure to finally meet all of you," Mother said, "thank you for joining us for this picnic."

"Thank you for inviting us," the Doctor said.

"Thank you," Samuel and Thomas echoed.

Having all been properly introduced, we then ventured into the private Gardens together to find a suitable place to picnic, where we were joined by a handful of Mother's ladies-in-waiting. The park landscape around us was lush and brimming with life- so much so that after the gates were out of sight, it was difficult to believe we were still in the middle of London.

Kensington Gardens is one of the most beautiful places I have ever known, and so as we roamed its paths, we were in no hurry to find a place to stop. Normally, my attention would have been entirely on the scenery, but today, we had the Wild Boy with us.

Peter did not have to do anything dramatic to attract attention- his very presence here in the Gardens was dramatic. The way he walked, how he stared, his smile, his wild hair, the green velvet clothing he wore... everything about him had a raw, natural feeling. He was every inch a boy, but a wonderful, unaffected boy.

My primary experience with boys up to this point was with my brothers, William and Frederick. William was perfectly innocent as an infant, and at his present age of five remained endearing a good portion of the time, but was beginning to lose the sublime glow of his early years. Frederick, at nineteen, was so sour that I wondered if he had ever been like William. Mother assured me he had, and said the sourness was a phase boys go through on their way to becoming men.

Peter was of indeterminate age. He was just my size, but no one knew how long ago he had been born. Surely he was more than double William's age, but to me, it seemed he still had all the innocence I remembered from William's early years.

There was something else about Peter, something that was unsettling, but also strangely attractive. He seemed to have an animal's awareness- or something akin to it. If you have ever seen the way a dog stands poised sniffing the wind, the way a cat treads over ground, or how a bird alights and perches upon a tree branch, that is the alert quality I saw in Peter. He appeared very calm and at ease, and at the same time I felt he was conscious of everything going on in the natural world around him. His clothes, though tailored to fit him fashionably, did not *fit* him, they restricted his motions and contained him- I imagined him free of them, as he had been in the Enchanted Forest.

When Peter looked at you, it was with savage, fresh eyes. There was nothing constructed in his mind yet to limit or focus his perceptions, no artificial knowledge of language or fashion. He had only his natural human senses and judgement. In one sense, Peter was ignorant. He was ignorant of all the prejudged values that we use to distinguish between things. But when Peter looked at you, if felt as if you were the ignorant one- because in the light of the sun, all of our worldly knowledge and prejudices seem to be mere vanity and vexation.

Walking with Peter in Kensington Gardens, I imagined a world where children never grew old, a place where the things that worry adults do not exist. This was how I imagined Peter saw things, and when he looked in my eyes, I believed I might begin to see things as he did. Gazing out at the trees and the fields full of flowers, I tried to see past the visible to the invisible, to the Fairy Realm, with which Peter was well-acquainted, if my grandfather was to be believed.

106

Then I saw Margaret take Peter's hand in hers, singing softly to him as she walked along. She must have done this out of habit, and perhaps to be comforting to him, but it bothered me. I can't say exactly why it bothered me, but it did. I hadn't known Peter long enough to feel possessive of him, but perhaps I wanted to feel possessive of him. It hadn't occurred to me, until I saw her take up his hand, that anyone else might have seen in Peter what I saw. I didn't know if Margaret saw what I saw, I didn't know if she knew more about Peter and his world than I did, but I imagined she did. She certainly seemed comfortable holding his hand. I had never held a boy's hand before, at least not any boy who was not my brother. Suddenly I felt jealous of this German country girl.

Margaret may not have known what thoughts and emotions were stirring in my mind- I certainly hope she didn't- but I think she saw a change in my expression. Being a good-natured girl, she smiled at me and said, "Peter likes music- that's why I sing to him. Do you know any nice songs Caroline?"

"What about 'Love Will Find Out The Way'?" Amelia asked.

Anne agreed that was a pleasant song, so the three of us began to sing:

"Over the mountains
And over the waves,
Under the fountains
And under the graves;
Under floods that are deepest,
Which Neptune obey,
Over rocks that are steepest,
Love will find out the way.

"When there is no place
For the glow-worm to lie,
When there is no space
For receipt of a fly;
When the midge dares not venture
Lest herself fast she lay,

107

If Love come, he will enter
And will find out the way.

"You may esteem him
A child for his might;
Or you may deem him
A coward for his flight;
But if she whom Love doth honour
Be conceal'd from the day—
Set a thousand guards upon her,
Love will find out the way.

"Some think to lose him
By having him confined;
And some do suppose him,
Poor heart! to be blind;
But if ne'er so close ye wall him,
Do the best that ye may,
Blind Love, if so ye call him,
He will find out his way.

"You may train the eagle
To stoop to your fist;
Or you may inveigle
The Phoenix of the east;
The lioness, you may move her
To give over her prey;
But you'll ne'er stop a lover—
He will find out the way.

"If the earth it should part him,
He would gallop it o'er;
If the seas should o'erthwart him,
He would swim to the shore;
Should his Love become a swallow,
Through the air to stray,
Love will lend wings to follow,
And will find out the way.

"There is no striving
To cross his intent;
There is no contriving
His plots to prevent;
But if once the message greet him
That his True Love doth stay,
If Death should come and meet him,
Love will find out the way!"

Margaret said at the end, "I should like to learn that song; the three of you sang it quite beautifully."

"Here children," Mother said, coming to a stop, "Let us make our picnic on this spot."

With the help of the ladies-in-waiting, the picnic cloth was spread out over the grass and we all sat down. The picnic baskets were opened and food was spread out for everyone to eat. Mother asked Anne to say Grace.

"Thank you, Lord, for the meal we are about to receive, for your many blessings, and for introducing us to these fine people. Thank you also for..." Anne continued, speaking, but Peter lost interest in listening, reaching for an apple instead. Mother cleared her throat, drawing Peter's eye, and she shook her head at him, trying to tell him this was not proper. Margaret put her hand on Peter's for a moment to delay him, and then, when Anne was finished, she indicated it was okay for him to eat the apple.

The picnic proceeded pleasantly from that point forward. There was plenty of delicious food for everyone to enjoy, and several parallel conversations sprang up quickly. Mother and John Arbuthnot conversed with Rose and the Doctor, Samuel and Thomas asked William about what life is like as a Prince, and Anne, Amelia and I inquired from Margaret about the Wild Boy.

"Is it true that before you found him, Peter lived with Fairies in the forest of Hamelin?" I asked Margaret after a while.

"Well, no one really knows the answer to that except Peter," Margaret said. "But it is called the Enchanted Forest, and Peter spent his whole childhood there. If there are such things as fairies, he must certainly have met them."

"Do you believe in fairies?" Amelia asked.

"Well of course I do," Margaret said. "But I've never seen one before. I mean- I'm not sure if I've seen one or not. Back home, we sometimes call the fireflies fairies. But a fairy is a magic thing- it can appear as a firefly, a butterfly, a bird, a squirrel, a flower, even as a rock. So fairies are difficult to recognize, most of the time."

"I wonder if it was a fairy, that led Peter to be separated from his parents and to live in the Enchanted Forest."

"Sure," said Anne, with a smile. "What other reasonable explanation could there be, besides fairies?"

"Our brother Frederick says there is no such thing."

"He wants to be a grown-up," Anne said. "Just because you've never seen something doesn't mean it isn't real."

"This place, the grounds of these gardens, is an ancient home of the Fairy folk," I told Margaret. "Thomas Tickell wrote a poem about it."

"Who is Thomas Tickell?" Margaret asked with a slight laugh.

"He's a poet," I said.

"He has a funny name."

"He does," Amelia said.

"Well, anyway," I said, "...This place was once like your Enchanted Forest is- home to tens of thousands of fairies. But that was many ages ago, before the Kingdom of Britain was established. In those early days, the fairies ruled over the land."

"Were there no people?" Margaret asked.

"Of course there were people," I said, "but they did not yet have dominion over the whole of the earth, as they do now. This was in the days when gods and fairies and all kinds of magical things were still powerful.

"In those days, fairies would sometimes sneak into nurseries and take human babies away from their homes, to be raised among the fairy folk. They would only do this, of course, if the child was very special, and also only if the child's parents did not look after him properly.

"Well it happened that there was a human boy named Albion in whose bloodline there was a trace of magic. He was descended from Neptune, God of the Sea. One of the fairies discovered this special boy- her name was Milkah, and she was skilled in fairy charms. She took Albion here, to the fairy kingdom, to raise him as her own.

"Milkah worked magic upon Albion, so that he never grew up to be a man, but remained a small and beautiful boy. He lived this way among the fairies for nineteen peaceful years, until he fell in love with a fairy princess named Kenna. The princess Kenna likewise fell in love with him and she wished to marry him and no other.

"When their love for each other was discovered, it caused great discord among the fairies. The fairy king Oberon sent a hundred chosen knights to slay Albion, each renowned for battle skill. But brave Albion was equal to their might, and so they could not slay him, but only drive him away. Albion was heartbroken to lose sight of Kenna, but had no choice in the face of this force other than to retreat. Afterward, the fairy king sent twenty myriads of troops to keep Albion away while he prepared to marry his daughter Kenna to the fairy prince Azuriel.

"Though the King of the Fairies was against him, many allies rallied to Albion's side, from all over this land and from many lands distant. Birds and beasts, fairies and dwarves, tree spirits and water spirits all rallied when they heard of Oberon's injustice. Brave Albion led all these assembled forces into battle against the myriads gathered against him, and proved an able commander in the field. Yet Albion's cunning adversary did wield his power swiftly and mercilessly, and also made use of bribes and bargains, so that either by fear or corruption, half the fairy realm was turned to his purposes overnight, and the other half was terrified into submission. Thus Albion came to despair, and on the banks of the stream that passes through these gardens, he prayed to his ancestor Neptune,

"'If true, ye watery powers, my lineage came,

"'From Neptune mingling with a mortal dame;

"'Down to his court, with coral garlands crown'd,

"'Through all your grottoes waft my plaintive sound,

"'And urge the God, whose trident shakes the earth,

"'To grace his off-spring, and assert my birth.'

"And indeed his impassioned words did reach Lord Neptune, in his palace beneath the sea, carried far by a sympathetic mermaid whose home was in this very stream where Albion stood. And Neptune, upon hearing of Albion's misfortune, was roused with indignation. He sent the mermaid back to Albion to foretell his coming and unite the fairy folk against the tyrant Oberon.

"She returned just in time, for the fairy legions then had Albion cornered. With her siren's call, the mermaid kindled a fire in the hearts of the great host, and confirmed the truth of Albion's ancestry. Further she pronounced Azuriel and Oberon doomed by the Fates and she directed the legions to heed the will of the sea god. Hearing the mermaid declare Neptune's will, the assembled legions raised their shields and saluted Albion as their new Emperor.

"Albion was filled with pride that his prayers had been answered justly, and called upon his new army to march. Riding on the back of a great white crane, he led them forward to seek battle. Their march was swift and quickly led them across the fairy empire to the Towers of the enemy's stronghold. There they were met by Azuriel's legions.

"At last, Albion stood and faced his rival, Azuriel, the fairy prince who wished to marry Kenna, and they fought a duel between them. At the start, Albion flung a spear dipped in hornet's poison at Azuriel but his shot was made in haste, and Azuriel dodged it easily. Then Azuriel cast a poisoned javelin of his own at Albion with deadly aim, and pierced Albion's shield, and further, passed through the armor protecting his chest.

"All the fairies gasped in horror to see Albion stagger with this terrible shaft stuck in his chest, and Azuriel rushed forward to claim victory by striking off Albion's head. But truthfully, Azuriel's javelin had only pricked the skin of Albion's chest, held back by his shield and armor, and in a moment, brave Albion recovered, casting aside his shield, and with it the shaft that had stung him.

"Then without a shield to defend himself, Albion stood his ground against his fairy foe, and Azuriel's attacks were turned by Albion's sword. With a keen stroke, Albion cleaved Azuriel from shoulder to waist, and Azuriel fell before him.

"Albion thought the battle was over then, and cast his sword aside. But Azuriel, the immortal fairy, put himself back together again, and rose to slay Albion in a cowardly attack. Poor Albion was pierced through the heart and had not the magic to heal himself, and so he died in the arms of his beloved Kenna. Her name was the last word he breathed. 'Oh Kenna, Kenna,' thrice he try'd to say, 'Kenna, farewell!'

"Albion's death was mourned by many, and the mermaid who lived in the stream swam away to Neptune's palace to report the tragic death of his descendant. Neptune was outraged at the conduct of the fairies, and rose from the sea to march on the fairy kingdom. The King of Storms advanced, and the sea came with him, with bursting tides sweeping ferociously over the land, even foaming over mountains as if they were mere boulders, and with a whirlwind's roar Neptune in his chariot landed in the heart of fairy empire. Summoning all his watery power with his trident in hand, he brought ruin to the fairy folk and wiped away their empire.

"And so, the power of the fairies was broken. Kenna, the fairy princess, was one of only a handful of fairies who survived the flood. She turned Albion's spirit into the snowdrop flower, and helped it to multiply over the land. Likewise did she look after the tribe of men, who were Albion's original kinsmen, and so their kingdom multiplied and grew. And many ages passed, from that time to this.

"It is said that Kenna still dwells here, with her kin, and it was by her charms that the architect of these gardens came upon his design. By her inspiration, he shaped these gardens in the image of the fairy kingdom as it was in the time of Albion, and in the light of the moon, the fairies do emerge to dance and remember their sweet adopted prince."

"That's a sad story," said Margaret.

Looking across at Peter, who had been listening intently as I told the tale of Kensington Gardens, I said, "...Well, it occurred to me that maybe the story isn't over yet." Peter smiled at me. "Like the song," I added, looking back at Margaret. "...Mortal forms may change and perish, or prosper and multiply, but as long as the spirit remains, love finds its way."

Margaret smiled, and a tear formed in her eyes. She reached into her handbag, and produced from it a book. Offering it to me, she said, "Here. Take this."

"What is it?" I asked, accepting it from her.

"It is Peter's story," she said. "I have been writing it since the day I met him, and I have just decided- I want you to have it."

Skipping through the book, I saw Margaret had filled many pages. "You've written a lot."

"I wish I were a better writer," Margaret said, "and I wish I had more time, but it's a start. I wrote down everything I knew about him, and things people told me. I wrote down stories that we made up about him too, but don't worry- you will know the difference. There are parts missing too- things your grandfather, the King, might be able to tell you about Peter that I don't know."

"What do you mean, stories you made up?"

"It started with Rose. She read stories to Peter everyday from books in your grandfather's library, like *Robinson Crusoe* and *The Legend of Melusine,* and she noticed he especially liked certain parts. So she began piecing together in her imagination a story about the adventures Peter had before he came into our lives.

"You must remember that Peter loves listening to stories," Margaret said, "...especially ones about him. He could sit and listen to Rose for hours.

"I want you to have that book," she continued, "because someone needs to keep telling Peter's story. He's not an ordinary boy, anyone will tell you that. He's a wonderful boy. But some people don't understand him. I believe in him- your grandfather believes in him- and I hope you will come to believe in him also."

I had never imagined writing a book before, and it impressed me that Margaret had taken this task upon herself. I recognized it meant something to her, that she was now asking me to take over her work, but I wasn't sure I could accept the responsibility. "I don't know if I am the right person to give this to. Maybe someone older, who knows how to write better..."

"No, a grown-up would spoil it."

"Rose is a grown-up, and you said she told wonderful stories."

"Rose is different. But she's not going to stay here with Peter, any more than I am. It must be you. You are a good storyteller, and you are the same age as Peter and me. Please? I'll help, if you want. I'll write you letters, and you can write me back, with Peter's latest adventures. It will be fun," she said, as fresh tears appeared in her eyes.

"All right," I said, "...I'll do it."

"Thank you," Margaret smiled.

We finished eating, and then Margaret suggested we play a game of chase with Peter and the boys. So we all got up and ran off together, leaving the adults to continue their discussion.

Our game of tag in the field eventually became a game of hide-and-go-seek amongst the trees, and later, after we had played for an hour or so, Mother called to us that it was time to go home. We said our goodbyes to each other, and prepared to leave. I asked Mother if we could have another picnic tomorrow, and she smiled.

"Perhaps not tomorrow, but certainly we can meet again here at Kensington some time this week."

"What is happening tomorrow?"

"We are going to go on a tour of the sights of London with Peter and the doctor's family."

❧ ❧ ❧

That week and the next passed very quickly for Anne, Amelia, William and me. Our days were spent in activities with Mother, Peter, and the Doctor's family, and our evenings were spent with our grandfather, telling him about the day's adventures. I showed King George the book Margaret had given me and told him how she had asked me to take over writing it. He seemed interested and said that it was a good project, but declined when I asked him if he wanted me to read some of it to him. "I think I know Peter's story well enough. But if you decide to add anything to the book, Caroline, then I would be happy to read it. And if you would like me to tell you anything about Peter for your work, please don't hesitate to ask."

❧ ❧ ❧

My grandfather's words encouraged me to begin reading the book at night, to familiarize myself with Peter's story. This led me to begin asking Margaret and my grandfather questions about the Wild Boy.

Apparently committed to passing on as much knowledge regarding Peter as she could, Margaret was patient with my questions and volunteered a great deal of information. Looking back at our time together, I recognize that all of our conversations put together would probably only fill three or four hours. But it seemed as if we spent a great deal of time talking together- and it is true that young girls are able to share a great deal of information with each other in a short period time.

One thing Margaret told me that made me curious was that Peter was sometimes restless in his sleep. In the daylight, Peter always seemed gentle, carefree, and happy, but at night, as he lay in bed dreaming, he occasionally wrestled and kicked and cried as if he were trying to fight off invisible adversaries. In the morning, as usual, he would be found not in his bed, but curled on the floor.

116

"I wonder if it is because he is troubled by memories of being captured," I said.

"Now that you mention it," Margaret said, "That does seem very logical. I remember how upset he was, when the hunters carried him out of the forest. But we can never really know for certain what Peter's thoughts and dreams are, because he cannot speak."

"I wish that he could," I said.

"Me too," said Margaret.

❖ ❖ ❖

My grandfather, in his private moments, was often tender and profound in his observations. I cannot adequately tell you what it was like to sit with him and listen when he was in such a mood. I hope that every child has a grandfather who inspires such respect and interest as my grandfather inspired in me. I was always thinking of some question to bring to him, in hopes that it would bring that twinkle of light to his eyes that always seemed to accompany his best discourses. One evening, I asked King George, "What will become of Peter, when he grows up?"

My grandfather smiled and answered, "Your mother hopes Peter will grow up to become the perfect English gentleman, a model of proper education and discipline. I, on the other hand, simply hope he is happy. We plucked him from the wild, and therefore we are responsible for what befalls him. It seems unlikely to me that Peter will grow up and accept a mundane life. There is too much of the flame of youth in him. He may learn things from us that will help him make his way in the world, but he will forever remain Peter the Wild Boy.

"Caroline, you must remember this, because although he is popular now, there will come times when Peter is ridiculed or diminished because he is different. But I did not bring the Wild Boy to England simply so he could learn from us. I also brought him here so we could learn from him; so we can remember what it means to be young- to be innocent. You are still young now, but there will come a time when you will be grown-up, and it is easy,

117

so easy, to forget how precious, how dear, life is. Then you forget to smile, to laugh, to cry, to dream. I hope knowing Peter will help you to hold on fiercely to your own innocence, to live joyfully, even in the midst of difficult times.

"Grace is that ability; to face adversity and be at ease, to enter into the suffering world and help others without losing yourself in the process. It is to be true to your most essential nature, and produce something good from that. To have grace is as close as we may come to perfection. Peter is not perfect, and neither are we. No human being is. But, with grace, Peter can be the very image of perfection, and so can you and I. And, if we can hold to grace long enough, we may come to recognize we belong to something greater- that our mortal lives are indeed mere reflections of something eternal.

"As a princess, you are free of many of the things that trouble ordinary men and women. But you should trouble yourself with this matter of grace, for if you do, eventually you will find your true purpose- the reason for which princes and princesses are granted so many luxuries. It is my hope, and indeed the hope of all the Empire, that we shall always have compassionate princes and princesses who are not only noble of blood, but also and more importantly noble of spirit."

❖   ❖   ❖

While I was learning about Peter, my mother was learning about him in her own way as well, both by observation, and by talking with the Doctor and Rose. One result of the discussions that took place between them was that Peter's baptism was postponed until July. My mother, the Princess of Wales, did not want Peter to cause a scene during the baptism, and there was some real concern that this might happen, because Peter was still adjusting to life in London. The mirthful story of Peter's escape from the bathtub at Herrenhausen Palace and how Rose and Peter had slipped in the soap was enough to convince Mother that a public baptism for Peter might not be something to be rushed into.

❖   ❖   ❖

Originally, Rose and the Doctor had only intended to remain in London for a month or so. Their stay became extended at Mother's request. Finally, however, the day came when the doctor's family was scheduled to say goodbye to Peter and return home to Germany. Margaret had told me in advance that this day was coming, and neither of us were looking forward to it, because we had become friends, but we promised each other we would stay in touch through letters.

On the banks of the Thames, they said their goodbyes to the Wild Boy. Amelia and I were both present, having received permission from our mother to go and see them depart. The doctor shook Peter's hand firmly, as did Samuel and Thomas. Margaret kissed Peter on the cheek, and said softly, "Goodbye Peter." Then Rose gave Peter a big hug.

After Rose released Peter, the Doctor said, "Come, we must go now."

Seeing the family walking onto the gangplank over to the boat that would carry them away, Peter stepped forward to follow them, but the doctor shook his head and said, "No Peter. Stay with King George."

"Peter," I called out, extending a hand to him.

Peter turned his head to look back at me, but quickly looked back toward the family upon the gangplank.

"Peter," Margaret called out with tears in her eyes, "...may I present Princess Caroline."

The Wild Boy then obediently came and took my hand, kissing it, before turning back to look at Margaret, Rose, Samuel, Thomas and the doctor. They were all aboard now, and the gangplank had been retracted.

Now tearful myself, I squeezed Peter's hand in mine, and said, "Wave Peter," and lifted my other hand to wave goodbye to Margaret and her family. Amelia, standing on the other side of Peter, wrapped one arm around him, and also waved at the ship.

On board the ship, Margaret and Rose smiled tearfully and waved farewell. Lifting his hand, Peter waved back at them.

119

I don't know if Peter understood why all of us girls had tears in our eyes, but Amelia and I were sorry to see the doctor's family go. We did not know then what the future held in store for any of us, but it was evident that one chapter had ended, and a new one would soon begin.

Chapter 10: The Talk of London

Peter was to begin his lessons with John Arbuthnot the next day. When Dr. Arbuthnot came to St. James' Palace that morning, he found Peter dressed smartly in a new tailored suit. However, the Wild Boy appeared uncomfortable in this new attire.

The doctor quickly realized why- the suit was specially made to restrict Peter's posture and movements, forcing him to stand, sit and walk in a manner befitting a proper English boy. This had been suggested to my mother by one of her trusted tailors, and in theory, it might have been a good idea, but Peter did not seem very happy about it.

Sighing sympathetically, he apologized to the Prince of the Enchanted Forest for this indignity being imposed on him. He told Peter that under the circumstances, the best thing he could do for him was to teach him the lessons that would help him make some sense of English society.

Peter may not have understood Dr. Arbuthnot's genial words, but he could sense his good intentions, and gave his attention to the day's lesson as much as possible. Peter showed signs of distraction at times, but the doctor could not really blame him for this, as he found himself sometimes becoming bored with his own words.

While reflecting that much of what he was saying to Peter lacked immediate context or emotional content, and was merely a recitation of intellectual debris, Dr. Arbuthnot struggled to follow through with his carefully plotted lesson plan. At times, his narrative gave way to impromptu observations about things he saw that caught Peter's attention.

Finally, he concluded it was better to talk to Peter about peacock feathers and silver broaches, if those things interested him, than to force Peter to listen to something that did not engage his attention. So, Dr. Arbuthnot fished some shiny coins from his pocket and set them on the table, to see if Peter would be interested in them. Peter reached out and inspected the coins curiously. Then he arranged the coins in groups, to teach Peter about numbers. This approach seemed more effective in holding Peter's attention, and the doctor resolved he would modify his lesson plans to take Peter's interests into consideration.

After the day's lesson, Peter and Dr. Arbuthnot were joined by Anne, Amelia, me and William. With our participation, the doctor reviewed the lesson for a few minutes, and then told us we would have some free time to do art, giving us each a paintbrush, paint, and a canvas to work on. This established a format of lessons that we followed for several weeks, with minor variations. Mostly, the idea was that by having the four of us briefly review Peter's lessons with him and Dr. Arbuthnot, it would reinforce what he was learning and encourage him to pay attention. Nothing that the Wild Boy was learning was new to any of us- not even to little William- but we enjoyed Peter's company, and Mother told us it was good for us to help him. Sometimes, Mother came to watch, and she encouraged us to play music and sing with Peter, having a harpsichord and other smaller instruments brought in for us to use.

Everyday, the doctor labored to teach Peter the fundamentals of language and vocabulary, of posture and manner, of music and dance and numbers ("1, 2, 3. 1, 2, 3.") and other basic building blocks of learning. Peter learned to mimic spoken words whenever Dr. Arbuthnot said, "Repeat after me," and he showed an interest in singing. The involvement of us children definitely helped Peter to understand better what was expected of him, but Dr. Arbuthnot also resorted to using toys and other objects in the lessons with Peter. Gradually, he began to show more signs of recognizing basic spoken language, and was able- with some difficulty- to repeat words spoken by his tutor, but still if he needed to communicate something, Peter would gesture and hum rather than trying to use words.

❊   ❊   ❊

As part of our own education, Anne, Amelia, William and I had all learned how to paint from master artists, and we enjoyed the freedom Dr. Arbuthnot provided for us to paint whatever we liked on our canvases. Peter of course, had no prior training, and did not produce what you would call fine art, but nevertheless he surprised us with his visualization abilities. He did not sketch his subject at all, but began immediately with color, applying a daub here and a daub there. At the start, his paintings would appear to be random, formless smudges of color. Gradually, however, dreamlike images would appear. Sometimes, Peter painted subjects we recognized, such as red-coated Palace guards chasing him, or King George in his royal raiment sitting on his throne, with Peter standing by, or all of us children running with our hair in the wind. Other times he painted things that seemed to be drawn from memories of life in the forest- riding on the back of a bear or a deer, or climbing in a tree. Interestingly, even in the forest scenes he painted himself in his green suit.

It was evident from his expressions Peter knew his paintings did not have the same realism as ours. He watched us paint with interest, and seemed frustrated when he returned to his own canvas. Sometimes, we tried to encourage him by collaborating on a painting, and he seemed to enjoy this.

Dr. Arbuthnot had to stay alert, because if Peter thought he was done painting a canvas, he would sometimes begin painting on the smock he was wearing. One day, King George happened into the middle of this scene, and laughed at the sight of Peter, covered in paint. "Peter, you have given me an idea. I would like to have you painted. Children, next weekend we shall take Peter to Kensington and have a portrait of him and Doctor Arbuthnot made by William Kent. I shall invite your mother to join us."

❊   ❊   ❊

The weekend arrived and Peter went with us to Kensington Palace to meet the man who would paint his portrait. William Kent was an accomplished architect, landscape designer and painter who was at that time decorating a staircase in Kensington Palace with portraits of my grandfather's favorite servants.

On his way to the Palace, Peter found an acorn and took it with him into the portrait session. Arbuthnot attempted to take the acorn from Peter so that Kent could pose him properly, but he resisted giving it up and Kent said, "That's all right. If he likes acorns, I see no reason not to include it in his portrait. Just let him stand naturally so I can get a sense of his features."

We watched with interest as Kent captured Peter's features, and our presence made it easier for Peter to be patient with the process. Afterward we all went to Kensington Gardens to have a picnic and enjoy the afternoon.

The party consisted of my grandfather King George, my mother, Dr. Arbuthnot, and all of us children- Frederick, Anne, Amelia, me, William, Mary and Louise. Frederick was there only because Mother had insisted on his presence- he would have preferred to be elsewhere, and I think most of us would not have minded if he had been.

When the meal was finished, Peter was allowed to take off the restrictive jacket he had been wearing and join us children at play. Freed of his restraints, the Wild Boy cried, "Yahoo!" and charged off into the grassy field. The adults laughed at his expression of joy and arranged their seating positions so they could watch us children play.

Keen to be thought of as an adult, Frederick remained seated when Peter and all of us children went to play, but then King George ordered him to join with us. Frederick was sullen about this at first, but once he got into the game of tag he seemed to enjoy himself.

The frolic continued for over an hour, while the adults discussed events of the day, until Anne suddenly stopped and asked, "Where is Peter?" and all of us looked around in surprise, because we had not noticed his disappearance.

"Peter!" Amelia called.

"Peter!" shouted Frederick.

"Oh no," I said. "...Peter is lost. We must tell Mother."

"Why? He can't have gone far," said Frederick. "Let's split up and search for him. Come on Will, you go with me." Without further discussion William and Frederick headed off in search of Peter, leaving us girls standing together still considering what to do.

"Frederick is right," said Amelia, "let's go. We know the layout of these gardens- there's no chance of us becoming lost. Mary, Louise, you two go back to Mother and King George, and tell them we are going hunting for Peter."

So young Mary and Louise joined hands and headed back toward the place where the adults sat. Looking off in the direction of the trees, Anne said, "...Right then; Amelia you go to the left, I'll go to the right and Caroline you search the center area. We'll meet you in the middle." We nodded, and then split up.

Once we had spread out and entered the wood, we could no longer see one another, but at least we could still hear each other's voices, calling out to Peter. This was a comfort as Kensington Gardens is a big place, and in spite of what Amelia had said, I was concerned we might become lost ourselves.

My fear became heightened as my sisters' voices grew more faint and distant. Could they still hear my voice? Could Peter? I called out as loudly as I could, and searched among the trees for signs of the Wild Boy. Where had he gone to, and why?

My calls became more plaintive. "Peter! Where are you! Peter!" but there was no answer from the wood. Was Peter playing hide-and-seek?

Abruptly, I caught sight of him, at a distance of perhaps thirty yards from where I stood. He was sitting beneath a tree, quite peacefully, and gathered around him was a large group of rabbits.

He was feeding them carrots, which he must have pocketed during the meal.

I remembered noticing rabbits on our walk earlier, before the picnic. Peter saw them too, and apparently had wanted to go off to find them. Obviously, he had found his opportunity while we were at play.

Now that the Wild Boy was in my sight, I did not call out anymore. I wanted to come closer, to see the rabbits myself. Would I be able to sit with him, amongst these usually shy creatures?

If Peter knew I was approaching, he did not let on. His gaze was on the rabbits, and theirs on him. It seemed almost as if he was speaking to them.

I was within ten yards of the place where Peter sat when it happened- I was staring at the rabbits and the Wild Boy so fixedly that I tripped over the root of a tree. As I fell, my knee landed on something hard. I cried out, and the startled rabbits scattered.

Rolling over and holding my knee, I sobbed in pain and embarrassment. Peter sprang to his feet, and was at my side in a moment. I sat up, still crying, but did not look him in the eyes, looking at the ground instead.

Sitting down beside me, Peter tried to catch my gaze by lowering his head to enter my line of sight, but I looked away, unhappy. Reaching into his pocket, he fished out the acorn he had found earlier, and then patted me on the sleeve to get my attention. Holding out the acorn, he offered it to me as a gift. I looked at the acorn with uncertainty for a moment or two, then at Peter, whose empathy showed clearly on his face.

Looking back at the acorn in his hand, I remembered how fiercely he had clung to it in the Palace, when Dr. Arbuthnot had tried to take it from him. Smiling, I accepted the acorn, realizing that for Peter, this was a meaningful gift. Seeing me smile, Peter grinned back at me and then stood up. I rose with him, and together we found our way back to the picnic site.

We returned home then, and we did not see each other again until Monday's lesson with Doctor Arbuthnot. On Monday, I arrived wearing the acorn on woven strands of thread around my neck. Peter saw this and smiled.

❖ ❖ ❖

In the weeks that followed, Peter continued to gradually expand his own verbal ability, and the number of spoken words he was able to recognize grew, which was encouraging to Dr. Arbuthnot. Mother or the King sometimes appeared and observed the lessons with interest, and on weekends, one or both of them would often take Peter and us children on outings in the park-these were happy times.

❖ ❖ ❖

After seeing him with the rabbits, I became alert to the fact that Peter had a natural ability to relate to animals. King George's dogs loved Peter, and attended him whenever he was present. Birds also were attracted to Peter, showing none of the fear that they exhibit normally around humans, and Peter talked to them as if he knew their language. Peter spoke with horses too, and made various sounds that seemed to calm them.

As a result, Amelia convinced Mother to let us teach Peter how to ride horseback, and though the English language still presented challenges for him, this was a skill he took to readily. In fact, he was so adept in the saddle, he was better than any of us.

❖ ❖ ❖

In July, under the supervision of Dr. Arbuthnot, Peter went to church and received his baptism from the priests there. Mother was gladdened by this event, and much was made publicly of the fact that the Wild Boy had now been baptized.

On the streets and in the coffeehouses of London, talk of Peter was spreading like fire, fueled by an unending supply of pamphlets being distributed by the popular presses. It seemed just about everyone wanted to be part of the discussion about Peter. One enterprising druggist, I am told, took to writing speculative articles about the Wild Boy's being raised by a bear in order to draw interest to his advertisements for various lotions used to cure unpleasant conditions.

127

The public gazettes were littered with articles about the Wild Boy of Hamelin, many claiming to share details of his origins or his new life in London, and the frenzy only intensified when a likeness of Peter was displayed in a waxworks museum on the Strand. The *Edinburgh Evening Courant* called Peter "a youth who is one of the greatest curiosities that has appeared in the world since the time of Adam... how he supported himself in comfortable solitude, is at present what takes up the conversation of the learned." Indeed, Mother's residence at Leiceister House, which had long been a gathering point for intellectuals and philosophers, played host to a number of writers who were interested in learning more about the Wild Boy.

Of what was written regarding Peter, we have some records, but of what was discussed at Leicester House, I have only what my mother told me. There were many unanswerable questions repeated from one night to the next by different guests, such as:

"Is it true the Wild Boy was raised by wolves?" or bears, deer, fairies, etc.

"How did Peter feed himself when he lived alone in the forest?"

"Before he was rescued from the forest, did Peter feed exclusively on leaves, moss, fruit, tree sap, honey, grasses, and herbs?"

"Was Peter suckled by a mother bear during his childhood?"

"Did Peter learn from the beasts how to prey on smaller animals?"

"Where did Peter take shelter when it snowed or rained in the wild?"

"Was the Wild Boy abandoned by his parents, or did he run away?"

For those who were present frequently, such questions became a source of amusement, as Mother grew so tired of saying "I don't know," that she began inventing answers. Eventually, the guest would be let in on the joke, and then everyone would share their own theories. Other times, guests would ask different questions such as:

"Does Peter fear anything?" *Correct Answer: Peter is brave, and occasionally reckless, but he is not stupid. Example: he has no fear of fire, and will sit right next to a blazing furnace, but will not let himself be burned.*

"Has Peter ever shown any tendency toward violence?" *Correct Answer: No, he is very gentle, though he seems capable of defending himself if necessary.*

"Is it that Peter simply does not know our language, or is he not able to understand? Is he capable of understanding God, or the concepts of science, or social structure?" *Correct answer: We do not know the depths of his understanding, but we can see he understands much more than he is currently able to express with words.*

"Can Peter communicate with animals?" *Correct answer: We don't know. He seems to understand them, and they seem to understand him, at least as well as he understands us.*

Mother enjoyed entertaining her guests and answering all of their questions, but eventually, she would say enough, and call for Peter to be brought in, so the guests could form their own impressions of him. "Just look into his eyes," she would say invitingly.

Peter's gaze had different effects on different people. When some people looked into his eyes, a smile would spread across their faces, and they would go on smiling for the rest of the evening. When asked what made them smile, everyone seemed to have their own answer. It was as if when looking into his eyes they recalled whatever memory was most sweet, pure and innocent.

A few people were frightened by Peter, and later could not explain exactly why. No one who met Peter believed him to be dangerous, but for some, meeting Peter's gaze evoked the sort of irrational fear one feels in the dark of night- it has no form or reason; it simply is. They tried to explain that Peter was human, but not human- they saw in his eyes no sign of a soul. He looked like a boy, walked like a boy and was dressed like a boy, but he was a creature of the wild.

Unlike these visitors, Mother had every confidence in the existence and health of Peter's soul, but felt he was like a mirror for people. "Society allows us to hide our nature in many ways," she said to me one day, "...with fashion, and language, and manner. But none of that matters to Peter. That is why I enjoy seeing different people's reactions in meeting him. People see in his eyes what lies beneath their own skins."

Sir Isaac Newton visited one evening, and said about Peter, "He is a fascinating case for scientific study. Some day, perhaps soon, we shall uncover as much about the workings of the mind as we are recently finding regarding the physical world, and a child such as Peter may help reveal much about our inner life- that part of us which exists beneath the surface."

❊   ❊   ❊

Regarding the general clamor about Peter, the famed satirist Jonathan Swift, who was a friend of Dr. Arbuthnot, remarked "...there is scarcely talk of anything else." Swift met with Peter briefly, long enough for him to form a generalized opinion of the Wild Boy. To my mother, Swift said, "He is a charming boy who has unfortunately become an icon. The idea of a noble savage is one that strikes a note in many hearts, including my own. But fame is seldom kind to the innocent. He will never be understood, nor will he ever understand us, I doubt. When we laugh, he neighs as a horse would. Who is to say which expression of passion is more noble? I don't want to put my friend Doctor Arbuthnot out of a job, but I think you might make the boy happier if you let him spend less time in the classroom and more time out of doors, out to pasture if you will. But this advice is from a once reluctant schoolboy who now makes his living at a desk, writing literature."

Though he derided much of the public sensation surrounding the Wild Boy, and the many pamphlets circulating about him, after meeting Peter, Swift could not resist authoring a pamphlet himself, entitled, *It Cannot Rain But It Pours; or London Strewed With Rarities.* Swift's work combined facts gleaned from Dr. Arbuthnot, together with hearsay and conjecture, to paint with words a popular image of Peter- that while uneducated and ignorant, Peter was an intuitive genius destined for greatness, superior in many respects to the society he had been drawn into, if only he could be taught human language to share his wisdom.

Swift found Peter to be an excellent device for poking fun at English society. He concluded, "Let us pray the Creator of all beings, wild and tame, that as this wild youth by being brought to court has been made a Christian, so such as are at court, and are no Christians, may lay aside their savage and rapacious nature, and return to the meekness of the Gospel."

❀ ❀ ❀

Dr. Arbuthnot also tried his hand at publishing a piece of satire involving Peter, with Swift's help. Titled, *The Most Wonderful Wonder that ever appeared to the Wonder of the British Nation*, the story involved a fictional reunion between Peter and the bear who had been his forest-mother, in which the two characters discuss the ways of the human race from an outsider's perspective, making a case that men were not the most civilized of creatures, but perhaps among the least civilized. I liked this story very much, and still keep a copy in my library. A quote from Dr. Arbuthnot's work:

"Peter: 'It is this I believe makes the Horse and Dogs suffer the Insults they meet from Man, for all things rightly consider'd, Man who provides for the Horse's Sustenance, who keeps him clean, carries away his Dung, and waits upon him when he has any Ailment, is no more than Slave to the generous Beast. As to the Dog, I have seen the She Men treat him with so much Care, Tenderness and Deference, that I am apt to think they worship him; they take him into their Bosoms, kiss, fondle and caress him, provide the best Entertainment for him, serve him before themselves; and never suffer him to set his Foot to the Ground, but carry him in their Arms and are diligent Attendants on him. They pay the same Respect to the Monkey. I was one Day in Conversation with one, who told me he thought himself happy that he had such a number of careful Slaves, who even prevented his Wishes, and provided so well for him not only all the Conveniences of Life, but also what might gratify the Senses, that he was satisfied, the rest of his species, had they a true Notion of Men, would condescend to converse with and take upon 'em the Government of that passive Animal. This is the Monkey's way of thinking; tho' the Man thinks quite differently, and boasts that the Monkey is his Slave.'"

I liked the story of Peter and the bear because it suggested how odd our culture might seem, to an outsider. That was one of the special things about Peter, he often caused us look at things in a different light.

* * *

Daniel Defoe- author of that book *Robinson Crusoe*, which Peter had so enjoyed during his time in Hanover- also wrote a satirical pamphlet about Peter, entitled *Mere Nature Delineated*, in which he addressed at length the character and story of the Wild Boy. I do not think that at the time of his writing, Mr. Defoe had actually met Peter, but that did not stop Defoe from writing prolifically about him in the assumed persona of a learned philosopher.

The narrator of Defoe's pamphlet considered it improbable that Peter had survived in the harsh German wilderness alone, overcoming the cold winters, feeding himself, and avoiding being killed by beasts of the forest, for man "cannot rest on the Ground, or roost in the Bushes; the Trees that are the Habitation of the Fowls, and which cover the other Creatures, scratch and hurt him. He must have a House to live in, or nothing; he cannot Burrow like a rabbit, or earth himself in a den like the Badger: They are warm and secure from the weather... but the poor naked tenderskin'd Brute of Human Kind, must have a House to keep him dry, Clothes to keep him warm, and a Door to shut him in, or he is lost." Defoe's narrator could not therefore dismiss altogether the possibility that Peter's story was true, but wished that more facts were available to explain how Peter had done it. Unfortunately for the narrator, and for other scholars, the wild beasts do not catalog their history as men do, so such facts may never be available.

Defoe's narrator was also troubled by the question of Peter's consciousness and the state of his soul. He applauded the efforts to educate Peter, and reflected on the implications of the Wild Boy's existence. He contemplated that "it would indeed be a terrible satire upon the present inspired Age, first to allow this Creature to have a Soul, and to have Power of thinking, qualified to make a right Judgment of Things, and then to see that under the Operation and Influence of that regular and well-ordered Judgment, he should see it reasonable to choose to continue silent and mute, to live and converse with the Quadripeds of the Forest, and retire again from human Society, rather than dwell among the informed of Mankind; for it must be confessed he takes a Leap in the Light if he has Eyes to see it, to leap from the Woods to the Court. from the Forest among Beasts, to the Assembly among the Beauties, from the Correction House at Celle, where at best, he had conversed among the meanest of Creation, viz. the Alms-taking Poor, the Vagabond Poor, to the Society of all the Wits and Beaus of the Age: The only Way that I see we have to come to this Part, is to grant this Creature to be Soul-less, his Judgment and Sense to be in a State of Non-Entity, and that he has no rational Faculties to make the Distinction. But even that remains upon our Hands to prove."

In other words, Mr. Defoe's narrator posed that there must be something wrong with Peter, or else there is something wrong with all of us. Indeed, the narrator suggested "a Plague of Dumbness" was presently afflicting the courts of England and Europe. "Can anyone learn Religion in this Town?" the narrator asked, "Shall he be taught Religion by its Contraries?"

❖   ❖   ❖

Later in the year, Jonathan Swift published *Gulliver's Travels*, which included, in the final parts of the book, a depiction of a race of crude, unsophisticated men, called Yahoos, contrasted with a noble race of intelligent, neighing horses, called Houynhnms. While obviously drawing some inspiration from Peter, the caricatures of the Yahoo and Houynhnms were in fact aimed at

133

exposing the crudeness that Swift saw in modern society. Again, Peter was being used as a mirror for the English to examine themselves. Mother enjoyed *Gulliver's Travels* very much, and gave me a copy to read.

❊ ❊ ❊

Peter continued to be the talk of London even as he gradually became more adapted to life in society. Sometimes all the attention was hard on him, and he began to show signs of frustration when amongst large groups of people.

King George liked the fact that Peter was a popular figure, and felt it was in the interest of the Royal Family to continue having him make public appearances. However, he did try to make arrangements so that Peter would not be made too uncomfortable by all the attention he was receiving.

❊ ❊ ❊

In general, the Royal Family was terribly fond of Peter. To the adults, he was a constant source of human innocence, and for us children he was a wonderful playmate, with whom anything seemed possible. Frederick was the only one who did not seem to have any appreciation for Peter.

Peter was an easy target for Frederick's overbearing, hostile teenage nature. Frederick may have been a bit jealous that everyone else was making such a big fuss over Peter, and he certainly wasn't overawed by the Wild Boy himself.

In the fall, during one of his visits to St. James' Palace, as Peter was exploring the halls, he had an encounter with my older brother, who was practicing swordsmanship alone. Frederick had seen Peter watching him on many occasions before, and decided to offer Peter a sword.

"Come on then," Frederick invited, when Peter accepted the sword. Stepping into the middle of the room, Frederick motioned for Peter to join him.

Lifting the sword in his hand, Peter approached Frederick. When Peter had come into range, Frederick parried his sword to the side. Then he put his sword out and said, "Now you do

134

it." Peter swung his sword back and knocked Frederick's sword aside. Frederick smiled. "That's the idea." A playful duel began between Frederick and Peter, and the sounds of swords clashing caught my attention.

When I came into the room and saw Peter and Frederick dueling, I exclaimed, "Frederick, what are you doing?"

"Just having a bit of fun with Peter," Frederick said.

"It isn't safe," I said, standing rigid with fear.

"Don't be such a girl, Caroline. Peter's been wanting to have a shot at me for a while now, and he's better at fencing than I thought."

"It isn't safe," I insisted.

"Relax, Caroline. I'm not going to hurt him, just teach him a lesson. Besides these swords aren't sharp. See?" With that he struck Peter on the wrist, making Peter drop his sword. I cried out. Frederick laughed. "I didn't hurt him, Caroline. See he's picking it up again."

"Frederick please don't be mean to him."

In the next clash, Peter managed to strike Frederick's wrist, causing the prince to drop his blade. "Ow!" Frederick exclaimed, "That actually hurt!"

"Okay, so why don't you stop now," I said.

"Are you kidding?" Frederick said, picking up his sword, "… This is just getting interesting! Look I swear I'll be nice."

"You'd better," I said. "If you hurt him, I'm telling." Peter and Frederick continued dueling for over an hour, with me watching pensively.

If only I were a boy I could certainly tell you better about their maneuvers and exchanges. Peter may have had trouble with his language lessons, but he learned his way about the sword very quickly from Frederick. Soon he was thrusting, parrying and slashing with authority. Their fencing match, which had begun as a joke, was now carried on in earnest. The two boys matched each other's strokes in clash after clash. Had I not been so afraid that

135

one of them would be hurt, I might have enjoyed watching their energetic display.

Finally Frederick said, "Stop." He lowered his sword, and when Peter did the same, he extended his hand for Peter to shake. Peter accepted it, and the two smiled at each other, shaking hands. "Look, don't tell Mother or Father or Grandfather about this, okay Caroline?"

"Promise you won't do it again?"

Frederick paused. "All right. I promise. Unless he starts it."

"Frederick!"

"Relax, Caroline," Frederick said, patting me on the shoulder. "It was fun to have a match with Peter, but once is enough for me. I promise I won't stir up any more trouble. Okay?"

So I did not seek to get my brother in any trouble with our parents or with King George. I kept an eye out, in case Frederick was inclined to cause any more mischief, but Frederick, to my surprise, stayed true to his word.

❁　❁　❁

Peter enjoyed his first Christmas in London with the Royal Family. He attended dinner on Christmas Eve, and showed himself much improved. He ate with proper utensils, and behaved more or less properly. He was well-behaved enough that the King decided to let him attend Christmas services at the Church. During the services, I held Peter's hand.

Then there was the Christmas gift-giving, and everyone, even Frederick, had a gift for Peter. Frederick's gift was a handsome new hat, which Peter wore proudly.

To Peter's delight, there was plenty of chocolate, and fruit and other sweet treats. After the Christmas holiday however, Peter fell sick and was not seen for several weeks. When Peter appeared again at St. James' Palace to resume his lessons, we were all much relieved.

136

Chapter 11: Crossing Over

The spring of 1727 was a happy period. Peter had become part of all our lives, to one extent or another, and the same effect that he'd had at Herrenhausen Palace was beginning to take hold throughout the English court. Of course there always are serious matters to be attended to at court, but during the in-between moments, smiles and laughter were more frequent, and the general atmosphere was more playful and humorous.

❖ ❖ ❖

There were a number of birthday parties in the spring, starting with Frederick's twentieth birthday in February. Peter was a lively and popular guest at these occasions. One never knew for certain what he might do, but usually it would be something interesting. When music was playing, Peter was likely to be on the dance floor, and if the group was singing, Peter would join in (he was better at vocalizing songs than sentences.)

I remember Frederick had a surprise for all of us at his birthday party, revealing that he and Peter had practiced singing together. Apparently the bout of fencing they'd done in the fall had warmed Frederick to the Wild Boy's character. I cannot recall the lyrics of the song he'd taught Peter, but it was a mischievous number that suited Frederick's character well. Frederick seemed pleased with himself as he sang beside Peter, and at the end of the song, as the people around them applauded, he tousled the Wild Boy's hair in a familiar, friendly way.

Lord Hervey was present for Frederick's party, and as usual was surrounded by ladies of the court. Though I had never interacted much with Hervey previously, I had always thought he was a handsome and clever man- much more charming than

137

Frederick was. However, that day I saw another side of him. He applauded Frederick's performance with Peter, as many others did, but then as he laughed and slapped Frederick on the back, he made a remark that soured any admiration I might have had toward him. He said, "…Who would have thought the idiot Peter could be taught to sing! Well done Frederick, well done."

"Peter's not an idiot," I said sharply, "…and Frederick didn't teach him to sing."

"Of course I taught the idiot to sing," Frederick replied, enjoying Hervey's praise and the attention of the young ladies gathered round. Frederick had a way of flipping in a moment from pleasant to unpleasant.

"You did not!"

"Who did then?" Hervey asked. "Obviously the idiot didn't teach himself. Was it the fairies of the Enchanted Forest that taught him?"

"Peter could sing when we met him, he's just been learning the words to our songs."

"Well," Frederick allowed, "…he could make some noises, but I wouldn't call it singing. Anyway Caroline, why don't you take Peter and go get something to eat? Peter is always hungry. Go on then, go get some food."

"Food?" Peter repeated, looking between Frederick and me hopefully. I did not appreciate Frederick's attitude, but was happy to take Peter's hand and move away from this group.

Frederick later apologized for calling Peter an idiot, after the party was over. "…It was a mean thing to say, even if Peter didn't understand what I said. I know you like Peter and I am sorry. I guess- I guess I was trying to impress the girls."

"Well, if they were impressed by that, then they are idiots," I said crossly.

Frederick laughed. "Here Caroline," he said, fishing something from his pocket. "I have a gift for you." It was a delicate silver chain. "For the acorn you sometimes wear around your neck. It was a gift from Peter, wasn't it? This way you can wear the acorn all the time, if you want. And Peter seems to like silver."

I was still somewhat upset, but Mother had taught us to be forgiving when someone apologized, and Frederick's gift was thoughtful and beautiful, so I thanked him, accepting the gift graciously.

"Can I get a hug from my sister on my birthday?" he asked, spreading his arms.

For me, it was impossible to hug someone if I was still upset. But I did not really want to be upset with my brother, especially not on his birthday, so I took a deep breath and gave him a hug. "Happy birthday Frederick."

"Thank you, Caroline."

❊ ❊ ❊

In March, Mother celebrated her forty-fourth birthday with a masquerade at Kensington. The theme of the party, taking inspiration from Thomas Tickell's poem, was fairies, and the Palace and Gardens were decorated accordingly. It was an extravagant, enchanted evening, and everyone who was anyone was there.

For Amelia and me, it was an opportunity to wander unattended through the Palace and Gardens with Peter, nibble on delightful morsels snatched from serving dishes, and play games of our own choosing. Anne was not with us- on that evening she decided to mingle with the adults. It was time for her to begin to grow up; Amelia and I knew that, and we did not hold it against her, though we hoped there would still be future days when she would play with us again.

Before letting us go to entertain ourselves, Mother introduced us to a special guest- Thomas Tickell himself. "Mr. Tickell, these are my daughters, Amelia and Caroline."

"It is an honor, Princesses," the poet said, bowing and kissing our hands.

"And this is the Wild Boy, whom you have heard so much about recently," Mother said, gesturing to Peter.

Shaking hands with Peter, he said, "…A pleasure to meet you Peter."

To my embarrassment, Mother told him, "Caroline is very fond of your poem about Kensington Gardens, and sees a parallel between your hero Albion, who was adopted by fairies as an infant, and Peter, who spent his childhood in the Enchanted Forest of Hamelin."

"Indeed," the poet responded with great seriousness, squatting down and looking into Peter's face, "…one can see plainly in his eyes that Peter has known fairy folk and lived among them. Perhaps he is Albion reborn." Tickell smiled. "If only you could tell us your secrets, Peter, what a wonder that would be."

"Do you believe in fairies, Mr. Tickell?" I asked.

"Of course!" he answered, rising. "…Don't you?"

"Yes, I do."

"Well don't ever stop believing. Perhaps one day, Peter will introduce you to their world."

"I would like that," I said. "Thank you, Mr. Tickell."

We took our leave of Mother then- Amelia, Peter and I- and set out to explore. As we wandered, Peter gazed wide-eyed at the spectacle around us, and being with him, Amelia and I found ourselves envisioning the costumes and illusions as being real. Holding hands, we imagined we were exploring an enchanted world with Peter.

Hidden, colored lights, strangely shaped lamps and a flickering sea of candles illuminated our surroundings. The trees and foliage were filled with these lights also, and upon the water of the Serpentine, a myriad of colored lamps floated merrily. Veils and garlands hung elegantly here and there, and cleverly crafted decorations transformed familiar landmarks into otherworldly marvels. All the guests at the party were dressed in imaginative costumes keeping with the theme of the Fairy Masquerade, and ballet dancers- also dressed as fairies- mingled amongst the attendees, elegantly striding, leaping, sinking, rising and pirouetting in time with the music that drifted through the air around us.

Of course, with few exceptions, most sensible adults do not believe in magic, but I believe that evening, something magical did occur between Peter, Amelia and I. Up until that day, though we had spent almost a year with him, Peter had been something of a friendly stranger to us. He came from a mysterious place that we might imagine, but might never go, and he surely had seen things that we might never see. But on that evening, holding hands with each other and with Peter, Amelia and I crossed over- from our world into his.

Poets and children sometimes see things that escape the eyes of common men. Thomas Tickell wrote that the land where Kensington Gardens was situated had once been a fairyland, and that by enchantment, the architect of these gardens had been guided to rebuild that land. Now we two Princesses walked in the midst of a fairy masquerade, with a Wild Boy who was said to have been raised by fairies.

Was it all simply make-believe, or was it true- that whether we know it or not, we are part of forces we may neither see nor hear but that operate around us and may influence our lives, and what is in our hearts adds gravity to such forces? Standing amongst the swirling crowd, I saw Peter still, unmoving, smiling.

I smiled back at Peter, and he squeezed my hand. Then he drew Amelia and me into a joyful dance, and the crowd gave way for us.

I realized then that not only on this surreal night, but every day, the magical world and the mundane exist in the same space. Peter was able to move from room to room between these worlds freely, and now so could we, as long as we remembered where to look. I looked at Amelia, and felt that she too sensed this- that we had broken through a barrier to another room tonight, and had woken in a field of dreams.

❊ ❊ ❊

My little sister Mary had her fourth birthday in March, and William had his sixth birthday in April. Peter attended these parties also, and added his usual energetic presence to the festivities. Then there was a farewell party for King George, who was returning to Hanover for another vacation.

My grandfather was not given to making large public gestures very often. Therefore, his farewell party was a small, private affair, with only a few hundred people present. Among other guests, Mother, Father, and all of us children were there, and Peter as well.

I remember dancing with King George that night- he danced with each of us granddaughters. He was so kind and gentle and great with me, and he said to me, "Caroline my dear, one day you will be such a young woman that every lad in the Empire should wish to marry you, and give you children. And I am certain you are capable of being as good a parent as your Mother is. But have a care not to rush into things too quickly. Your childhood is precious- it is a time of freedom, and a time to pursue excellence. See how nicely your sister Anne has matured- she did not hurry things along."

Smiling, I told him, "...I am in no hurry to grow up, Grandfather."

He nodded. "I know. And I am proud of you for that. I just wanted to let you know that my hope is for you to be happy and not to rush anything. So- continue, continue..." he said, smiling back at me. We danced together for several minutes more, until the melody concluded and a new dance began. This was a faster paced tune. With my hand held in his, King George began to exit the dance floor.

"King George!" Peter called, causing my grandfather's head to turn. He saw Peter standing a short distance away on the dance floor. As soon as Peter saw him look, the Wild Boy broke into a fast-footed dance, shuffling, tapping, kicking and stomping his shoes on the dance floor. My grandfather laughed. "King George!" Peter beckoned.

King George could not resist the call of the Wild Boy. Striding back onto the dance floor, he imitated Peter's fast-footed steps, adding a bit of style of his own. The dance was reminiscent of a Celtic step-dance. Peter was delighted, and spun himself in a circle, with his arms extended out and his head thrown back.

King George mimicked Peter again, whirling about beside the Wild Boy who stopped to watch him. King George added a classically-trained flourish to his spin. Peter applauded.

By now other people had become aware of what was going on, and were spreading out to give Peter and King George room as the two figures now circled each other. There was a joyful intensity in their eyes as they challenged each other with dance moves. Peter's expressive movements, for the most part, were conjured from his imagination, while King George's style was informed by years of practicing different forms of dance, but King George did his best to find movements that matched Peter's, and Peter likewise took notes from King George's style.

The dance between the sixty-seven year-old monarch and the fourteen year-old Wild Boy went for some time, with everyone else standing by watching, and then King George called out to Anne, Amelia and me to join in.

We stepped out together and joined hands with Peter and our grandfather at the center of the room, dancing in a circle. We did our best to match them step for step, and then at my grandfather's word, we all stopped and let go of each other's hands.

Peter continued dancing for several moments after we had halted, and then he stopped too. As soon as he stopped, King George pointed at Anne. "Anne!" he said, prompting her to dance. She did not miss a beat, but immediately performed a short exquisite solo dance, halting when she heard our grandfather say, "Amelia!" Anne held her pose then, as Amelia went into motion. Like Anne, Amelia was an excellent dancer, but her style was different, more muscular and aggressive. When King George called out "Caroline!" she too froze in a dance pose, yielding the floor to me. Free to dance however I wished, I pirouetted briefly and then opened a ballet routine I had been practicing lately.

I was in the midst of a particularly difficult move when I heard Peter call out, "King George!" and then, being a good sport, I had to hold my posture while my grandfather danced. Thankfully, he chose to only make a very brief effort, concluding his dance at an opportune moment during the melody that was playing. Laughing, he called us together and we all hugged, then exited the dance floor together.

❖ ❖ ❖

The illness that had afflicted Peter over the winter returned in full force after that party, so Peter was unable to be present when King George boarded his ship again at Whitehall and sailed away. As Peter had been an almost constant presence since his arrival the year before, people noted his absence with some concern.

Peter was also absent from Amelia's sixteenth birthday celebration in May- an event that the Wild Boy surely would not have wished to miss. Amelia was disappointed that Peter would not be there, but it was said that he was terribly ill, and could not get out of bed to attend the event.

Soon afterward, reports surfaced in the newspapers that Peter the Wild Boy had died, leading many who had been charmed by the sight of him at public events to grieve. The British Journal ran an epitaph in Peter's memory, penned by Jonathan Swift. It went like this:

"Ye Yahoos mourn,
For in this Place lies dead the Glory of your Race,
One, who from Adam had Descent,
Yet ne'er did what he might repent;
But liv'd, unblemish'd, to fifteen,
And yet, O strange, a Court had seen,
Was solely rul'd by Nature's Laws,
And dy'd a Martyr in her Cause!
Now reign, ye Houynhnms, for Mankind,
Have no such Peter left behind,

None like the dear departed Youth,
Renown'd for Purity and Truth,
He was your Rival, and our Boast,
For ever, ever, ever lost!"

But, Peter was not dead yet. Sick perhaps, but not dead. Thankfully our mother kept us informed about Peter's health during this period, and though it was too soon to pronounce him cured, it seemed the British Journal and the other papers had been premature in reporting his demise. If Swift, the satirist, knew this through his connection with Arbuthnot, he certainly didn't let on.

Peter appeared healthy again in time for my fourteenth birthday party in June at Kensington Palace. This was a lavish New World costumed spectacle that Mother had organized. She was fond of throwing grand events, and in my opinion, the New World celebration outdid the Fairy Masquerade.

There were real Indians at the party, performing their traditional folk music. There were also Pirates, or at least men dressed to look the part, and they performed mock duels with British navymen. There were also exotic characters borrowed from the Orient, such as sword-swallowers, veiled dancing women and firebreathing men. There were even Mermaids and Mermen who swam and sang in the waters of the Serpentine pond, around a small sailing ship that had been outfitted for this occasion.

Peter arrived in one of his trademark outfits of green and red. I was very pleased to see him, and waved for him to join me. It was my party, but many of the people there were friends of my parents, not mine.

❁ ❁ ❁

Peter and I wandered together around the Palace and in the Gardens, taking in the sights of the party. By chance, during our wandering, we came across Daniel Defoe, and I recognized him from a portrait I had seen previously. "Mr. Defoe!" I said, pleasantly surprised, "…I did not realize you had been invited to our party. Welcome."

145

"Princess Caroline?" Defoe asked. "Happy birthday to you, Your Highness. This is quite a party. Are you enjoying yourself?"

I nodded. "Peter and I are just taking a walk and enjoying the sights."

"Is this the famous Wild Boy then?"

"Yes."

"You know I wrote a rather silly pamphlet about him, having never actually met him."

"Yes I know. Don't worry, I never read it to Peter. But he does like your book *Robinson Crusoe*."

"Really? I didn't know he had learned to read."

"He hasn't yet, but he can listen to others read. And he likes the pictures."

Defoe took a deep breath. "You know, I actually have a great respect for Peter, from the little that I do know about him. He is every bit as much of a survivor as Robinson Crusoe, and his challenges have not ended upon being returned to civilization after a long absence. Perhaps I should write a novel about him- what do you think?"

"Too late, Mr. Defoe- I am already working on one."

"Ah- then I wish you the best of luck in writing," Defoe said, bowing. "And a happy fourteenth birthday as well."

"Thank you," I said smiling.

❖ ❖ ❖

I received good wishes from everyone we encountered, until we met Lord Hervey by the water dressed as a pirate. He was drunk, and alone. Seeing the two of us holding hands, he made a remark about the two of us looking like a young Romeo and Juliet. I let go of Peter's hand and stepped forward saying, "Peter and I are friends, Lord Hervey."

"You and I are also friends, are we not?"

"I suppose."

"Will you hold my hand, Caroline?"

"I don't feel like holding your hand."

Lord Hervey reached out and snatched up my hand. "Come on, Caroline. Dance with me." He pulled me close to him and began to dance.

"Stop!" I said, protesting, "Let me go! Stop it!"

Peter ran forward and tried to separate the two of us. Hervey tried to push the Wild Boy away, and Peter resisted for a moment, then fell back, but as Peter fell, Hervey heard a sound that got his attention. Peter had seized hold of the hilt of one of Hervey's swords and as he fell back had drawn the sword from its scabbard.

Hervey saw Peter rising and pushed me aside, to the ground, muttering to himself, "Oh God, now the idiot has himself a sword." He drew his other sword from its scabbard and said, "Have at thee, thou irrepressible youth!"

The two of them clashed several times, with neither scoring a strike, and much to Hervey's surprise, Peter seemed to know what he was doing. Hervey thought he would easily overwhelm and frighten the Wild Boy into submission, but instead, he found himself focused as much on defense as on attack. Peter dodged, lunged, parried, and struck with the natural deftness of an experienced fencer. Hervey, warming to the challenge, unleashed a blazing offensive, shouting and slashing with such ferocity that I thought he meant to do real harm to Peter, but still the Wild Boy matched him move for move.

Then, with an understated gesture that took Hervey off guard, Peter succeeded in striking Hervey's wrist, just as Frederick had done to him in their duel the previous year. But the swords they were playing with now were sharp, and Hervey cried out in fear and pain as the strike landed. His hand fell to his side and his sword clattered to the ground and then bounced into the water with a splash.

Peter advanced on him, sword pointed and eyes blazing. Hervey took a step back, then another, holding his wrist in pain. When Peter continued to press forward, Hervey jumped into the water to save himself. Then I ran over to where Peter stood, took the sword from Peter's hand and cast it into the water.

"Are you all right?" I asked Hervey, who had surfaced in the water. "Your hand, is it okay?"

"It's still attached if that's what you mean, but I'll need to see a doctor. Help me out of the water, will you?"

"You have two hands," I said, "…you can help yourself."

"I'll ruin that boy," Hervey cried from the water, raging at the indignity of his defeat. "I'll tell everyone what he did to me. They'll lock him up."

"You do that," I said coldly, "and I'll tell everyone what you tried to do. We'll see who gets locked up." Turning, I said, "Come on Peter, let's go."

Peter and I returned to the Palace and tried to enjoy the remainder of the party. Lord Hervey, as it turned out, decided it would be better form to keep his complaints to himself.

❖   ❖   ❖

And so things carried on more or less pleasantly in the days that followed, until news reached London that King George had suffered a stroke on June 9th while traveling from Delden to Nordhorn and had died on June 11ᴬ at the Prince-Bishop's palace at Osnabrück. This news came as a great shock for all of us. Anne, Amelia, Mother and I spent the better part of a day in tears. We didn't tell William or Mary at once, but waited several days, because our own emotions were still too fresh, and we did not want to make the news any more upsetting for them.

❖   ❖   ❖

Over the next few months, the adults of the Royal Court would be engaged in many political meetings and public events, culminating in October in the coronation of my father, George Augustus, as the new King of England. Leading up to this event, we moved our residence to Kensington Palace, and the Wild Boy came along with us. Frederick, meanwhile, was established as the new Prince of Wales and took up residence in Leicester House, the home our parents had just vacated.

Up to this point, we had been living separately from Peter, with King George keeping Frederick, Anne, Amelia, me and William at

St. James' Palace, while Peter and the youngest children Mary and Louise stayed with Father and Mother at Leicester house. Now, all of us except Frederick were together under one roof. Though our hearts were still heavy with past memories of our dear grandfather, ahead of us summer gleamed with prospects of adventure.

❊   ❊   ❊

In the days leading up to the coronation, the adults were so busy making preparations that we children and Peter were left more or less to our own devices and had the run of the Palace and its private Gardens. The five of us (Anne, Amelia, William and I) quickly came to know every room, corridor and staircase, as well as all the wonderful spots to play in the Gardens. We chased each other, played games of hide-and-seek, made believe we were brave explorers in the Gardens, and took expeditions in a boat upon the Serpentine, sometimes visiting an island together, where we imagined ourselves castaways like Robinson Crusoe.

Being eighteen and sixteen respectively, Anne and Amelia were old enough to have other interests besides our grand childhood adventures, so they did not always go with us. Anne for instance was continuing to take music lessons from George Friedrich Händel- who considered her a prodigy. She filled her spare moments with practice on the harpsichord, so that throughout the day, music drifted through the Palace like a summer fragrance. Amelia, on the other hand, had a great passion for horseback riding- more so than any of the rest of us. Nonetheless, both girls knew that childhood was fleeting and so they were happy to take opportunities to play with me, William and Peter from time to time.

❊   ❊   ❊

One day, Peter and I went venturing in Kensington Gardens together and stayed out late. It was just the two of us.

I said many things to Peter on that evening, about the future, about growing up, about marriage, about the responsibilities of being a member of the Royal family... I emptied out my heart to

149

Peter, knowing he could not understand most of what I said and would never share my secrets with anyone.

Peter listened respectfully, sometimes looking at me, sometimes looking at the pond. I did not want to grow up- I did not want anything to change- but I knew it would happen. My grandfather had died, my brother was becoming a man, my father and mother were becoming King and Queen, and soon I would be expected to become a woman and take my place in society.

I told Peter, "I know that some people disparage you for your lack of knowledge, and I know you may not understand me, Peter, but I wish you could, because you might be the only person who would. I feel that I can tell you anything Peter." I laughed, and tears appeared in my eyes.

Peter saw this and looked concerned, reaching out and touching my face to wipe away the tears. I took his hand and held it to my cheek. After a moment I brought his hand down to my lap and continued to hold it. "You are my best friend, Peter. Do you know that word? Friend?"

"Friend."

I smiled. "…You and I will always be friends."

A voice called out in the dark, "Caroline! Peter! Where are you? It is late." It was Mrs. Titchbourn, who was one of Mother's bedchamber women and lately a caregiver for Peter and us children.

I squeezed Peter's hand, then released it. "Come on, Peter. Let's go."

❧   ❧   ❧

The next day, in Westminster Abbey, with the music of George Friedrich Händel filling the air, George Augustus was crowned King of Great Britain. It was a lucky day for Sir Robert Walpole, who was expected to be dismissed from his position as Prime Minister when George II became King, but was instead kept on, upon the advice of the new Queen, Caroline of Ansbach.

Peter was there, with Doctor Arbuthnot watching over him, and Arbuthnot commented to a friend later that the coronation of

150

George II was a lucky event for Peter too, because he would not have to learn a new name for the King.

❊ ❊ ❊

After the coronation, Peter saw less of Anne, Amelia and me. We were still present around Kensington Palace, and took any opportunities we could to visit with Peter, but our schedules were much fuller than they had been over the summer, and the Queen was also interested in spending more personal time with us herself, so Peter became better acquainted with young Prince William and Princess Mary.

By now, Peter knew enough of our games that he did not need us older princesses around to help him understand how to play. William and Mary, for their part, loved Peter dearly, and spent many afternoons playing with him.

Chapter 12: Axter's End

Gradually, the public fascination with Peter had settled down, so that by the fall of 1727 there were relatively few stories being told about him in the papers. Mother also felt less attached to Peter, because after King George's death she now had all of her own children in her home, and she had many new responsibilities to be concerned with as Queen. She still cared for Peter, but saw that he was becoming increasingly marginalized, and she understood from speaking with Doctor Arbuthnot that in spite of his progress, it seemed unlikely Peter would ever become fully educated.

And so at the Christmas holiday, Mother announced that come spring, Peter would be going to live in a new home in the country, where he could live a more peaceful existence away from all the hectic difficulties of the city, and that we would all be able to go and visit him out there whenever we wished.

We all took this news hard, particularly me, but the Queen's decision was final. So in the next few months, we all had a lingering tension about us, which Peter did not understand. As spring drew closer, Peter was filled with the usual hopefulness of the season, and was perplexed to see us looking awkward more and more often.

❖ ❖ ❖

Finally the appointed time came. Early in the day, the family climbed into a carriage with Peter and rode out to Axter's End in the parish of Northchurch, in Hertfordshire, to the farmhouse of James Fenn, where Peter was to stay. We spent several days there, helping Peter to become acquainted with the place and with his new caregiver, Mr. Fenn, who was a friend of Mrs. Titchbourn.

Mr Fenn would be paid a generous crown pension of thirty-five pounds per year to look after Peter.

It was a pleasant place, with woods nearby, and even we children, who were unhappy that Peter would not be staying with us any longer, felt that it was a good choice for him. Also, Mr. Fenn seemed like a genuinely good man, who could be trusted to care for Peter and keep him out of harm's way.

So one morning, all too soon from my perspective, our family said our goodbyes to Peter, and rode away in our carriage, leaving Peter standing beside Mr. Fenn, waving. Once out of sight, all of us children broke into tears, and though she tried to comfort us, Mother also cried. She reassured us saying, "Don't worry children; we'll come back to visit when summer comes."

Peter meanwhile, looked up at Mr. Fenn curiously. Mr. Fenn, who had been informed that Peter liked chocolate, produced a chunk from his pocket. "Come on Peter," he said, "let's go visit the horses."

※ ※ ※

Mr. Fenn quickly learned Peter had a way with animals. They were drawn to him- liked him. Though it seemed difficult for many people to understand him, he could whinny just like a colt, bark like a dog, mew like a cat, whistle like a bird and make other noises that were incomprehensible to humans but that the animals seemed to comprehend as if he were indeed speaking their language. Mr. Fenn was surprised by how easily Peter adjusted to his new life in Northchurch.

The neighbors soon learned that the famous Wild Boy was now living in their parish, and insisted that Mr. Fenn let them throw Peter a welcoming party. All the locals gathered together, bringing with them food, drink and song, and the party lasted well into the night. Peter clapped and danced with the music and charmed all the girls with his natural smile. It became apparent to Mr. Fenn that Peter's life on the farm was unlikely to be a solitary existence.

※ ※ ※

Soon, local boys and girls began to appear regularly at the farm to visit with Peter. Peter was the most exciting thing that had come to Northchurch in many a season, and the children rallied around him. They would take him on adventures into the woods, chase around the farm, play hide-and-go-seek, and engage in other games. They even helped Peter do his chores, because it was more fun helping him than doing their own chores at home.

It was hard for Mr. Fenn to keep track of the names of all these children who followed Peter around, but in those first few months, there were four children who seemed to be almost always present. There was Sean, a natural-born ringleader just a couple years younger than Peter, who became Peter's right hand and spokesperson, and helped mastermind all kinds of excitement. There was Jessica, a girl of thirteen who preferred bows and arrows over needle and thread, and took every opportunity she could to escape with Peter and Sean into the wilderness. There was little red-haired Luke, who was only six years old with a handsome round face and a mischievous grin, who was seen around Axter's End more often than at his own home. Though small, Luke was very quick. Then there was Colin, a tall, slightly awkward twelve-year old boy who admired Peter's strength, agility and courage, and followed the Wild Boy on many adventures into the woods. These four children formed a nucleus around Peter and drew many friends to join them.

When children band together, inevitably they seek their own place to hold council and make plans, away from the eyes and ears of adults. So it was with Sean, Jessica, Luke, Colin, Peter and the other children. Within a few weeks of Peter's arrival, they had found a place in the woods to hold as their own, and on that spot they began to build a hideout. Of course, they had many other competing interests, and so the hideout did not come together all at once, but was to be a work-in-progress for a long time to come. Still it served as an alternate gathering point for the children, when they needed a place to conspire.

Peter seemed to enjoy life on the farm, whether he had company or not. On a few occasions he wandered off alone, leaving Mr. Fenn worried whether he would return, but he always came back refreshed and happy to see Mr. Fenn, and so it seemed he had accepted that this was his new home.

❁　❁　❁

Mrs. Titchbourn had originally proposed that Peter continue his education at a local schoolhouse in Berkhamsted. I am told Peter did visit that schoolhouse on some number of occasions. However, it seems these visits had little effect on our Wild Boy, and so became more infrequent as time went on.

❁　❁　❁

Summer arrived, and Mother came with Anne, Amelia, me, William, Mary and Louise to visit Peter. When we arrived, Peter looked the same as he had on the day we left him here. Peter was overjoyed to see us all, and hugged everyone as soon as we stepped out of the carriage.

The visit would last a fortnight. In that time, Peter led us all over the farm and the nearby wood; showed us his favorite trees to climb in, taught us how to eat acorns and the sweet sap that comes from certain trees (skills he had acquired while living free in the Enchanted Forest of Hamelin), introduced us to the horses and the dogs, laughed and danced with us, chased and played games from morning until night. He also got on the back of a horse he called Cuckow and went riding with us. Cuckow was Peter's horse, Mr. Fenn informed us.

We met some of Peter's local friends, and pretended that we were commoners, like them. We probably seemed a bit odd to them, with some of our speech and manners, but we were not dressed in the fancy clothes we wore at court, and Mr. Fenn had been instructed not to reveal our identities, so I think they may have never known that we were princes and princesses.

❁　❁　❁

At one point, while we were out on an adventure, we saw a group of older boys taking turns wrestling each other in a field.

155

Peter stopped at the side of the road and leaned on the rock fence to watch. After a short time, the group noticed us watching them, and several of the boys came over to where we were standing. They were bare-chested, and looked very strong. "We're having a wrestling contest. Anybody can challenge anybody. Whoever wins the contest is the Chief."

"Who's winning now?" Sean asked.

"Well we just started, but I usually end up the winner. Any of you want to try your luck?"

"No."

"Well…" the older boy looked around, unsure of what to say or do. He saw Peter looking out into the field, watching the wrestling going on, and snatched the hat from Peter's head. "…Maybe this will change your mind."

"Hey!" Sean said angrily, "that's Peter's hat. Leave it alone."

Smiling because he was getting the response he was looking for, the bully said, "You want the hat, come and get it."

Sean jumped over the fence and rushed at the bully. But the older boy just grabbed Sean and threw him to the ground, laughing. When Sean got up to try again, the bully just tossed him down a second time, holding Peter's hat up in the air and laughing. Sean rose and tried a third time to recover the hat, and was again thrown down in front of all of us.

As all this was transpiring, I saw Peter out of the corner of my eye taking off his shirt. As Sean fell for the third time, Peter flew over the fence and tackled the older boy, knocking him over and wrenching the hat from his hands. Leaping off, Peter landed a short distance away and put his hat back on his head.

Getting to his feet, the older boy turned and faced Peter. Red-faced and angry at being caught off guard, he tried to charge Peter and tackle him the same way he'd been tackled. But the Wild Boy sprang up in the air like a cat and avoided the tackle, then came down with his feet on top of the bully's head and back, sending the older boy crashing into the ground.

By now the whole gang of older boys had gathered round, and as the bully rose again, growling with frustration, I was fearful that they would hurt Peter. But then they all rushed forward, and it was not Peter who was pressed to the ground, but the boy he had been fighting. The other boys held him down for several moments until he promised to be calm, then they let him up, and he offered his hand to Peter and said, "I'm sorry."

Peter graciously accepted the older boy's hand and shook it. Then the boys all gathered around him and lifted him up in the air, declaring him their new Chief. As far as I know, that was the only time Peter ever participated in any wrestling contests, but his status as Chief Boy of the region was firmly cemented after that day, and as word of his victory spread, his band of followers grew more numerous.

❖ ❖ ❖

When you are waiting for something, a fortnight seems like a long time, but when you are enjoying yourself, a fortnight passes by all too quickly. We wished we could stay longer, but Mother insisted that we needed to get back to London, promising another visit at the end of summer. As we departed, Peter stood beside Mr. Fenn and waived goodbye to us again. Amelia and I watched out the back window until Peter disappeared, and then we looked at each other sadly.

❖ ❖ ❖

Mr. Fenn wrote letters to the Queen, informing her about Peter's welfare, and she read these to us. Listening to Mother read these letters was bittersweet for me, however.

Summer on the farm was glorious. Peter spent as much time out of doors as possible, and he had many playmates, since all the children were free from their spring and autumn duties of tending crops or going to school. Peter had become the leader of a merry band of youngsters, aged six to fourteen, who followed the Wild Boy wherever he went and seemed to understand his unintelligible noises. If they did not understand, then they pretended to.

The life of a princess has many advantages, but I envied those children for their time with Peter and for what seemed to me to be a simple, carefree existence. Listening to Mr. Fenn's letters, I tried to imagine myself as a part of their company. Unfortunately, Mr. Fenn's letters were missing many details one might hope for regarding what Peter and his company were doing on their adventures, but one would not expect that the children would reveal all of their secrets to an adult.

I greatly admired Jessica, as Mr. Fenn described her, and from what I had observed about her when we met. The boys all treated her as if she were one of them, for indeed she could leap as high and as far as anyone but Peter, she could run and climb quite well, she knew how to fight, wasn't afraid to get dirty, and spoke her mind freely. If I had been able to stay there, I imagined Jessica and I would have become best friends.

❖   ❖   ❖

As promised, we visited Peter again for a week at the end of summer. By then, Peter had regained the tan he had lost during his time in London, but aside from that, everything about him was the same as it had been when he left. We children, for the most part, slipped easily back into our old routines of playing with Peter, except for Anne and Amelia. I noticed that my two older sisters seemed less comfortable running about and playing with the Wild Boy now. They were looking more like young women everyday. Considering this, I feared that one day soon, I too would grow up, but I tried to put that unhappy thought out of my mind.

❖   ❖   ❖

One day, Amelia and I were out in the woods with Peter, Sean, Colin and Jessica. We had just been officially introduced to the children's hideout when the Wild Boy made a noise to call us to attention, and then he put a finger to his lips, and led us deeper into the woods. We did not know what he was up to, but of course we were eager to find out.

Noiselessly, Peter pushed onward through the trees, and we did our best to keep up, while regretting every twig snap, every crunch of a leaf, every shift of a rock under foot. How Peter was able to move without a sound was a mystery in itself.

Finally, he brought us to a halt and gestured for us to stay where we were. We obediently did so, and he disappeared for a several moments.

Just when we were beginning to wonder if Peter had forgotten us, he came back, riding on the back of a great antlered deer. We gasped. Peter held his finger to his lips, and gently stroked the deer's neck and flank. Then he carefully dismounted, and producing a bit of food from his pocket, he led the deer forward to where we stood.

Peter reached out and beckoned for me to come forward. Taking my hand, he put a bit of grain in it, and then had me hold it out for the deer to take. The deer hesitated at first, but Peter breathed a gentle sound, and the deer advanced a step and accepted the food from my hand.

Each of us took a turn silently feeding the deer, and we all were filled with wonder by how calm it was. Then, when all the food was spent, Peter said goodbye in his own way to the deer, and the deer turned and moved as silently as Peter back into the woods.

When the deer was gone, Colin said, "I've seen rabbits, and foxes, and birds approach Peter and stay with him calmly like that before, but never a deer. And he rode on its back!"

Jessica said, "...My father likes to hunt deer. I can never tell him about this." Pausing, she added, "We mustn't tell any adults about this," and we all agreed.

❖   ❖   ❖

The week was over before any of us were ready for it to end. Anne, Amelia, William, Mary, Louise and I were all reluctant to leave, and Mother herself seemed sorry that we had to go. Mother could not resist kissing Peter on his cheek before boarding the carriage, and this gave all of us girls a perfect excuse to do the same, leaving Peter's cheeks looking quite rosy.

Drawing up beside Peter, Mr. Fenn put a hand on the Wild Boy's shoulder and said, "You're a lucky boy, Peter." Peter waved at the gradually disappearing wagon, until it was finally gone, and then sighed and went inside with Mr. Fenn.

❖ ❖ ❖

There was work to be done about the farm, particularly as autumn began. Peter did his best to be helpful, although Mr. Fenn did not require too much of him. The local children were also busier, so that Peter's band of boys and girls was diminished in size, but still Peter could often be seen around the area with an intrepid group of explorers following him.

❖ ❖ ❖

Before Christmas, we returned to Northchurch again to visit Peter at the farm. The ground was covered in a blanket of snow, and so we came in a horse-drawn sleigh.

Peter was fascinated by the sleigh, and so we took him for a ride through the countryside. When we came upon a suitable hill, we disembarked, and Anne, Amelia, William, Mary and I ran up the hill, carrying three sleds. The Queen also climbed the hill with a sled in one hand and her other hand leading young Louise. Peter followed along, unsure of what the game was, until Anne took one of the sleds, sat down on it with William, and took off down the slope. Amelia sat down next with Mary and took off down the slope crying out, "Yahoo!" as they went.

I sat down on the third sled, and beckoned for Peter to sit down behind me. When he was properly seated and had wrapped his arms around me, I leaned forward and scooted the sled over the edge of the slope. As we went, Peter cried out joyfully. Louise and Mother followed shortly behind.

Once at the bottom, we were all eager to climb the slope again. We repeated this loop a number of times before the Queen finally said enough. "I am tired children, and we don't want little Louise to catch a cold from being outside too long. Let us go back to the farm."

And so we did, but over the next few days, we made further use of the sleds, and Peter learned how to steer one himself, enabling us to race each other down slopes. A number of members of Peter's merry band ended up joining in the fun, and we spent many hours at play together. During our visit, we also built snowforts in the field and had snowball fights, and worked together to construct a great snowman.

❀ ❀ ❀

As always, Mr. Fenn played host for the family, providing meals and entertaining the Queen and all of us with stories of Peter's life on the farm. In the evenings, Anne played music on a small harp she brought with her from London and the family all sang and danced together with Peter.

On the last evening of our visit, however, a snowstorm struck, and before anyone knew what was happening, Peter was out of doors. Mr. Fenn called to him from the porch, but Peter did not come. Instead, Peter lay down in the snow and rolled around, laughing and tossing the snow into the air. With the snow falling heavily, Mr. Fenn fetched his warmest coat and put on his boots and went out into the field to get Peter. Peter, however, had other ideas. As soon as he saw Mr. Fenn coming, Peter scooped up two handfuls of snow and packed them into a snowball, which he hurled with great accuracy at Mr. Fenn's head, knocking the farmer's cap off. Perceiving an event in the making, we children rushed out into the snow, over Mother's objections, and began scooping up snowballs of our own to toss at Peter and at each other.

Mr. Fenn, meanwhile, shouted and snatched up his cap, but then seeing Peter laughing and scooping together another snowball, he put back on his cap and bent over, making a snowball of his own as another shot from Peter landed on his shoulder. Mr. Fenn roared and tossed his snowball back at Peter, but Peter ducked, and so Mr. Fenn had to arm himself quickly.

We all stood in the field, pelting each other with snowballs (or at least trying to) for several minutes, and then Mr. Fenn, laughing and out of breath, said, "All right, Peter, all right. You won. Come in now. You may have grown accustomed to running around in the snow when you lived wild and free in Germany, but here I am in my warmest coat, and I am freezing cold. It is time to go inside."

❧ ❧ ❧

The next morning, the ground was so covered in snow that it did not seem possible for us to leave. Anne, Amelia, William, Mary, Louise and I certainly hoped it would not be possible. Mother was inclined to go, but then she saw that the sleigh had been buried in snow and decided to wait a day or two. We children were happy about this and immediately set out to make the most of our extra time with Peter.

So another two days passed before we finally did leave. We filled our hours as much as possible with time spend out of doors in the snow.

On the appointed morning, we all presented Peter with Christmas gifts, and gave him big hugs before departing on our sleigh. As always, Peter and Mr. Fenn stood at the gate, waving goodbye as our family drove away.

❧ ❧ ❧

All of the gifts given to Peter were thoughtful, but some were more obviously useful for Peter than others. I had given Peter a new hat, which he put on immediately and did not take off for several days after I left. We also left one of the sleds with Peter, and reportedly, he made considerable use of this with the other children after our departure.

Chapter 13: Childhood Farewell

Winter was long and cold, but eventually spring came around, and our family appeared at the farm again. This time, however, Anne did not come, and all of the rest of us children had grown a little bit bigger than we had been the previous year- all except Peter, who looked the same as he had the day we brought him to the farm. I fretted about this, but I seemed to be the only one who noticed.

The visit in spring was shorter than I would have liked- I was beginning to sense that time was racing forward, and the fact that my sixteenth birthday was fast approaching also bothered me. No one knew exactly how old Peter was, but to me, it seemed that Peter did not look much different than he had three years earlier, when we had first met. All of my worrying about the passage of time only made it harder for me to enjoy the bit of time I did have with Peter, and before I was ready, the time was gone, and I was sitting again at the back of the carriage, looking out the rear window at Peter.

❖ ❖ ❖

On my sixteenth birthday, I asked Mother to take me and the other children on a longer summer holiday in Northchurch. Mother asked why I wanted to visit Peter so much.

I said, "Because all of us are growing up Mother, except Peter. Haven't you noticed? When we first met, he was just my size. Now I am taller than him, and... and I am changing. I won't be a child much longer. Whereas Peter..."

Mother looked into my eyes and smiled sympathetically. "... Whereas Peter will always remain a wonderful boy." Nodding, I burst into tears and hugged her. Holding me close, she said,

"Peter is a dear friend to all of us, and I know you have grown attached to him. You know that I love you dearly Caroline and would do anything to make you happy. But are you sure you want to go back to the farm again, knowing that inevitably you will outgrow your friend Peter? You understand Peter as few people do- certainly better than I do, and perhaps you always will, but there will come a time, maybe soon, when he does not understand you anymore, when perhaps he may not even recognize you." I sobbed, and Mother patted my head gently. "...Do you think that it might be better to make a clean break of it now, rather than stretching things out?"

"No!" I said, separating from my mother enough to look into her eyes. "I want to see him again. I want to stay with him this summer, as long as I can."

"All right," Mother said, nodding. "I will make arrangements."

❖ ❖ ❖

So Mother went again to the farm with me, William, Mary and Louise. Peter was happy to see us, and gave everyone a big hug when we arrived. As soon as Mother allowed us to, we followed Peter off on an adventure.

The summer days were long, but somehow passed quickly. Five days went by, and Mother was ready to leave. I was allowed to stay, which led William, Mary and Louise to protest and beg that they be allowed to stay too. But Mother shook her head, and said, "No, you all will come home with me. But we shall return in three weeks, and you will have another chance to visit with Peter." Then Prince William, Princess Mary, Princess Louise, and our mother, the Queen, all boarded the carriage, and set out for Kensington Palace, leaving me and Peter standing together beside Mr. Fenn, waving happily.

❖ ❖ ❖

The next three weeks were packed with golden memories. Peter and I were out of doors from morning until night. We ran over the fields together with the neighboring boys and girls, and tromped through the woods, we splashed in the stream and lay out in the grass, we rode Mr. Fenn's horses far and wide, and ate our lunches out of a sack. Everything was perfectly wonderful. I did not count the days that passed- I did not want to. I wished that things could always remain like this.

One night, Peter woke me, and led me by the hand out of the farmhouse quickly, pointing to the moonlit sky. I looked up, and gasped, as I saw the stars falling from the heavens. It was a meteor shower. Peter squeezed my hand.

We stood together and watched until it was over, and then went back inside. I thanked Peter for waking me, and then climbed back into bed. Peter curled up on the floor, as was his habit, and fell fast asleep.

        ❊   ❊   ❊

The next day, the Queen arrived, along with William, Mary and Louise. I smiled and hugged my mother and siblings, but inside, I was troubled, knowing that my time was almost up. However, I resolved not to let this keep me from enjoying what time I had left, or spoil the other children's visit with Peter. Putting on a brave face, I made it my aim in the next five days to help the younger children come to understand Peter as well as I did.

Finally the day came when we had to leave. I hugged Peter tightly, and did not let go for several moments. Then I released him and with tears in my eyes, I smiled and said, "Goodbye Peter."

Chapter 14: Five Years Apart

Peter did not see me again for a long time. Part of me longed to go to the farm and visit him, but another part resisted, unwilling to face the reality that I was growing up and he was not. He received semiannual visits each spring and winter for several years from William, Mary, Louise, and sometimes Amelia, but I did not come with them. After three years, the semiannual visits became annual visits, taking place each spring.

Peter continued to enjoy the attention of the local children, and from time to time he was visited by curious travelers who had heard stories of about the Wild Boy and wanted a chance to see him first hand. A common question asked of Mr. Fenn was, "How old is the boy?" to which Mr. Fenn's reply, year after year, was, "He has been somewhere between twelve and thirteen since the day I laid eyes on him."

❖ ❖ ❖

Peter's gentle personality manifested itself differently depending on the company he was in. Among children, or with people he was very familiar with, Peter could be quite lively. But among most adults, Peter was often more subdued, and so some people did not get a chance to see his intelligence at work, and therefore assumed he was nothing more than a handsome idiot who had been made much of by the London press. Mr. Fenn listened to people's impressions of Peter, but rarely commented, as it was not his place to do so.

❖ ❖ ❖

One day, in the summer of 1734, there was a knock on the door of the farmhouse. Mr. Fenn opened the door to find a young woman standing on the porch. "Hello, Mr. Fenn?"

"Yes ma'am? Can I help you?"

The young woman bit her lip, "You don't remember me do you?"

"Begging your pardon ma'am, we've received a lot of visitors here, but I should think I would have wanted to remember a young lady as pretty as yourself. Perhaps you could jog my memory?" Seeing tears form in the young woman's eyes, Mr. Fenn shook his head, and said, "Please ma'am, won't you come inside and sit down? I'm sure it'll come to me."

"Thank you," the young woman said, entering. She brought a travel bag with her inside and then set it down. "I came here when I was younger, to visit with the Wild Boy, Peter."

"Ah, of course. You were one of his merry band, then."

"Yes, along with my brother and sisters."

"Forgive me, dear. It is hard to keep track of all the boys and girls who played with him over the years."

"How is he?"

"Oh, he is fine. I don't know where he is at the moment. Peter!"

"Mr Fenn! You needn't call him," the young woman said.

Mr. Fenn turned his head, "You came all this way and you don't want to see him?"

"I do," the young woman said, wiping away her tears. "...I do want to see him. But I am also afraid," she added, sinking from the chair to the floor and drawing her knees up to her chest.

"Afraid of what, ma'am?"

"That he won't recognize me." At that moment, Peter entered the room, and she took a sudden breath. He looked the same as he had the first day they'd met.

"Ah, there you are, Peter. You have a visitor today," Mr. Fenn said, smiling. Peter by now had laid eyes on the young woman, and was staring fixedly at her. "I've never understood the effect you have on the ladies, Peter, but there you have it." Looking over at the young woman sitting on the floor, who was staring back at Peter, Mr. Fenn took a deep breath and said, "Well I'll give you two a bit of privacy now."

167

When Mr. Fenn had stepped out of the room and closed the door, the young woman said to the Wild Boy, "Hello Peter. Do you remember me?" Peter said nothing, but approached her, his eyes shifting from her face to the silver chain that hung from her neck. At the end of the chain, there was an acorn. Peter's eyes widened. "...I'm so sorry that I didn't come sooner. Peter, please say something. Please?"

Peter looked up into the young woman's eyes again, which were now welling fresh tears, and he smiled slightly. "Friend," he said, putting his hand on my knee.

I nodded, smiling. Suddenly his arms were around me, holding me tightly. I hugged him back, then after a few moments, we separated and Peter took my hand. He pulled and hummed, wanting me to get up from the floor and come with him. I hesitated for a moment, and then stood. Peter felt something different and turned his head to look back at me. Lifting his head, he saw that I was now several inches taller than he remembered. He smiled, and then began to head for the door again.

We passed Mr. Fenn on our way out the back of the house, and Mr. Fenn smiled seeing the two of us holding hands, "I gather he remembered you, Miss?" I looked back, smiled and nodded as Peter dragged me onward, out of the house.

Peter neighed, and the grazing horses came over to the fence to greet us. Picking up two apples, Peter handed one to me and gave the other to one of the horses. I offered my apple to the other horse, and the horse gladly accepted it from me. Then Peter barked, and Mr. Fenn's dogs came running. They sniffed around me for a moment or two, and sat down. Peter squatted and gave them all a good rub, and I joined him.

Standing up again, Peter hummed, and led me walking across the field with the dogs. Sometimes the dogs ran ahead, and sometimes they lingered behind, but in general it seemed they were quite happy to go wherever Peter and I were going. I did not yet know where I was being led, but it didn't really matter, I was just so glad to be together with Peter again.

168

In a few minutes we were at the edge of the wood, and I saw we had come to a familiar place. "...I remember this tree!" I exclaimed. "We used to climb it all the time." Peter seemed to have this in mind also, because as I spoke he was already starting to climb the tree. "You don't expect me to climb that tree in this dress, do you," I said, looking up at him. He smiled down at me. "Of course you do," I said, shaking my head. "Of course." Taking off my boots, I began to climb up after Peter.

Once up high in the branches of the tree, Peter stretched himself out along the length of a strong branch and watched me climb. Eventually I got up to where he was, and found a branch to lie down on beside his. He smiled.

We lay there in the tree branches for a short while, and then Peter got up and leaped down to the ground. I looked down at him and shook my head, then began to carefully climb my way back down to the ground. Peter watched me climb down, and then turned to go, but I said, "Wait! I still have to put my boots on." And so Peter waited for me to be ready.

❖   ❖   ❖

Our tour of the farm and surrounding territory continued until nightfall, when we sat down outside the farmhouse and gazed up at the moon and the stars. "You know you haven't changed one bit," I said, looking over at Peter after we had sat for a while in silence. "You are as changeless as the stars, Peter. I always thought my grandfather was joking when he said you had been adopted by fairies as a child, but now- it wouldn't surprise me to learn that was true. How I wish you could talk. There are many men in London who never seem to stop talking, and yet when I listen to them I find they have very little of value to say. You on the other hand, speak very little- but if you could talk with the same endurance as those other fellows, I think that I would never tire of listening to you." Peter hummed.

"Excuse me, ma'am," said Mr. Fenn. "But it is getting late. Peter needs to get some rest, and you too, most likely. I am sorry, by the way, but I haven't been able to place your face with a name."

I stood, and turning to face Mr. Fenn, I said, "Sorry for not introducing myself properly earlier, Mr. Fenn. I am Princess Caroline."

Mr. Fenn quickly took off his hat, "Your Royal Highness! No need for any apologies. Ah- will you be staying with us for a while?"

"Yes- I think I will."

"I'll have one of the stable-hands bring your horse around and take his saddle off, then."

I gasped. "I forgot all about my horse!"

"Well, I made sure he got some food and water, so he's all right. But you two must be hungry. Can I invite you in for some dinner?"

For the next week, I remained in Northchurch and visited with Peter and Mr. Fenn. I enjoyed hearing from Mr. Fenn about some of the adventures Peter had had in my absence, and I was happy to spend time with Peter again. But as the week progressed, a sadness gradually came over me, and I said to Peter, when we were alone in the field, "Peter, I have to go away again soon. The farm is your world and you fit into it so well." Peter looked at me questioningly. "I wish that I could stay here with you always, but I can't always stay in your world. But we will always be friends, Peter, and-" I hesitated, "…and I will always love you." Peter, who had been listening intently as I spoke, stepped close and hugged me.

❄ ❄ ❄

The next day, I made ready to depart early in the morning. Peter and Mr. Fenn came to the gate to wish me farewell. I shook Mr. Fenn's hand, and gave Peter a hug goodbye, telling him, "I will visit you again, before long."

Chapter 15: Among Savages

A few days after returning from Axter's End, I had an encounter
with Lord Hervey, whom I had carefully avoided speaking to since
my fourteenth birthday. We met by chance in one of the corridors
of Kensington Palace, and he took it as an opportunity to break
the silence between us. I was carrying a book with me at the time,
and held on it as if it could shield me from him.

"Princess Caroline, may I speak with you?"

"I have nothing to say to you, Hervey."

"Then do me the honor of listening, for a moment at least. I
have been plagued with guilt since the night your Wild Boy Peter
and I crossed swords."

"As well you ought to be."

"I deserve your mistrust and contempt; I know that. I was
drunk beyond my wits, and crossed the bounds of propriety. It
was terribly bad form on my part."

"Bad form indeed."

"For a gentleman such as myself there is nothing more vital
than good form. Without it I am less than nothing- I am a savage
lie and an affront to the notion of dignity. Your friend Peter may
not know the meaning of such words, but just the same, he showed
a great deal more character than I did that night, and that stings
worst of all.

"I don't expect you to forgive me, but you are the sweetest,
gentlest, most honest and good lady at court, besides your mother
the Queen, and it is a blot on my conscience that I have offended
you. If I must spend the rest of my life trying to make amends for
that offense, my time will not have been spent in vain." Hervey
paused, "...Yes, I have a conscience- don't look so surprised."

171

I shook my head, "You speak well, Lord Hervey, there is no denying that."

"But?"

"But eloquence and charm have never been your problem. It is constancy."

"Constancy? My dear, what do you mean?"

"Your reputation as a libertine and a political agent is not unknown to me. If half of what I have heard is true-"

"Half of it might be," Hervey said, "but the trouble in dealing with half-truths is knowing which half to believe. I am not a perfect man, Caroline- nor do I pretend to be. That much you know already. But I hope that one day, you will understand that you can trust me to be what I am- a daring coward, an honest liar, and a God-forsaken scoundrel, trying with every fiber of my corrupted nature to be something better, to serve a higher purpose."

"Why?"

"Because you and your mother have made me believe salvation is possible."

"So go and be a monk."

"I could never be a good monk, and that is not the sort of salvation I am talking about. I am talking about what rests in the heart. Have you not seen yet through the gaudy trappings of high society? We are all dirty, grasping Yahoos pretending to be civilized, and most of us will never acknowledge our hypocrisy. Our only hope is to find something truly good in this world and hang on to it, to serve and protect and uphold it. That is why I serve your mother, the Queen, and why I hope to serve you also, in any way I can."

"My mother may have use for your political wit, Hervey, but I am not interested in intrigues."

"Perhaps not. But perhaps there are other things you would like to know. There is much I could tell you about men and women- things that would serve you well to know, now that you are grown up to adulthood."

I swallowed, clutching my journal to my chest. "I am not interested in what you have to say about such things, Lord Hervey."

"As you like, Princess. But a beautiful young woman such as yourself will have many suitors. Not all of them will be perfect gentlemen, and it can difficult for one who is inexperienced to know the difference."

"I am not interested in choosing between suitors."

"You would have your parents choose for you?"

"My mother would never!"

"Your father might. He wants you to be happy, and in typical male fashion, he thinks he knows how to fix everything."

"Are you speculating, Hervey- or do you know something I do not?"

"As a courtier, one hears things, from time to time."

"What have you heard?"

"Only that your father is concerned you have not yet found a suitable life-partner. A maiden reaches a certain age, and her options begin to narrow. Now there are plenty of eligible men who would be happy to marry you and give you children, but you don't seem interested." Pointing at the journal held in my arms, Hervey said, "You spend all your time buried in your books or in the gardens. At parties you are the unapproachable girl every lad has eyes for, but can never hope to woo. Tell me one thing, and I will leave you alone. What is in that book that is more interesting than the world around you?"

I replied, "Like you said, Hervey, the world is full of gaudy, dirty hypocrites."

"And what do you find in that book that is different? Is it not the writing of one of those hypocrites you shun?"

"It is my own writing, from my heart."

"Ah-ha! So even in literature, no man has found a pathway into your heart. But at least you have found a means of self-expression. And what, pray tell, do you write about?"

I responded accusingly, "You said that if I told you one thing, you would leave me alone."

"I also confessed to being a liar. Please Caroline, I am sincerely interested to know what someone like you would write about. I myself occupy spare moments writing my memoirs. They are extremely private, of course. I would never wish anyone to know their full contents- at least not until I am dead- but from time to time I write something so splendidly clever that I cannot help but share it with someone else. Does that happen for you also? Perhaps there is some snippet you might share with me?"

"No."

"Well we can't all be clever, I suppose," Hervey sighed. "At least you have your beauty, and your youth."

"I didn't say I never wrote anything clever- just nothing I would share with you."

"Oh- dear me. My charm isn't working at all today is it? Forgive me for troubling you, Caroline. I shall leave you to your solitary pursuits." Bowing, Hervey turned and began to walk away.

"...I saw Peter again, recently," I said. I didn't know why I blurted this out, and I regretted saying this as soon as the words had left my mouth, but there it was.

Hervey stopped, and turned around. "Really? How is Peter? I've heard it said that he remains youthful in his appearance."

I smiled, "He hasn't aged a day."

"Is he still good with a sword?"

"I imagine he is."

"Has he learned to speak yet? Or is he still incomprehensible?"

"Peter was never incomprehensible to me. But he remains a boy of few words. Unlike certain men I know."

"So is he in there?" Hervey asked, pointing again to the book.

"Yes," I said. "So is my mother, my father, my siblings... even you. You have immortalized yourself as a pirate who lost his hand in a duel with the Wild Boy."

Hervey smiled. "Who taught Peter to fence like that?"

"Frederick. At the time I was afraid he would hurt Peter, but now I look back on it as one of the few good deeds my brother did."

"Frederick may yet come around. I hope he does. He and I have many things in common. We were friends once, you know. We had a falling out because we both fancied a girl named Anne Vane. Turns out she fancied another fellow, William Stanhope, and all of our jealousy was for naught. But it soured our friendship all the same, and I came to see Frederick in a different light." Hervey paused, "So, like me, you are writing your memoirs."

"...I started writing when I met Peter," I said. "A girl named Margaret, from Germany, got me started. Her father was the man who had discovered Peter, and introduced him to my grandfather, King George. She gave me a book she had written, about the adventures Peter had, before he came to London. It was fantastic- I couldn't believe someone my own age had written a book. Anne, Amelia and I read it to William, Mary and Louise until we all knew it by heart, and then we began to add stories of our own. Sometimes they were true stories, sometimes they were fanciful things we dreamed up while playing in Kensington Gardens. Of course, eventually we all grew up, all of us except Peter, and the book sat and collected dust, while I did my best to become a mature young woman. I didn't look at it for years, because I was afraid that in hindsight, our stories would seem quaint and childish. I tried to write other things instead, journal entries about the mundaneness of being a Princess and serious, weighty essays about life, womanhood and God's role in the modern world. But now I have begun to look back on the things I wrote as a child, and I think the little girl that was me had more to say. I think it's too bad she didn't get to finish, and I am more interested in her story, than the words of the woman I was trying so hard to become. So I have dusted off the old book, and I am carrying it with me again."

"Interesting." Hervey paused, looking thoughtful. "Well, thank you Caroline, for sharing that with me. I did not expect so much from this conversation- I really only wanted to apologize for my past behavior and perhaps establish a more civil dialogue. Perhaps another day, you will relent and read some of your writing to me?"

"You have been very charming today, Lord Hervey," I said. "But I still remember you as a pirate."

"Fair enough," Hervey replied, bowing and withdrawing.

❧ ❧ ❧

Lord Hervey may have withdrawn at that time, but he certainly was not done with me yet. In the following months he would continue, through small gestures, to try and show his good intentions. I was not ready to count him as a friend, but I began to see him as a more complete character than I had previously.

I understood he traded to some extent on his connections, his relationships, and his influence. More than most other courtiers, Hervey seemed aware that this made his conduct appear superficial and hollow, but this awareness also increased his desire to show good form, and to win earnest appreciation and genuine affection. My mother was fond of Hervey, because he tried so hard. My brother Frederick, on the other hand, had come to hate Hervey in recent years, because of jealousies between them, and because of ugly things that Hervey had said and done. But to be fair in accounting, where Hervey had done wrong by anyone, including Frederick, he had certainly tried to make up for it later.

I remained uncertain of whether to trust Hervey or not, but I no longer kept a wall of silence between us. Whether this was a mistake or not, I cannot say.

❧ ❧ ❧

Still considering how he could make amends with me for his past conduct, Hervey took an opportunity one day in July to recommend to the Queen that Peter be brought into London for a special visit. At the time a delegation of Creek Indians from the American Colonies were visiting London and preparing to meet my father, King George II, and Hervey thought it would be entertaining to see how the Wild Boy would interact "with other savages like himself."

For a man who was supposed to be an expert at diplomacy, Hervey's choice of words showed a surprising lack of tact, but it was nevertheless an intriguing thought, and my mother agreed to send for the Wild Boy. So I went to Axter's End in a carriage to fetch Peter.

Peter had not ridden in a carriage in many years, and seemed delighted as he sat down beside me at the window. I had brought with me a basket full of provisions, and as we rode through the countryside together, we dug into this supply happily. When all the food was gone, Peter stretched out on the floor with one contented hand on his belly and the other behind his head. Looking up at me, he smiled and hummed. I smiled back, and began to sing.

I sang to Peter until he fell asleep, and then we rode the rest of the way into London in peaceful silence. Peter was very happy and at ease. When we reached St. James' Palace, my current residence, I woke Peter, and we went inside to have dinner. The next day, we would meet the Indians.

❊ ❊ ❊

On August 1, 1734, King Tomochichi of the Yamacraw tribe, together with his consort Senawki, his nephew and heir Toonakawi, his war captain Hillipilli, and five other chiefs of the Creek Nation, Apakowtski, Stimalechi, Sintouchi, Hinguithi, and Umphychi, all assembled at Kensington Palace and greeted George II. Tomochichi spoke in clear English, to the surprise of many. He said:

"Great king; this day I see the majesty of your person, the greatness of your house, and the number of your people. I am come in my old days; so I cannot expect to obtain any advantage to myself; but I come for the good of the Creeks, that they may be informed about the English, and be instructed in your language and religion. I present to you, in their name, the feathers of an eagle, which is the swiftest of birds, and flieth around our nations. These feathers are emblems of peace in our land, and have been carried from town to town, to witness it. We have brought them to you, to be a token and pledge of peace, on our part, to be kept on yours. O great king! whatsoever you shall say to me, I will faithfully tell to all the chiefs of the Creek nation."

To which my father replied, "I am glad of this opportunity of assuring you of my regard for the people from whom you came; and I am extremely well pleased with the assurance which you have brought me from them. I accept, very gratefully, this present, as an indication of their good dispositions towards me and my people; and shall always be ready to show them marks of favor, and purposes to promote their welfare."

James Oglethorpe, the founder of the colony of Georgia, who had brought the Creek here on this day, then introduced Tomochichi to my mother, Queen Caroline. Tomochichi said respectfully, "I am glad to see you this day, and to have the opportunity of beholding the mother of this great nation. As our people are now joined with yours, we hope that you will be a common mother, and a protectress of us and our children."

The Queen was moved by Tomochichi's eloquence, and said, "I am touched by your words, and as long as I live, the Creek shall have my sympathy and care."

Oglethorpe then introduced Frederick, Prince of Wales, William, Duke of Cumberland, Anne, Princess of Orange, Princess Amelia, Princess Mary, Princess Louise and me.

The Indian chief had a stern but kindly expression, and bright, alert eyes. He greeted each of us respectfully in turn, and then asked Oglethorpe, "And who is this handsome youth, who puts on a hat in the Great King's presence?" While everyone had been talking, Peter had been amusing himself by playing with his hat, and had just now put it on.

Peter had never fully understood the need to take off one's hat at certain times, or put it on at other times, but he liked hats. He smiled at Tomochichi, doffed his hat and bowed respectfully, and then replaced it on his head.

"That is Peter," said Frederick, "the Wild Boy."

"Pe-ter," Tomochichi pronounced carefully. "...Why is he called Wild?"

"Because he lived in the forest alone until the age of twelve, with no one to care for him but wild beasts and fairies," Frederick said.

"Fairies?" Tomochichi asked, looking at Oglethorpe.

"Spirits of the forest," Oglethorpe said.

Tomochichi turned and told the other chiefs something in the Creek language, and they all made a sound of awareness and understanding. "…I have told them about the Spirit Boy," he said, turning back to face us. "We could all see there was something unusual about him- now we know, it is because of the spirits."

"Perhaps you would enjoy visiting Kensington Gardens," Mother said to Tomochichi, "…Peter is very fond of the Gardens."

Tomochichi conversed briefly with the other chiefs, and then nodded, "We are happy to accept your invitation."

❖ ❖ ❖

Mother, Anne, Amelia, William and I spent the afternoon and evening together with Peter and the Indians, roaming the Gardens. I found the company of the Indians to be very calming. It seemed to me that what my grandfather had said to me in the past about the Indians was true- each of them, to one extent or another, possessed the same soulful quality that we saw in Peter. It wasn't necessary to understand their language to sense this about them, because unlike so many modern men, they were not practiced in deception. Their genuine nature was evident in every gesture.

Peter got along well with the Indian boy Toonakawi, as with the chiefs, and showed curiosity in examining the Indians' costumes and personal articles. I was accustomed to seeing men condescend toward Peter, but all of the Indians submitted to the Wild Boy's inspections good-humoredly, and indeed, seemed to treat him seriously, as if he were an equal- something only my grandfather and the good doctor from Germany had done.

We had a picnic in the grass, and afterward, William, Toonakawi and Peter ran off to play together in the field, chasing each other. "When I am gone," Tomochichi said to me, as he looked out at his nephew playing with the Wild Boy and the young Duke,

179

"Toonakawi will be lead the Yamacraw. I want him to learn the ways of the English, so that he will be a capable leader."

"You are wise to want this for Toonakawi," I said. "Because Peter has never fully learned our ways, some people look down on him. They call him a savage."

The Chief stroked his chin. "…Some English call Tomochichi a savage."

"Yes, but the English also say that Tomochichi is wise, and has made great efforts for his people."

"This is true."

"Peter is different. He has no people- he is all alone, and many English do not understand him. They call Peter an idiot."

"What is an idiot?"

"An idiot is unable to learn. Peter is not an idiot. He is able, but he does not wish to learn. He wishes to remain a Wild Boy forever."

The chief laughed, and then told the other chiefs what had been said. They laughed too. "We also," Tomochichi said, "…wish to remain boys forever. But this is not the fate of a chief, and it shall not be the fate of my nephew Toonakawi. So, he will learn, and the English will respect him." Tomochichi paused. "In Georgia, Peter would be welcome among my people. We would not look down on him, as you say many English do. The spirits have touched him. Among my people, he would be treated with respect."

"Peter has friends here, people whom he cares for, and who care for him. I think it would be difficult for him to go."

Tomochichi nodded. "Difficult."

❊ ❊ ❊

When the Indians were ready to leave Kensington Gardens, Tomochichi produced a feather from his belongings and held it before Peter. It was not of the same kind as had been given to my father, but it was, nevertheless, an attractive feather. "I present this to the Spirit Boy as a token of friendship," he said. Then he touched Peter's head and gently inserted the feather into Peter's hat. "May God and the spirits of nature watch over him, bring him good friends and let him remain forever young."

❁　❁　❁

The next day, I returned Peter to Axter's End and said my goodbye there, promising to come and visit again soon. The promise I made, to visit again soon, was as much to reassure myself, as it was Peter.

Chapter 16: To Meet a Fairy

After the encounter with the Indians, I resumed the practice of visiting Peter at Axter's End regularly. I saw Peter on a number of occasions each year, and sometimes brought with me Amelia, William, Mary or Louise. Mr. Fenn always greeted me kindly, and informed me about life on the farm.

Peter continued to be a well-known and popular figure in the region, as he sometimes wandered in a wide range, visiting with people he knew. Over time, Mr. Fenn had pieced together reports of Peter's wanderings, and surmised that Peter was capable of traveling as much as seventy to eighty miles in a day. Of course he did not always travel this far- there were many periods of time when he did not even leave the farm, but Mr. Fenn never knew when Peter might disappear for a day or two.

Local children continued to make frequent visits to Axter's End to see Peter, and he always played a lively host for them. At the local pub, Peter would sometimes make appearances, and join in the singing and dancing that took place there, sometimes with Mr. Fenn, and sometimes on his own. The local people were friendly and knew him well.

To the best of my knowledge, no one from the region ever took advantage of Peter's innocence by stealing from him or involving him in anything improper. It seemed that Peter had indeed found some friends in the countryside, and I was glad of this.

❖ ❖ ❖

Things continued in this way for several years. Then one day in November of 1737, an empty carriage came for Peter and Mr. Fenn. Thinking that one of us had come to visit him, Peter ran out of the farmhouse to see who it was. James Fenn followed behind him, at a slower pace. Both were surprised to see the carriage was empty. The driver presented Mr. Fenn with a letter, and after reading this letter, Mr. Fenn immediately indicated to Peter that they were required to enter the carriage and set out for London.

Mr. Fenn was nervous on the ride to London. His hands were restless, sometimes folded in his lap, sometimes on his knees, sometimes tapping on the seat, or on the edge of the window. He smiled at Peter, but Peter could tell something was bothering him. It had something to do with the letter Mr. Fenn was holding, but Peter could not read. Every time Mr. Fenn looked at the letter, his expression froze, and afterward, he appeared anxious. Peter looked into his eyes, hoping to read some hint there of what was troubling the old farmer, but what he saw in Mr. Fenn's eyes was something he did not understand, and Mr. Fenn quickly broke eye contact.

❖   ❖   ❖

When they reached Kensington Palace, Mr. Fenn was shown to a waiting room, and Peter was taken to the Queen's bedchambers. There he saw the Queen, lying in bed, looking very pale, and my father, the King, sitting beside her holding her hand.

"Come in Peter," said the King. My father, George II, had never really related to Peter very much, but now his voice was tender- almost trembling with emotion. "...The Queen has asked to see you. My dear, Peter is here." Squeezing Peter's shoulders gently, Father held the boy in Mother's line of sight. She smiled, and reached out to him. The King put Peter's hand in hers, and she squeezed it tenderly.

Peter's eyes were wide with concern. "Dear Peter," the Queen said, smiling softly, "...Caroline told the truth about you. You haven't aged a day. Too bad I called an end to Doctor Arbuthnot's lessons; I'd love to hear you tell your secrets. Were you raised by fairies after all? I have always wanted to meet a fairy." With a smile on her face, Mother closed her eyes and released Peter's hand.

❖   ❖   ❖

The funeral for the Queen took place approximately one month after her death, at Westminster Abbey. Peter was there, having stayed at Kensington Palace during that time as a comfort to the younger children of the Royal Family. Mr. Fenn meanwhile, had gone back to the farm.

❁ ❁ ❁

After the funeral, Peter was returned to Axter's End, where Mr. Fenn was waiting for him. It would be six months before they received any further visits from members of the Royal Family. Then I came, and brought Amelia, Mary and Louise with me (Anne had married the Prince of Orange several years earlier, and no longer had time for such outings). We stayed at Mr. Fenn's house and visited with Peter for the week that summer, just as we had when our mother had brought us, years earlier, and then took our leave.

Following Mother's death, I had dedicated myself to charity, and supported a number of causes around London, including children's hospitals, schools, and other worthy endeavors. This pursuit helped me feel a sense of purpose in life, and it was easier for me then to see Peter and not feel sorry for having grown up. Adults could do important things also, and Peter and Mother had given me the inspiration to take action to give help to children and others who needed it.

Chapter 17: The Parting Glass

Amelia, Mary, Louise and I came again in the winter time and spent the week visiting with Peter, wandering with him in the snowy woods and going sledding as we had done when we were young. We repeated this schedule of visits again the following year.

Then, early in the summer of 1740, Mary became married to Landgrave Frederick of Hesse-Kassel. It was an arranged marriage, which Mary was not very happy about, but she was obligated to go through with it, and travel to Germany to live with Landgrave Frederick for the good of Britain. So when we visited Peter next, it was the winter of 1740 and Mary was not with us.

Amelia, Louise and I continued making semiannual visits to the farm in Northchurch together for the next two years. Then, in 1743, Louise entered into an arranged marriage with Prince Frederick of Denmark and Norway, and had to travel to be with her new husband. During that year, Amelia and Louise did not visit Northchurch. However, I came alone to see Peter for several weeks in the summer.

❀   ❀   ❀

While I was visiting, Mr. Fenn who was becoming advanced in his years, fell ill, and his brother, Thomas, came to help around the farm. Sadly, James Fenn died within a few days of his brother's arrival. Peter was alarmed, but fortunately I was there to reassure him.

I attended the funeral with Peter, and spoke with Thomas Fenn at some length about the responsibilities of caring for Peter. Thomas Fenn was already familiar with Peter to some extent, having seen Peter on various occasions over the years, and he agreed to take over James Fenn's role as Peter's caregiver, moving Peter to Broadway Farm to stay with him.

❖   ❖   ❖

I stayed on with them for several days afterward, to be sure that Peter was comfortable in his new home. During that time I found myself telling Thomas Fenn many, many stories about Peter. When I returned to St. James' Palace in London, I sat down and began reviewing everything Margaret and I had written down about Peter over the years, with the aim of composing all these fragments into a book, like *Gulliver's Travels* or *Robinson Crusoe*, that would tell Peter's life story.

My intention was to make a short composition, to help Thomas Fenn understand and appreciate the Wild Boy. It became a larger project, which would occupy my attention for a period of years. There were stretches of weeks where I could not make any progress at all, but then there were also times when the words seemed to flow from my quill onto the page as easily as if they had written themselves.

❖   ❖   ❖

Making matters more complicated, in the fall of 1743, I developed a persistent cough that the doctors said made it unsafe for me to travel. I could have sent for Peter, but I did not want him to see me sick. I remembered how he had seen the Queen on her deathbed, and I did not want Peter to be frightened. Being only thirty years old at the time, I thought that I would soon recover my health. Unfortunately, the disease I had contracted did not go away.

My health did not allow me to see Peter more than once a year, in the hot, dry days of summer when the doctors said visits to the country would be good for me. Then I spent weeks at the farm, enjoying the sun and visiting with Peter. While I was there, I would read to Mr. Fenn and Peter from the manuscript I was writing about Peter's life.

Amelia came with me, and also visited Peter at other times of the year, ensuring that he was being properly looked after.

186

Sometimes she came alone, and sometimes she brought the King's grandchildren, our nephews and nieces, with her.

❖ ❖ ❖

For the next eight years, things continued in this way, until in the summer of 1751, while visiting Peter, my illness took a turn for the worse. I collapsed while in the field with Peter, and was confined to a bed at Broadway Farm for several days before I was able to make a return journey to London.

Poor Peter had never appeared more grave, and not even I could make him smile. He had seen me fall, and saw me lying in bed looking pale and weak, and he knew something was wrong, but could do nothing to fix it.

Peter stayed by my bedside morning and night until I left for London in a carriage, attended by a doctor. Then he stood solemn-faced with Thomas Fenn at the gate of Broadway Farm, waving goodbye to me.

❖ ❖ ❖

After I left, Peter spent two days in the farmhouse sitting, staring out the window. He was so sad that he did not eat or drink. Then on the morning of the third day after I left, Peter got up and left the farmhouse. Thomas Fenn was still asleep when Peter took off.

It was not the first time Peter had gone off wandering, but in the past, Peter had always returned within a few days. This time, Peter did not. He traveled far from home, driven by a storm of emotions that would not give him peace. For the first time in his life, Peter was filled with adult feelings of anger, grief, and helplessness. He had seen sickness and death before, and now it seemed those things were threatening me.

❖ ❖ ❖

Peter wandered for over a month and traveled over one hundred miles. Sometimes he traveled by night, sometimes by day. He wandered when the unwelcome thoughts and feelings began to gather in his heart, and he rested in the branches of trees or on the ground near trees as he had as a child when fatigue overtook him.

As the days passed, a change of appearance came over Peter. His hair grew longer, but also, he began to grow a thick beard. He began to look less like a Wild Boy and more like a Wild Man.

Eventually, Peter came to a point where he was calm, where he no longer was driven, and he was able to sit down beneath a tree and be still. I don't know exactly how long he sat there or how many trees he sat under but gradually the storm within him subsided, and his heart became clear again.

Out of the darkness, a firefly came to find Peter. The firefly danced in the air before Peter until he took notice of it and smiled. Then it danced a little bit further away from him. Peter got to his feet and followed. It led him out of the forest toward the town of Norwich, then disappeared.

Peter looked around for the firefly but it was nowhere to be found, and he heard sounds of music and song. Wandering toward the source of the sounds, he found a small pub, where a number of local townfolk were concluding an evening's festivities. As he reached the door of the pub, they began their last song of the evening, a popular tune called *The Parting Glass*. Peter did not necessarily understand all the lyrics, but the song nevertheless stirred his heart.

As the song concluded, the pub's patrons began to file out, and some of them took note of the strangely dressed vagabond standing outside. When they questioned him, he smiled and hummed the melody of *The Parting Glass*, unable to answer them more appropriately, so they called for the local constable to come and investigate.

❈ ❈ ❈

The constable was not an unkind man, but since vagrancy was against the law, and Peter could not answer for himself, the constable arrested him and took him into the police station. The police concluded that Peter was probably drunk, and that a bit of time in jail would help clear his head. So they cast him into a cell in the local house of correction, known as the Bridewell. Two months later, however, Peter was no more able to communicate with his jailers than he had been at the time of his imprisonment, and the authorities were uncertain of what to do with him.

❖   ❖   ❖

Peter might have remained locked up in the Bridewell for much longer, if not for a fire that broke out at two in the morning in a nearby furniture warehouse. The fire spread quickly uphill toward the Bridewell and threatened to swallow the jail with its inmates still locked inside. Under the circumstances, there was nothing that the keepers of the Bridewell could do except release the prisoners before they perished in the fire. The prisoners in turn helped the townspeople to fight back against the fire with buckets of water. In the midst of all the commotion, someone noticed that Peter was still inside the burning prison, and the jailers went back inside the burning Bridewell to rescue him.

They called to Peter to come out of his jail cell, but he sat still, captivated by the sight of the fire all around. Thankfully one man was brave enough to go all the way inside and drag Peter out, or else he might have died that night. As it was, the drama of the fire and Peter's rescue led everyone in town to ask who this wild-haired man was, and in the days that followed, someone pointed out an advertisement in the London Evening Post that ran like this:

LOST, or Stray'd away, From BROADWAY in the Parish of NORTH-CHURCH, near Barkhamstead in the County of Hertford, About three Months ago,

PETER, the WILD YOUTH, dark haired, of medium size, he cannot speak to be understood, but makes a kind of humming-Noise, and answers in that manner to the Name of PETER.

Whoever will bring him to Mr. Thomas Fenn's, at the Place abovesaid, shall receive all reasonable Charges, and a handsome Gratuity.

When the jailers called Peter by his name, he responded immediately. So within a short time, Peter was returned to Broadway Farm. Afterward, Mr. Fenn decided to put a collar on Peter's neck, with his name and address printed on it, in case he wandered off a second time. However, Peter did not go wandering again.

❖ ❖ ❖

Princess Amelia came to see Peter soon after he was returned to Broadway Farm. She did not plan to stay long, but she confirmed that he was in good health, and she insisted that Mr. Fenn shave off Peter's beard at once. When the beard was removed, Peter once again looked like himself, and Amelia took him out horseback riding for an afternoon. Then she took her leave of Peter and Mr. Fenn, and returned to London.

Amelia was very fond of the outdoor life. Recently, she had become a ranger of Richmond Park southwest of London, a great Natural Reserve and the largest of the Royal Parks, full of deer and other wildlife. Following my collapse, she decided to close the park to the public, and made plans for Peter to visit me there in the spring.

❖ ❖ ❖

Before Christmas, Amelia returned in a horse-drawn sleigh with six of her nieces and nephews: Augusta, George William Frederick, Edward, Elisabeth, William Henry, and Henry. Peter greeted Amelia and the children happily, and gave everyone hugs, then ran inside the farmhouse, leaving the group slightly puzzled. A moment later, Peter emerged, holding the sled he had been given so many years ago. Everyone laughed, for they too had sleds with them, and they welcomed Peter aboard the sleigh. They spent the afternoon playing with their sleds on the local hill, and then returned to the farmhouse in the evening for dinner. Keeping with tradition, they stayed at the farmhouse for the week, and played all the old games with Peter, and then, much to the children's dismay, Amelia said it was time to go, promising a return visit in the year to come.

190

Spring came and Amelia took me to meet Peter in Richmond Park. He had been transported there separately by my brother William, who had a residence nearby in Berkhamsted. Though he was often preoccupied with his military duties, William liked to look in on Peter at the farm whenever an opportunity presented itself, and was happy in this case to help make it possible for me to see Peter.

The four of us spent a fortnight together in Richmond- Amelia, William, Peter and I. Inside the high wall and gates that surrounded the park land, there was no one to disturb us. Our lodge there was quite comfortable, but Amelia swore she would have it expanded. We rode horses together, or hiked on days when I felt strong enough, enjoyed the gardens and the woods, idled by the ponds and streams, caught sight of the free-roaming deer, and had wonderful picnics in the grassy open spaces. As he had when we were children, Peter displayed an amazing ability to connect with all animals, and soon befriended the herd of deer that inhabited Richmond Park, as well as the rabbits, squirrels and other creatures. We enjoyed ourselves so much we were reluctant to say farewell to Richmond, when the appointed time came, but resolved to come again soon.

❋ ❋ ❋

In the summer, Amelia and the children came back, and they brought me with them. Thanks to my influence, they stayed longer than they had in wintertime. I was unable to run about as much as I had in the past, but I still enjoyed Peter's company, and felt sorry for what had happened the year before. So it was a good two weeks before we finally boarded their carriage and headed back to London.

For the next four years, things continued in this pattern- with both Amelia and I visiting with Peter several times in the course of the year, either at the farm or at Richmond Park. Anne and William participated in a few of these visits, and once, at White Lodge in Richmond, Frederick also came to join with us.

In the summer we would take the children to stay for a few weeks, and in the winter Amelia would take them for a shorter visit, while I remained home at St. James Palace. The children all looked forward to these visits with Peter, and I was glad to see my nieces and nephews becoming as fond of the Wild Boy as we had been, when we were children.

❊   ❊   ❊

Peter continued to be popular in his local community. Children he had played with years before now came to Peter with boys and girls of their own, and they all wondered how he could still appear as youthful and energetic as he had been when they were children. But they did notice there was something different about him- ever since he had gone missing and been returned, his eyes appeared older, wiser.

Chapter 18: The Story of Us

In the fall of 1757, the carriage that always brought Royal visitors arrived at the farm, and Thomas Fenn went out with Peter to greet the arrivals. The carriage was empty.

Thomas Fenn was puzzled by this, but Peter gazed at the empty carriage with a look of recognition on his face. Twenty years ago, with James Fenn at his side, he had looked into an empty carriage like this.

When the driver handed over a letter for Mr. Fenn to read and the expression of puzzlement on Mr. Fenn's face changed to concern, Peter was not surprised. He quickly jumped up into the carriage, and looked at Mr. Fenn expectantly. Taking a deep breath, Mr. Fenn climbed up into the carriage after Peter.

As soon as the driver had resumed his position at the front, the wheels were in motion. Not a word was spoken, but nothing needed to be said. Solemn-faced, Peter gazed out the window on their way to London.

As they drew near to the city, the sun was going down, and out in the field beside the road, Peter saw a host of fireflies rising into the air. He stared at them for several moments, and then suddenly got up from his seat and jumped out of the carriage, running into the field toward the fireflies.

Mr. Fenn called for the driver to stop, and then he stepped out on to the road to follow Peter. But out in the field, amongst the fireflies, Peter had stopped running. He was standing very still, facing away from the road.

Mr. Fenn decided to let Peter have a few moments to himself, to work out whatever emotions he was dealing with. This seemed to be a wise decision, because after a minute or so, Peter turned around and headed back to the carriage, seeming to be much calmer.

❖ ❖ ❖

They continued on their way into London then, to St. James' Palace. Once they arrived, Thomas Fenn was directed to a waiting room, and Peter was ushered deeper into the Palace, to a bedroom where I lay in my bed, coughing.

"Hello Peter," I said, propping myself into a sitting position. "Will everyone but my sister Amelia please leave us now?" The physicians and serving staff filed out of the room, past Peter, who stood staring with tearful eyes at me, his hands clenched tightly.

When the door was closed, I asked Peter, "What is it Peter? Why don't you come over here?"

Peter took two steps toward the bed, and then stopped and shook himself vigorously.

I lifted my eyebrows and asked, "Peter, what-?" and then I gasped, as the air was filled with glowing fireflies who had hidden themselves away in his pockets. Amelia too gasped at the sight of the fireflies swirling around the room.

Coming over to my bedside, Peter opened up his clenched hands and released two more fireflies that rose up and danced in the air before me.

Amelia and I both were speechless for a moment, and then began to laugh. Peter laughed too, and I extended my arms to him. Jumping up on the bed, Peter gave me a hug, then Amelia joined in, and Peter was crushed between the two of us women, with the fireflies circling around us.

"Peter, thank you so much!" I exclaimed, smiling as my eyes filled up with tears. "Thank you for being the best friend I ever had." When Amelia let go of the two of us, I settled back into the cushions of the bed, still holding Peter close.

For several moments I did not say anything- I shut my eyes and just held Peter in my arms. Then I took a deep breath, and said to him, "I am sorry that I can't go on any adventures with you right now, but I want to share something with you. It's something

194

I've been working on for a number of years, and you just gave me the perfect conclusion for it.

"Amelia will you please hand me the manuscript?" Taking a leather bound book from my sister and opening it my lap, I squeezed Peter and said, "Peter, this is the story of us."

❊   ❊   ❊

Peter stayed with me, listening to me tell the story by candlelight, until night turned to morning, and I said at last, "... And that is where our story ends, my dear Peter." I hugged Peter tightly, and broke out in fresh tears.

Peter buried his face against me for several moments, and then I heard him begin to sing. In a moment, he lifted his eyes to look into mine. The song he sang to me was *The Parting Glass*. The lyrics go like this:

"Of all the money e'er I had,
I spent it in good company.
And all the harm I've ever done,
Alas! it was to none but me.
And all I've done for want of wit
To mem'ry now I can't recall
So fill to me the parting glass
Good night and joy be with you all.

"Oh, all the comrades e'er I had,
They're sorry for my going away,
And all the sweethearts e'er I had,
They'd wish me one more day to stay,
But since it falls unto my lot,
That I should rise and you should not,
I gently rise and softly call,
Good night and joy be with you all.

"If I had money enough to spend,
And leisure time to sit awhile,
There is a fair maid in this town,
That sorely has my heart beguiled.

195

Her rosy cheeks and ruby lips,
I own she has my heart in thrall,
Then fill to me the parting glass,
Good night and joy be with you all. "

I smiled and cried as Peter sang. "Where did you learn that song Peter?" I asked, when he was done. Peter smiled sadly. "Never mind," I said. "Thank you, for being my friend." Then I turned my head to Amelia and said, "Amelia, please take Peter back to the farm with Mr. Fenn and stay with him for a few days, so he does not worry about me."

And so I gave Peter over to my sister to look after, and Amelia led Peter out of the room. Peter stopped at the door to wave to me. I smiled back at him and waved goodbye.

Act III:
Amelia

Chapter 19: Immortal Youth

Caroline left her book unfinished in my hands, along with a collection of journals and letters that contained her thoughts and tales of Peter, as well as stories from Margaret's family in Germany. She told me to give a copy of her book to Mr. Fenn, because she had always intended for him to read it, and she also asked me to continue writing Peter's story. There was more that she had intended to write- chapters which did not make it into the book.

I wish that I had Caroline's gift as a writer. She took the stories Margaret gave her, the things our Grandfather told her, and all of her own years knowing Peter, and told the story you have now read- at most I could only add a handful of tales to the collection. Caroline knew Peter best, better than Margaret, and better than me. But there is more to the story than what has been told thus far. Someday, perhaps, all of our tales of Peter may be brought together. For now, I will tell you what became of our dear Wild Boy, after my sister passed away.

The Princess Amelia of Great Britain
St. James' Palace, London

That was the last time that my sister Caroline and Peter saw each other- she died only a few months later, and was mourned by all who knew her, except Peter, who was not present at the funeral. Caroline wanted Peter to remember her always as a living friend, and so that last visit was the end of Caroline's part in Peter's story.

Though her life was marked with a sadness that increased as she grew older, Caroline was remembered as a gentle, truthful, kindhearted and accomplished soul, devoted to her family and generous in her actions. Lord Hervey, who had passed away fourteen years before her, wrote in his memoirs, "Princess Caroline had affability without meanness, dignity without pride, cheerfulness without levity, and prudence without falsehood." My friend Horace Walpole, son of the late Prime Minister, said of Caroline, "though her state of health has been dangerous for years, and her absolute confinement for many of them, her disorder was in a manner new and sudden, and her death was unexpected by herself... Her goodness was constant and uniform, her generosity immense, her charities most extensive- in short I, no royalist, could be lavish in her praise."

Never was a princess more fair or good than my sister Caroline. If personally unhappy, she sought to increase the happiness of others, and in so doing, Caroline relieved her own spirit. This courage, I believe, she got from Peter.

❖ ❖ ❖

Peter lived on for many more years, and had many further adventures. He did not go back to Richmond- after my sister's passing I allowed the Park to be opened to the public again, but we still visited him on the farm.

The next year, a new little princess came to see him, wearing the same acorn necklace that Princess Caroline had worn in her lifetime, and though Peter's eyes filled up with tears seeing this, he also smiled. Her name was Caroline Matilda, she was seven years old, and she was beautiful.

❖ ❖ ❖

Peter lived long- twice as long as the average person of his century, and inspired many generations of children. Every year new children from around the area of Northchurch, as well as new Princes and Princesses from London, came to see the immortal Wild Boy at his home on Broadway Farm. And Peter lived to see the coronation of another king, a grandchild of George II, who as fortune would have it was also called King George. George III was happy to have Peter among the guests at his coronation and marriage, and continued the generous pension that the two previous Kings had provided for Peter. Throughout his days, even into his seventies, Peter's face retained its youthful appearance, and his body remained strong. Perhaps he was kept young by the attentions of all the children. The only thing that changed in his later years was that his hair turned silver-white.

❖ ❖ ❖

In June 1782, the philosopher, linguist, and natural scientist Lord Monboddo visited Broadway Farm to investigate reports of the Wild Boy. He met Peter personally, and also spoke with local people who knew him. Lord Monboddo observed Peter was "of low stature, not exceeding five feet three inches: and though he must be now about 70 years of age, has a fresh, healthy look.

"His face is not at all ugly or disagreeable; and he has a look that may be called sensible and sagacious for a savage. About twenty years ago, he often wandered, and used to be missing for several days, and once, as I was told, he wandered as far as Norfolk: but of late he has been quite tame, and either keeps the house or saunters about the farm.

"The farmer told me that he had been out to school... but had only learned to articulate his own name, Peter, and the name of King George; both of which I heard him pronounce very distinctly. But the woman of the house... told me that he understood everything that was said to him concerning the common affairs of life; and I saw that he readily understood several things she said to him while I was present. Among other things, she desired him to sing *Nancy Dawson*, which he accordingly did, and another tune she named.

"He was never mischievous, but had always that gentleness of nature, which I hold to be characteristical of our nature, at least until we become carnivorous, and hunters or warriors. He retains so much of his natural instinct, that he has a fore feeling of bad weather, growling and showing great disorder before it comes on.

"If he hears any music, he will clap his hands and throw his head about in a frantic manner. He has a very quick sense of music and will often remember a tune after once hearing. When he has heard a tune which is difficult, he continues humming it for a long time and is very uneasy till he is master of it. He can sing a great

200

many tunes and will always change the tune when the name only of another tune with which he is acquainted is mentioned to him.

"He understands everything that is said to him by his master and mistress. He has a quick eye, and is still very robust and muscular. In his youth he was very remarkable for his strength. He is said to have sometimes run seventy or eighty miles a day.

"His strength always appeared so superior that the strongest young men were afraid to contend with him and this strength continued almost unimpaired till about a year and a half ago, when he was suddenly taken ill, fell down before the fire, and for a time lost the use of his right side; since which it has been visibly less than before.

"It is evident that he is not an idiot, as some people are willing to believe him to be. What alone can induce anyone to believe him an idiot is, that he has not learned to speak, though he was sent to school, and as it is said, much pains taken upon him. But in the first place, it is to be considered that he was about fifteen, as the newspapers say, when he was catched and brought to England.

"...The schooling that Peter got was not such as, I think, could have taught him to speak when he was so far advanced in life, if he had the best natural parts, and a greater disposition to learn than can be expected from any savage, who, not perceiving the immediate utility of speech, either for sustenance or self defense, will not be disposed to take so much trouble as is necessary to learn an art so difficult to be learned, especially at an advanced time of life. And therefore I rather wonder that he has learned so many words, many more than I thought he had known, and it appears he has also the use of numbers to a certain degree; and his progress in music would appear to me very wonderful. I can have no doubt that if he had been taught by such a master as Mr. Braidwood, he would long before now have spoken very perfectly."

Such was Lord Monboddo's impression of the Wild Boy, which validates many of Caroline's long-held beliefs.

Chapter 20: The Firefly

In February of 1785, along with other members of the Royal Family, I came to visit Peter on the farm, and we sent a messenger ahead, to make sure Peter had time to prepare for the visit. So Peter was able to get dressed in one of his fancier green and red outfits, then he sat down in his favorite chair facing the window and waited.

The sun was setting then, and the sky was full of colors. In the fields, fireflies danced in great numbers. As the carriage rolled up in front of Broadway farm, a single firefly meandered its way to the window and looked in at the white-haired Wild Boy Peter, who smiled softly and held out his hand to it. Needing no further invitation, the firefly entered the room, and came to settle in Peter's hand. Peter looked down at it and his smile spread wider.

A moment later, we came into the room together, just in time to see the firefly rise from the immortal youth's hand, fly out the window and disappear.

THE END

Things Worth Believing In -
(Excerpted from a Response to a Reader)

Since publishing Peter: The Untold True Story, I have received messages from many readers about my book, and about Peter Pan. Some messages are public, many others are personal. I enjoy hearing from my readers, and have been happy to respond as much as I am able.

I recently received a moving personal message from a reader who shared how books like Peter Pan and Harry Potter had provided an escape for her at difficult times in her childhood. As a girl, she had imagined Neverland and Hogwarts as being real places. She also shared how in growing up, it became harder for her to find that same magic in books. She now finds solace in music. When she saw my book, Peter: The Untold True Story, it sparked her interest to think there had once been a real Boy Who Never Grew Up. Her message was well-written, and while everyone's personal trials are different, I think her experience in childhood and in growing up is more universal than she may realize. What she wrote inspired me to write a lengthy response, and I would like to share some of that response here today.

❖ ❖ ❖

Thank you for writing to me and sharing your personal experiences. It is always moving to receive a message like this from a reader- to know how a book can impact someone's life.

From one, unimaginative point of view, writing is empty, meaningless. "Peter Pan is just make-believe. There's no such thing as magic." And yet, across space and time, the written word allows us to know that things we cannot see or touch do exist, because if we can decipher the text, if we can read what another human being has written, and if that message tallies with things we have seen and felt ourselves, then there is some truth in it, even if it is hidden in fiction. What if Peter Pan was real, and this was your letter from Hogwarts?

204

You seem to have some writing ability- have you tried your own hand at writing? Not for school or work, but for yourself, and for the ones you love? Ray Bradbury suggested that fantasy and science fiction are not simply an escape; he compared writing fantasy and science fiction to the means by which Perseus confronted Medusa. We look at the monsters in our lives indirectly, through the mirror of our writing, and in this way we take aim and strike.

If you love music, and Peter Pan, and Harry Potter, then don't let the world convince you that it is all just make-believe. Believe. Create. Fill your life with the things you love, and seek the truth in them. Don't give up on your dreams. Dream bigger, and be willing to put in the effort to make your dreams come true.

Life is right here, in the middle of the dust and decay of the world. If you can't find anyone else like yourself, keep doing what you love anyway- flowers don't find each other until they rise out of the dust and bloom. And if you are the only flower to bloom in the midst of a desert- what a sight to behold!

There are some things that are worth believing in, no matter what.

❊   ❊   ❊

The reader responded and confirmed, among other things, that indeed she did enjoy writing, and had dreamed of becoming an author, but the task seemed daunting for a number of reasons, including some practical concerns from family members about career stability, as well as the artistic challenges of creating a rich fantasy world, filling it with vibrant, vital characters, and finding the magic words to transport her readers into that world. She asked me if I could share some advice for someone starting out at novel-writing, understanding that there is not one specific method, and everyone has their own techniques.

I resolved immediately to write a further response to the reader, but also reflected that other readers might benefit from this. So I will be addressing my next response not only to her, but to any readers who may hold an abiding interest in writing.

In discussing the art of writing, I can only speak from my own experience. I hope that this will be helpful to you. I intend to follow up with several more installments on this theme through my blog and future books.

Reader Questions and Answers

One place where I frequently interact with readers online is Goodreads. Recently we held a public Q&A session, where readers were free to ask me questions about my writing. Many inquired about the inspiration for this book, and there were also questions about the art of writing. Below is a transcript of that event:

Erin, Age 25, wrote:
"...What made you want to further explore Peter's world?"
They say that truth can be stranger than fiction. James Barrie's Peter Pan is a wonderful fantasy, that I have loved since childhood. What moved me to write this novel is the idea that there were real-life characters and events that inspired Barrie's work, and that the true historical tale was even richer and more poignant than the fairy tale it inspired. Also, the fact that no one had written about this before was both surprising and compelling.

In reading a fairy tale, we suspend disbelief and discriminating thinking and return, at least for a while, to a state of innocence. But sooner or later we know we must return to the "real world," and with that thought, the fairies perish, the colors fade, and the lights all dim.

What if Peter Pan existed in the real world? What if the Boy Who Never Grew Up were flesh and blood? What if he in fact lived, and never lost his innocence? Wouldn't that be a tale worth telling- a tale worth reading?

Besides, Peter, King George, Princess Caroline, Amelia, Lord Hervey, and Tomochichi would never let me rest if I did not tell their story.

Claudia, Age 23, from Chile, wrote:
"The story is very original encounter as most authors do another version of the story but you tell the story before the original story. Therefore I wanted to ask what inspired him to create the story, as did the idea, and how was the process of writing the book?"

I have always liked Peter Pan, and when I learned about Peter the Wild Boy, I made an instant mental connection between the two characters. I was surprised no one had made this connection before, and the more I read, the more I became convinced that I had discovered the true story behind Peter Pan. So at that point, it became inevitable that I would write this novel, to introduce the real Boy Who Never Grew Up to the world.

Marine, Age 21, from France, wrote:
"What are you the most proud of in this book?"

I love all the poignant little moments that enrich the story, and how the larger emotional arc is maintained. I really appreciate when readers share the scenes that made them laugh out loud or cry. Many readers have described becoming attached to Peter through the course of the book, and the fact that I was able to evoke such feelings for a character who does not speak much throughout the story is something I am proud of. That was one of the central challenges of writing this book- Peter the Wild Boy is known to have been only spoken a few words through the course of his life in the eighteenth century, and yet he did communicate in very intuitive, human ways, and inspired deep interest and attachment from the people who knew him.

Book Affectionist, Age 18, wrote:
"Is any of this book inspired from your childhood or a child in your life? "

The novel is about Peter, as I have come to know him. When an immortal youth sits down on top of your desk and tells you his life story, you listen carefully. Now when I think of Peter, am I reminded of my own childhood, and of other children I've known? Of course. But I imagine my readers are similarly reminded of their own experiences. Barrie had it right when he had Peter Pan say, "I'm youth, I'm joy, I'm a little bird that has broken out of the egg." Peter springs from a place in all of our hearts.

Book Affectionist wrote:
"How did you come upon this story? Do you intend to do more books like this novel, exploring the history of such beloved tales that inspire us?"

Discovering the origin of Peter Pan and then writing a novel about it was an unexpected joy. I did not set out to find Peter's story- Peter found me.

Book Affectionist wrote:
"What other stories have you written?"

Peter: The Untold True Story is the first book I've published, but not the first I've written. I have many more books to share, and look forward to announcing my next title. When that time comes, my Goodreads fans will certainly be among the first to know. Until then, however, I hope you will patient with my silence.

Book Affectionist wrote:
"What authors inspire you to write?"

There are many authors whose work has inspired me. In the preface to my book, I give thanks to Ray Bradbury in particular, because I was fortunate enough to have known him personally.

Book Affectionist wrote:
"What do you think is the best portrayal of peter pan in social media (disney, etc.) and why? Did that have any influence on the book as well?"

I enjoyed the 2003 live action film version of Peter Pan, as well as Finding Neverland (2004). I've watched both these movies several times over the years. However, as I've said, the inspiration for my book was Peter himself.

Beverly, Age 31, from New York, wrote:
"What was it about the original Peter Pan that spoke to you the most? Was there a moment or a scene that made you think "I need to tell his story"? As far as writing in general goes, what is the most useful advice anyone has given you about the craft, and what would you tell other aspiring writers (such as myself)?"

Peter Pan is innocence triumphing over all. I always liked the story, but I never had any inclination to write another version of it, until I found there was a real Peter, who similarly retained his innocence throughout his life.

Advice on writing… one of the things that my father has always suggested to me is to write out my idea first, and edit afterward. I have found this to be very good advice. It's easy to get stuck when you overanalyze your work in process. There will be plenty of time to do that later.

Outside of my immediate family, the person who gave me the best advice about writing was Ray Bradbury. I wrote something about my experiences with him in my preface to *Peter: The Untold True Story*. Ray was a great inspiration for me.

On the day I first met Ray, I remember he said to the group, "Now, I know that you've all come to hear me talk about the Art of Writing, but I am going to talk to you about Love…" Ray believed we should do what we love, love what we do, and fill our lives to the point of overflowing with the things that inspire us.

From conversations we had, Ray knew I was working on finishing some large projects, and recommended to me that I publish some short stories in the meantime, to introduce myself as an author. He wanted me to get my work out there. *Peter: The Untold True Story* is 220 pages long, so it's not exactly short by Ray's standards, but just the same, I am glad to have begun introducing readers to my work.

To any aspiring writers reading this, I would say start today. Write what is in your heart. Persist, day after day.

Aleksandr Solzhenitsyn had to write his novels on cigarette wrappers and other scraps of paper while imprisoned in the gulag, and then the guards found the papers and burned them, so that he had to write it all out again. But writing sustained his spirit through that difficult period, when others perished. He survived, and so did his writings. Do not give up.

Jamie, Age 24, wrote:
"What made you decide to write about Peter Pan?"

They say that luck is what happens when preparation meets opportunity. I felt very lucky to have discovered the true story of Peter, and to have had enough prior experience writing to feel ready to tackle such a subject.

Belinda (TheBookBuddies), Age 21, from New York, wrote:
"What was the hardest part of writing this novel for you?"

Finding the time to write was probably the hardest part. Besides that… portraying Peter's character while having him say very little was a challenge, but also there was the challenge of capturing a sense of the magic of a fairy tale within the constraints of a story based on true historical events. Yet, truth can indeed be stranger than fiction, and I found I did not have to try too hard to bring the tale I envisioned to life.

Charity, Age 25, from Texas, wrote:
"When you began writing your book, how many first sentences did you go through till your mind slipped away and your first page started coming together?"

My earliest draft of this story was in screenplay form. Regarding how many first sentences I went through- as I recall, I slipped into that other place pretty quickly. The very first words I wrote were from the narrator,

"All children grow up, all but one."

Then I wrote a description of the scene to be visualized…

We see a covered wagon passing along a road in the German countryside. Ahead there is an ancient forest. It is the time of fireflies, and the air is filled with their colorful wings. One particular firefly meanders its way toward the wagon. We hear he voices of a married German couple arguing.

(In the Q&A session, I shared an excerpt from the opening scene of the book for comparison. As you now hold the complete book in your hands, you can flip back to the beginning and compare with the lines above, if you are so inclined.)

Traci, Age 36, from Wyoming, wrote:
"What makes your twist unique to other stories retold out there and how did you come up with the concept?"

Well, there are a lot of authors out there today that are reimagining the stories of popular fictional characters, but I haven't heard of as many novels being written about the real-life people who inspired those fictional characters, and I am not aware of any other books written on the premise that Peter the Wild Boy was the true-life inspiration for Peter Pan. As for how I came up with the concept, as I've said, I didn't set out to find Peter, Peter found me.

Michelle, from Nevada, wrote:
"When writing this book, did you only research Peter, or did you also read about other feral children that have studied throughout the ages? "

When I was young I learned about a girl who was found in the wild, and the experiences researchers had trying to help her acclimate to normal life. One thing that stood out in my memory was hearing how happy she was to run out of doors naked in the freezing snow, while her guardians stood by in heavy coats. In writing this book, I certainly did take an interest in the stories of other feral children, but the primary focus of my research was on Peter himself.

Kirsty, Age 23, from South Africa, wrote:
"My question is, what made you decide to write this book?"
Love.

Jan, Age 35, from Washington, wrote:
"What made you decide to write the true story versus writing a retelling of the Disney version?"
I had no specific desire to write a Peter Pan story, although I loved the book and the movies. But when I encountered Peter the Wild Boy, it was like a light turning on. After discovering the true story, how could I not write this book?

Joanne, Age 61, from Oregon, wrote:
"Do you wish you could be Peter Pan???? Hopefully we can all have a bit of Peter Pan in us, right?"
Yes- I would be very happy to never grow old but always remain young, and yes- Peter is there, in all of us, if we care to pay attention.

Tyler, Age 24, from Tennessee, wrote:
"What are your viewpoints on life, death, and immortality, especially when writing?"
I'm tempted by your question to write something esoteric, theoretic and vaguely poetic about how one can achieve immortality through writing, but the truth is that life is more precious than any words written on a page, and I hope you live every day of your life to the fullest.

My mother died of cancer a few years ago, and I am grateful for every moment I spent with her. There were difficult times, to be sure, but we made the most of what we had together. If you want to be a great writer, go and do your best to live a great life. Sooner or later, you will find the meaning of the words you are looking for.

Linda, Age 52, wrote:
"I believe there is a bit of Peter in all of us and I am curious as to the 'untold story'."

The appeal of the untold story for me, is how the flesh-and-blood Peter managed to live into his seventies and remain an innocent Wild Youth. We see his journey through the eyes of the people who knew him, and we feel how he touched their lives. There is love, action, and adventure, but at the heart of the story is this conflict- how does Peter endure in our world? In the fairy-tale of Neverland, Peter Pan did not have to face certain realities, but in real-life, Peter did have to face them, and still, his innocence triumphed.

JoAnne, Age 53, from Canada, wrote:
"I would like to know what inspired you to write your version of Peter Pan??"

I've answered this question in several ways already, but I'll try to inject something new here, to keep the conversation fresh. Do you know the song *Hurt*, by Johnny Cash? I love that song, and I never connected it particularly with this book before- but some of the verses fit in well with the theme. Peter does not change, but everyone around him does. Eventually he loses people dear to him, an experience which threatens to claim the very thing that defines him- his innocence- yet in the face of it all, Peter finds a way to bring light, joy, and hope, not only for himself, but for the ones he loves.

Jenna, Age 25, from New Mexico, wrote:
"Were you always fascinated with the story of Peter Pan as a kid? Did you have other favorite characters besides Peter Pan?"

I am very eclectic in my choice of heroes. Alongside Peter Pan, you will find a monkey, a seagull, a ragtag band of rabbits, a Terminator, a wandering samurai, Joan of Arc, William Wallace, and many others.

Supranee, Age 26, from Thailand, wrote:
"How do you feel the secondary characters (Lost Boys, Tiger Lily, Captain Smee) have contributed to the development (and/or idolization) of Peter Pan within Neverland?"

In my own book, the supporting cast of characters is very important. Peter is defined by his interactions with others, and by their perceptions of him. The same is true in Neverland.

Barrie conjured eighteenth century pirates, Indians, lost boys, and the fairies of Kensington Gardens, into Neverland along with Peter to create a children's fantasy adventure that marked the Boy Who Never Grew Up as a hero, a leader, and the very ideal of wild youth. And then, having set the stage, Barrie laid the course for Peter to be undone with the introduction of Wendy Darling.

Sarah, from Australia, wrote:
"How did your own personal feelings affect the way you wrote your book and the evolution of the characters as the book progressed?"

Funny thing about that- as the author I generally know the plan of things well before they are written, but occasionally my characters do something unexpected. In this project, two characters surprised me by falling in love with each other and getting married. I could not deny their happiness. With the help of King George, we were able to arrange a suitable wedding and reception, and it turned out to be a wonderful event, but it was not something we discussed ahead of time.

This was not the only occasion when my cast took the script into their own hands. Peter, as you might expect, proved himself to be quite the rascal, and I love Princess Caroline too much to question any unexpected choices she might have made. In the process of writing, I typically feel what the characters feel and so, if Lord Hervey decides to ad-lib his lines a bit, I give him some rope. It keeps everybody on their toes.

The relationships between the characters are at the heart of this book, and I see bits of myself in all of them. Someone else asked me this week what I am most proud of in my book- I guess the relationships are a part of the answer to that question. Peter and the Firefly, Peter and the Doctor's Family, Peter and Rose, Peter and King George, Peter and the Deer, King George and Princess Caroline, Princess Caroline and her mother and sisters, Princess Caroline and Peter, Peter and the Queen, Peter and Frederick, Peter and Hervey, Caroline and Hervey, Peter and Tomochichi, Peter and his band of kids, etc.

Sara, Age 22, from Sweden, wrote:
"...what drove you to write about Peter? What were the external and internal forces that made you decide that Peter Pan was your thing? "
Well for starters I wasn't driven or forced to write about Peter- generally I never write from that perspective. Sometimes I write from my imagination, sometimes I write about things I encounter. I learned about the historical life of Peter the Wild Boy, made a connection between it and the fairy tale of Peter Pan, and decided this was something I wanted to share. So, I wrote a novel to capture the feeling I had about this character.

Destiny, Age 16, wrote:
"Hello. What I want to know is where did you come up with the idea for your book and why you decided it would make a good story?"
The book is based on the true life adventures of Peter the Wild Boy. When I learned about him, I immediately made a connection with the character of Peter Pan, and I was fascinated by the idea that a real-life Boy Who Never Grew Up could have existed in England a century before the fairy tale was written. So I read more, and started putting more pieces of the story together, and I am more convinced now than when I began that the true story of Peter the Wild Boy is the origin of the fairy tale of Peter Pan. Barrie himself hinted that the characters in his stories were drawn from real-life. Of course, J.M. Barrie is responsible for writing his classic work, but I believe he drew inspiration from this poignant 18th century story, and that is why I wrote the novel.

215

...Oh, one more thing!

My next book, *Tales of Peter,* is coming soon.

Best Wishes

Chris

Exclusive Sneak Peak:

Tales of Peter

ONCE MORE

To the dear ones who have written me, asking for more tales of our Wild Boy Peter, I offer this volume. It is a collection of stories from Margaret, Rose, Caroline, Jessica and myself. Some of what you will find here are our personal memories, and some are what might be called legends. For as long as we knew him, there were mysteries about the Wild Boy that were never answered, and as much as he lived in our presence, he also lived in our imaginations. A tradition began with Margaret and Rose, that was passed from one generation of young people to the next, of adventures that crossed from our world into the realms of the fantastic unknown, where Peter originated from, and where we knew he was destined to return.

This then is the last that I shall write, but certainly not the last that shall be written about our friend Peter. Perhaps one of you shall add to our tales with some of your own. Perhaps the next volume shall be written by one who is not yet born.

In any event, I hope you will enjoy reading our tales of Peter, and then not fail to go out and seek your own adventures. There is no telling how far you may go, when you remain young at heart.

The Princess Amelia of Great Britain

Coming Soon

CPSIA information can be obtained
at www.ICGtesting.com
Printed in the USA
LVOW08s1829310317
529201LV00002B/311/P

9 780989 127028